THE HIDDEN

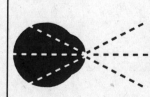

THE HIDDEN

HEATHER GRAHAM

THORNDIKE PRESS

A part of Gale, Cengage Learning

GALE
CENGAGE Learning·

Farmington Hills, Mich • San Francisco • New York • Waterville, Maine
Meriden, Conn • Mason, Ohio • Chicago

LIBRARY OF CONGRESS CATALOGING-IN-PUBLICATION DATA

Graham, Heather.
  The hidden / Heather Graham. — Large print edition.
    pages cm. — (Krewe of hunters) (Thorndike Press large print core)
   ISBN 978-1-4104-8030-9 (hardback) — ISBN 1-4104-8030-5 (hardcover)
   1. Paranormal romance stories. 2. Large type books. I. Title.
PS3557.R198H53 2014
813'.54—dc23   2015030780

Published in 2015 by arrangement with Harlequin Books S. A.

Printed in the United States of America
1 2 3 4 5 6 7 19 18 17 16 15

For family and family trips.
Road trips!
Dennis, Jason, Shayne, Derek, D.J.,
Bryee-Annon and Chynna.
Ghost tours along the way . . .
And a precious journey through time
and American history.

In memory of Shirley Dougherty,
Harpers Ferry, West Virginia —
one of the most entertaining and
informative guides I have ever had the
privilege to know.

And to ghost stories . . .
History isn't so much a list of dates and
times as it is the tales of those who
came before us, their failures and their
triumphs, and their place in the time
that led us to our world today.

PROLOGUE

The Colorado Territory
Fall 1870

Nathan Kendall woke in the middle of the night, aware that something wasn't right. He tried to tell himself that he was imagining the sudden sense of danger that had roused him from a deep sleep; he had done his best to leave the past behind, to embrace his new life.

And the woman he loved.

She lay at his side, still sleeping peacefully. Jillian Vickers Kendall, whose smile truly seemed to radiate light, whose every movement was silk and grace. The miracle was that she loved him — and that their child slept in a cradle at their side.

Jillian . . . and their child. Fear swept over him like a tidal wave.

He was instantly alert, afraid to move until he recognized the source of danger.

He wished to hell he'd thought to get

7

himself a good guard dog. But at first there had been no reason to fear anyone, nothing to worry about except an angry bear.

There still shouldn't have been anything to worry about.

He lay in the darkness, listening. He felt as he had sometimes during the brutal years of the Civil War, as he lay asleep in his tent on the cold earth, where the men slept wherever they had fallen in exhaustion after retreat had been sounded.

He felt as if the enemy might come at any minute, guns blazing and bayonets ready.

All his fears then had been of the enemy, of battle, guns and swords, the sound of horses shrieking, caught in the fire, dying in the mud. The sound of men screaming, the scent of burning flesh that coincided with horrible pain and despair.

But the enemy was no longer the enemy, at least not on paper. And not according to the greatest general the United States — and the Confederacy — had ever nurtured, Robert E. Lee.

When they'd lain down their arms, Lee had urged that they all sue for peace.

It had taken Nathan a few years to truly understand the concept.

His own home had been razed in the fighting. His parents had passed away during the war years. His only brother had been killed at Shiloh.

Peace, General Robert E. Lee had said. They were beaten. No more blood, no more horror. Find peace. But for some, many of them in Nathan's company, drawn from what had become West Virginia during the middle of the war, the war hadn't ended. For a while he'd fallen in with them. Brian Gleason's home at Front Royal had been burned to the ground, Jeff Bay's wife had died in childbirth while they'd been away fighting and Billie Merton's father had sided with the North. All had felt they had nothing left but to keep fighting, which meant stealing anything that belonged to the hated Northerners.

He hadn't thought it such a bad thing to rob banks owned by carpetbaggers. Or even to hold up stagecoaches as they moved westward, filled with more carpetbaggers from the North. He'd had no problem joining up with a few of the other men from his infantry company to become bandits — like Robin Hood, of course, stealing from those who had descended on the broken and bleeding South like a horde of vultures.

But then they had killed someone during a bank robbery.

And Nathan had wanted out. War was one

thing — it was horrible and ugly, killing men with different ideals who just wanted to go home as much as he did. But that was kill or be killed.

Cold-blooded murder was another thing, and more than he could bear at this stage of his life.

Peace.

He had found it in the Colorado Territory.

A little bit of money had purchased a nice piece of land from old Rollo Conway, a worn-out prospector who hadn't done so well, up on a plateau that looked out on the majestic peaks of the Rockies. The ranch still bore his name.

A fellow named Joel Estes had founded Estes Park, the nearby community that bore his name, around 1859, and since then, rich Europeans and inquisitive naturalists had come to marvel at the place, along with prospectors determined to search for riches in the nearby multitude of mountain streams.

Nathan panned for gold himself, but he kept quiet about his discoveries, because he didn't really want to be a gold miner. He wanted to be a rancher. He wanted simple things. The precious gold bits he'd found were nothing but a means to an end. He

10

wanted a stable and a home, both of which he was more than willing to build by hand. Hard labor, working to erase his painful memories, was his way of finding a new life.

And then he'd met Jillian at the little church just down the mountain. She'd been there with her father, United States Marshal Tom Vickers, and though Vickers hadn't liked him, Jillian had fallen head over heels in love with Nathan. When Marshal Vickers had left town to do his duty in the surrounding countryside, Jillian had talked Father Ferguson into marrying them. After all, they were both of legal age, so that had been that.

After all those brutal years, he'd found peace.

Peace and that rare, elusive feeling called happiness.

But tonight . . .

What in God's name was it? The slight difference in the breeze, the rustle as it moved through leaves just beginning to hint of fall . . .

The bugles were silent now.

But there was something out there . . .

He jumped out of bed and grabbed his Colt. It wasn't as cumbersome as the the Enfield rifle he'd carried during the war. No, it had come from his outlaw days, an

11

army rifle manufactured at the end of the war, and offering precision aim and six bullets that could be fired in quick succession.

He looked at his wife, his precious wife, where she still lay sleeping. And he looked at his child, *his son,* sleeping just as peacefully.

He walked to the window of their upstairs bedroom and looked out on the world he had forged on the little mountaintop plateau. Storage and stables to his right, smokehouse and bunkhouse to his left. So far, no one was sleeping in the bunkhouse; he was just getting to where he could afford to hire the ranch hands who would fill it.

Great trees stretched high to the heavens in the night sky, visible by the light of a slightly waning moon. He heard a horse neigh and that seemed like another warning.

He wished again that he'd gotten dogs; the cats he kept as ratters in the stables wouldn't be much of an alarm.

What was spooking him? he wondered.

Indians suddenly creeping back to reclaim the area? No, not now, not here.

The ghost of a dead Yankee soldier he might have killed, back to seek his revenge?

Or a living man? His father-in-law, ready

to kill them both for defying his edict not to marry?

Who else?

The outlaws he had ridden with until theft had become murder? Jeff Bay, who had led them all? Jeff had become so filled with hatred that he hadn't understood Nathan's anger that he'd shot a man in cold blood simply because the victim had come from the North.

Or were Brian Gleason, Billie Merton and the other outlaws he'd ridden with angry because he had opted out?

He jumped suddenly as his wife slipped her arms around him. He'd been so lost in his thoughts that he hadn't heard her come up behind him.

"Nathan," she said softly. "What is it?"

He turned, holding her close, feeling the beat of her heart and the warmth of her body. "I don't know," he said. "I thought something was out there."

"It's nothing, my love," she told him. "Come back to bed."

He nodded and turned back to the window for one last look.

And then he saw it, a shadow slipping from the storage shed next door.

"Stay here," he told Jillian. "Look after the baby."

13

Nathan crept quietly down the stairs. He unbolted the front door as silently as he could, then slid outside, using the wall as cover, straining to see in the darkness.

The shadow was still there by the storage shed. It seemed to be lumbering.

He almost laughed out loud.

A bear.

He stepped out on the porch, thinking to fire a warning shot, so the creature would amble off without doing any harm.

Without warning, he was hit. A blow to the head sent him stumbling forward, tripping over the steps to the porch, and he landed hard in the dirt with his head spinning so wildly that he saw stars in the sky that weren't there.

He blinked to clear his eyes and realized that he'd been attacked by a monster.

No, not a monster.

A man.

A man in a bizarre mask and hat.

"Coward," Nathan whispered. "Show yourself."

And then he knew. He'd never really found peace.

And he was going to die.

CHAPTER ONE

Colorado, Present Day

A majestic elk stood stock-still on the hill, long neck arched to the sky in the sunset, antlers large and proud. Scattered wildflowers nestled within the long grass, and the colors of the horizon were almost whimsical in their beauty.

Scarlet Barlow kept her distance, though the animal didn't seem to be the least bit afraid of her. The elk in the area were accustomed to people who came to hike the mountainous country, the crests and valleys and little plateau where the onetime Conway Ranch was now a bed-and-breakfast, complete with a gift shop and museum. No one disturbed the elk that came here to graze the lush meadows, and the elk apparently knew that. The B and B was a mere stone's throw from the eastern entrance to Rocky Mountain National Park, so those who came to admire the animal life there meant it no harm.

The big bull elk seemed to be aware that he was posing like a model; it was almost as if he was happy to offer her the photo op.

She snapped several pictures, paused and glanced at them on the screen, then smiled, pleased with what she had captured.

"Thank you, sir," she said to him, then turned away and looked out over the natural splendor of the Rockies and the town of Estes Park, nestled among them.

People came here for many reasons.

One of the biggies was The Stanley Hotel. Stephen King had been staying there when he'd been inspired to write *The Shining.* The hotel offered both ghost and historical tours, and Scarlet loved it. She liked to imagine what the author had thought and to hear the staff talk about how the events in the book related to what had really happened there.

The Conway Ranch, where she'd been working as a researcher and curator for the past two months, had a history just as unique and intriguing, even if not as well-known. She loved knowing that her contributions to the small on-site museum were helping it to become more and more of an attraction on its own. The ranch had been founded in the 1860s, just a few years after Joel Estes had established the town and a few months after Welsh explorer Griffith Evans had opened a dude ranch in the area. Ranching was no easy matter in this mountainous country seventy-five hundred feet above sea level. And as far as the Conway Ranch went, "ranching" had long meant guided trail rides for the tourists.

Scarlet smiled. She couldn't get over the awe she always felt as she looked at the towering snowcapped peaks of the Rockies.

She'd been told nothing compared to the Canadian Rockies, but she couldn't imagine that any scenery could be more beautiful than this.

Even the town felt special to her, with its unique shops and restaurants, everything nestled in a natural paradise of mountain peaks and forests cut through by brooks that were bubbling and bright in the sunlight, cool and mysterious by night. Hikers, horseback riders and tubers and rafters, who took their chances with the rapids, came year-round to enjoy the scenery.

This place was as different from her native South Florida as it could get, but both were natural playgrounds, and this was a perfect place to be. At least for now.

Her apartment was on the top floor of

what had once been a storage barn for feed and ranching equipment. Now it housed the museum on the ground floor and her two-bedroom apartment on the second. The museum had actually come about accidentally. The original builder had started out organizing his own Civil War and Native American memorabilia, then added more pieces as he acquired them. Over the years various people had taken a stab at cataloging everything, but finally the current owner had decided it was time for a professional to come in and make sense of it all.

And that was where Scarlet had entered the picture.

She'd been a bookworm all her life, with a particular interest in history. At college she'd majored in history and minored in archaeology, going on to get master's degrees in both. What she loved most wasn't the bare bones of dates and places but the stories that went along with events, stories about the people who'd actually lived at the time and whose experiences provided a unique perspective.

After college she had worked in New York for several years before she had been invited to come home to South Florida to work a new dig in the field she considered her specialty, eighteenth and nineteenth century America, at the mouth of the Miami River. She had followed both the lure of the job and her heart, taking the position not only for itself, but also to be closer to the man she'd loved, FBI agent Diego McCullough. And now, thanks to the current owner of the ranch, Ben Kendall, she was here in Colorado.

Ben, a descendant of the original owner, Nathan Kendall, and his wife, Trisha, had purchased the place five years ago. For them, restoring the Conway Ranch was a labor of love. They'd refurbished it with the money he'd made as a New York stockbroker, having given up the city life to return to his family roots.

A history buff from way back, he had tracked down Scarlet in New York City after discovering that she, too, had a family connection to the ranch and to him, and they'd stayed in touch when she went back to Florida, where she'd eventually married Diego. And he'd been right there with a job offer after the divorce, when she'd wanted and needed to get away.

"Scarlet! Afternoon!" Ben called out to her now from the wide porch of the main house, breaking into her thoughts.

Given the time, she realized he must have

19

just returned from leading the afternoon trail ride, just as he did six days a week. Angus Fillmore — the quintessential cowboy, with his long white hair and beard, solid shoulders and strong arms — was still leading horses into the stables. One of the guests, Terry Ballantree, thirtyish and another descendant of Nathan Kendall, was talking animatedly to Angus, who was nodding politely but didn't seem to be saying much. Gwen and Charles Barton, newlyweds from Mississippi, were waiting for their chance to say something to Angus, but Terry seemed to be nothing if not long-winded.

"Scarlet, I'm glad to run into you," Ben told her, just as the head housekeeper, Linda Reagan, tall, slim and very pretty, stepped out on the porch behind him.

"Don't forget to wipe your boots off before you come inside," Linda said, then waved to Scarlet.

"I will, I will!" Ben promised, then joined Scarlet on the wide front lawn.

She smiled, wondering how he had ever been a stockbroker. He was fifty-five and blessed with a full head of snow-white hair that he liked to keep long. He always had a smile on his face now, which he hadn't had when she'd first met him. The stress of working on Wall Street had kept him looking harried and worn, but now he was a happy man. He'd told her once that he was certain he'd really been made for the great outdoors.

"You're welcome on the ride anytime," he told her. "I know you love the horses."

"Believe it or not, Ben, I grew up around horses."

"South Florida? That's beach country."

"There are lots of horses all over the state," she said. "I grew up in Davie. We had horses there, and my folks still do."

"Well, I'll be damned," he said. "So how's it going? Are you liking the job?"

"I love it here," she assured him. "Your collection is amazing. Colts from just about every era from the 1850s onward, Spencer repeating rifles, Smith & Wesson revolvers, Winchesters, you name it. Worth a fortune, if you wanted to sell."

He shook his head. "My selling days are over. I'm looking forward to spending every day here, sharing all this with our guests, for the rest of my life."

"You're a happy man," she said.

He grinned. "Best wife in the world and this little piece of heaven. How can I not be happy? Looks like you appreciate the place, too." He nodded toward her camera.

21

"I just got a terrific picture of an elk. Big guy with a huge set of antlers."

"Can't bring yourself to say 'big rack,' huh?" he teased.

She laughed. "Honestly, it never occurred to me. One thing we don't have in Florida are elk. Especially not elk that like to pose for you."

"Let me see," Ben said.

She produced her camera and hit the little button to show her stored photos.

Ben took the camera from her with a grin on his face, but his grin froze as he stared at the screen and then at her. "Where the hell were you? What is this?" he demanded, handing the camera back to her.

Startled, Scarlet took the camera and stared at the screen. There was no bull elk with majestic antlers. It was the same spot, but the picture was of a man. A man hanging from a branch of a mighty oak, blood dripping from his body to the ground.

She stared at it, stunned.

"I — I didn't take this!" she said.

She hit the button to switch to the next picture. That one showed two people, the same man and a woman, on the ground, tangled together in a pool of blood.

She flicked backward and saw a picture of the woman while she was still alive, though just barely. A large red stain covered her midriff, her arms were thrown back and her mouth was open in an O of agony and shock. It looked as if a bullet had just ripped through her body.

Dead people. Her pictures were of dead people.

She flicked back to the shot of the couple. It was hard to tell exactly which limbs belonged to which person as they embraced in a pool of blood.

"Honestly, Scarlet, what the hell?"

"I — I don't know," she said. "I didn't take these. I never saw any of this. I — I was right over there," she said, pointing.

He looked at her for a moment as if she was severely disturbed. Scarlet looked back at the camera, flicking through the many shots she had taken in search of the elk.

It wasn't there anywhere.

Just the man and the woman . . .

Perhaps her stunned expression had an effect on Ben, who asked, "Can a camera be hacked?"

"I don't think so," she said. "But I just don't get it. I didn't see anything like that, and I never would have taken pictures of it if I had." She shook her head and handed the camera back to Ben, as if she couldn't bear to touch it.

Ben studied the camera and scrolled through the shots, then stared at her, frowning. "What did you do that for?"

"Do what?"

"Erase them all."

"I didn't erase anything!"

"Well, they're gone. I admit your elk is fantastic, but why on earth would you fake pictures of corpses on my property?" Ben said.

She stared at him, angry now, and totally confused. How could those vile shots have disappeared and the elk have reappeared in their place? "Really, Ben? You think I could do something like that? Because I didn't take those pictures, and I didn't erase them, either. I don't know how they got there, but I had nothing to do with it."

"I'm sorry, Scarlet. But they *were* there, and it was a real shock to see them."

He stared at her, puzzled, but she thought he believed her.

"We should just take your camera in to Marty Decker. He runs a great camera shop in town. I'm sure he can figure out what's going on. You know, even if it's just a camera, I think anything and everything can be hacked these days. I wouldn't even have a computer if we didn't need the damned thing for the business. Leave it with me. I'll get it to him, and I'll make sure he saves your pictures of the elk. They're really beautiful."

"Thanks, Ben," she told him. "I use computers and cameras all the time while I'm working, but I've never seen anything like this."

Ben shrugged, then asked, "You going to join us for dinner?"

She was still offended that he could even think she would do something like that, but on the other hand, she couldn't really blame him. She forced a smile. "No, I've got some paperwork to finish, but thank you for the invitation. You're sure you don't mind taking the camera to your friend?"

"Not at all."

"Okay, thanks." She gave him a little wave and walked away. Terry Ballantree and the Bartons crossed her path, so she paused to say hello, even though she longed to get away and try to sort out what had happened.

"Scarlet, thanks so much for the tour yesterday," Terry said. "Any way I can get another look before dinner? I'd love another look at some of those old photos."

"We loved it, too," Gwen said.

"I'm glad you enjoyed yourselves," Scarlet said. "Ben is kind of strict about the museum. It's only open Thursday to Sunday, and this is Monday, but if you're all here for a few more days, I'll ask him if I can take you back through for a private tour tomorrow or Wednesday."

"Thanks," Terry said.

"That would be great," Gwen said. She and Charles were both in their twenties, and they almost looked like children playing at marriage, but Scarlet had found them both to be open and friendly. Charles had been a football player at Ole Miss, and Gwen had been a cheerleader. Now he had just started his own law practice. Gwen was blonde and blue-eyed, a perfect contrast to his tall, dark and handsome.

Terry was a nice guy, too, though his never-ending enthusiasm was a bit exhausting. He was good-looking, with sandy-brown hair and large hazel eyes, a generous mouth and a perfect nose. While he was only medium height, he was in good shape.

But with her nerves completely frayed right now, she just wasn't up to dealing with any of them.

"I'll talk to Ben and let you know," Scarlet said, then quickly made her escape. "See you all later," she called over her shoulder.

The old storage barn had been given windows sometime at the end of the

Victorian era, and though plain shades were drawn over the museum windows, those upstairs boasted pretty drapes.

Scarlet unlocked the door and stepped inside. The security lights, added to the last of the daylight seeping in, created an eerie glow, but it didn't bother her in the least. She was in love with the place. Many of the displays were the originals, over a hundred years old, as were the placards they held, written in cursive by a gentle hand almost a hundred and fifty years ago.

There were life-size figures on pedestals arranged throughout the room, ranging from Ute chiefs in full battle regalia to Yankee and Rebel soldiers, fur trappers, gunslingers and frontier women, along with excellent re-creations of real people like Teddy Roosevelt and John Muir. There were twenty-two of them altogether, the oldest nearly as old as the ranch itself. Her favorite was a Ute woman holding a child and looking skyward. There was something so beautiful in her expression that Scarlet was certain she had been modeled from life by an artist who adored her.

The stairs to her apartment were to the far left. A sign hanging from a velvet rope advised No Admittance. She unhooked the rope and walked upstairs.

The whole second floor was hers. She had a kitchen, dining room, living room, bedroom and even a guest room. It wasn't fancy, but to be honest, she preferred it to the main house, which had been fully renovated to offer the rustic, frontier look guests expected.

In the main house, the parlor was spacious, and boasted Victorian furniture, period portraits and paintings, and a number of mounted animal heads, all of them at least a hundred years' old. The dining room offered more massive heads, including a giant moose head that stared down at the large central table, which seated twelve.

The animal heads actually made Scarlet a little sad, but Trisha had told her that they were part of the tradition of the West and the guests expected them. Even so, Scarlet had never quite gotten used to them, and she had actually declined several meals at the main house because she felt so uncomfortable eating with the dead moose looking down at her.

Her place, however, was, in her opinion, just as nice as the main house, not to mention it was her own.

And neither her apartment nor the museum had trophy heads anywhere on the walls.

The apartment had been recently remodeled and refurbished. The master bedroom held two antique dressers, a washstand with a pitcher and bowl and an antique bed frame that held a very modern and comfortable queen-size mattress.

Scarlet loved her job here and was enjoying the emphasis on the Civil War, Reconstruction and westward expansion. It was so different from her work in Florida, which had focused on the Seminole Wars.

She walked into the kitchen and decided to brew tea while debating whether to go into town for dinner. She hadn't actually left the property in a few days, so getting out and about was probably a good thing to do. She could become reclusive all too easily, she knew.

She was mulling over the strange pictures on the camera and pouring hot water over a tea bag when she heard a thump.

It was a loud thump. Loud enough to make her nearly spill scalding water over her hand.

She quickly set down the kettle and frowned. The sound had come from downstairs, where there shouldn't have been anyone. She was certain she'd locked the door behind her.

Unease filled her. There wasn't even a door between her and the downstairs, something she'd never thought about before.

She dug in her pocket quickly for her cell phone. After the camera incident, she didn't want to sound like a paranoid idiot, but she didn't want to take any chances, either.

She dialed the main house. "Hey," she said when Ben picked up, "I'm just checking. Is anyone supposed to be downstairs in the museum? I just heard . . . something down there."

"Not to worry, I'll be right there," he told her.

"I hate to bother you."

"It's a bother of about thirty steps. I'll see you in two minutes."

As soon as Scarlet heard Ben's key in the door she ran down the steps to meet him.

He hit the switch that turned on all the overhead lights. "Let's see what's up, okay?" he asked.

"Thanks. I didn't know — I thought maybe someone was supposed to be in here."

He shook his head. "You, Trisha and I have keys. No one else. So what did you hear?"

"A thump."

"A thump. Hmm. Well, let's look around."

The museum consisted of a single large room, with the platform holding Teddy Roosevelt and John Muir right in the middle.

They began to walk from one end to the other and found one of the frontiersmen on the floor.

"I'll be darned. My great-great-whatever fell down," Ben said.

"Poor Nathan Kendall," Scarlet murmured. The mannequin was a handsome one; Nathan's father-in-law had commissioned it — along with one of his daughter, which had disappeared at some time over the years — because he'd wanted them for his grandchild. Scarlet had never been sure whether she'd thought that was nice or creepy.

He grinned and hunkered down by the fallen figure. "I guess he wants to be sure we remember him. Well, we should. We're both his descendants, after all. Give me a hand, will you?"

Scarlet helped him lift the mannequin. It was heavy, which made sense, since it had been carved from solid wood, then painted with care and dressed in period clothing. She assessed the handsome features for damage, thinking the nose might have been broken in the fall, but it was unharmed.

"Why would a statue just fall over?" she ventured.

"Who knows? So much mining went on around here, the earth is always adjusting. You okay?"

"Of course. The noise just startled me, that's all."

"I should probably install a security system out here. I never really thought that much about it. Locks on the doors. I didn't even buy a gun and learn how to shoot until a few months ago. They frown on stockbrokers packing heat on the streets of New York."

"I know how to shoot," Scarlet said quietly. "But I don't own a gun."

"That's right, I forgot. Your ex-husband was a cop."

"Agent," Scarlet said. "Federal agent."

"I remember meeting him in New York one time, before you took that job in Florida. He seemed like a nice guy. But . . . none of my business. His loss is our gain, I say."

"He *is* a nice guy," Scarlet said. "Sometimes things just don't work. Anyway, yes, he taught me how to use a gun."

"Well, there you go — you've got a room full of guns right here," Ben said. "Of course, half of these are older than the war between the States."

"But most of them are in good working order," she said. "Anyway, I'm fine. I think I'm going to head into town, but I'll make sure I lock up when I go and when I get back."

" 'Night, then," he said and left, locking the door carefully behind him.

Scarlet looked at the handsome face of Nathan Kendall. He and his wife had both been killed soon after he'd built the place, though their infant son had been spared. No one had ever been brought to justice for the murders. Some believed that the marauders he'd once ridden with had murdered them for revenge. Others said that Nathan's father-in-law — a United States marshal who had taken over the ranch and raised the child, and who had opposed the marriage — had been responsible. Scarlet hated to think that a father might have killed his own daughter, but she knew that such things still happened to this day.

Back then, there had been no way to find the killer or killers. Forensic science had barely existed, and this little plateau had been truly isolated. Estes Park had been a tiny town in the middle of nowhere, and The Stanley had yet to rise on the mountaintop across the way.

"You behave," she told the statue, wagging a finger at it. "I've been here two months and you've been good so far. Keep it up. I'm going out, and I don't want to find that you've messed up the place when I get back, okay?"

She ran upstairs and grabbed a sweatshirt and her shoulder bag, then went back down.

She looked around the museum before leaving. Everything was quiet, just as it should have been.

But she was still spooked by the fallen mannequin.

Maybe it bugged her so much because it had come right after she'd seen those horrible pictures on her camera. *Could* a camera be hacked? She simply didn't know.

She *did* know that she hadn't taken those pictures.

If only Diego was here, maybe she wouldn't feel so uneasy.

But Diego *wasn't* with her. She had made that choice, and now . . .

She regretted it every day.

But this was her life now. And she loved Estes Park and the museum and the Conway Ranch. Okay, a mannequin had fallen over. No biggie. Maybe someone had bumped into it the other day and it had been unsteady ever since, so her walking around upstairs was all it had taken to tip it over.

And the pictures . . .

Ben had undoubtedly been right. She'd been hacked or tricked or played for a fool, somehow. She had just bought it on impulse at the electronics shop at the Miami airport, so some jerk there had probably fooled with it.

But how would anyone at the airport have known that she would be staying in the mountains, much less right here at this very ranch? She was certain she hadn't said anything.

She let out a groan of self-disgust.

Getting shaky over this was ridiculous.

Scarlet stepped outside and started to close the door, but she paused and looked back, then said, "You all behave in here, do you understand me? I'm your best friend, preserving your history for posterity, so you need to listen to me, okay?"

Naturally, the mannequins did not reply.

She closed and locked the door and headed for her car, determined to think only about which restaurant to choose in town.

CHAPTER TWO

"The invitation will always stand," FBI agent Brett Cody said, glancing over at Diego. "I've got to say, amigo, you're the best partner I've ever had. So," he added, "even if you don't accept right now, we'll always want you in the Krewe. And that really means something. No one gets into the Krewe by asking — it's invitation only."

Diego looked over at his partner. Brett was finishing out his last day at the Miami field office; he'd transferred in to the FBI's Krewe of Hunters — the elite unit that investigated crimes that crossed over into the supernatural — when they'd closed a recent major case, a series of "zombie" murders that had rocked Miami.

Not only that, but Brett was also now engaged to Lara Mayhew, who'd been key in helping them solve the case — in part by calling in longtime friends who were part of the Krewe — after a truly whirlwind romance. Not that he should comment on that. He and Scarlet had gotten married less than two months after meeting.

Would they have made it, if not for the accident?

He didn't know. And there was no reason for him to doubt Brett and Lara just because of his own failure.

His mind returned to the recent case, when they'd been aided by the ghosts of several of the victims. Brett had actually been visited by them, and though he'd balked, he'd finally come to believe.

Diego wondered why he himself really had no problem believing in ghosts. He'd seen the murdered couple — Miguel and Maria Gomez — and never questioned the reality of the experience.

Then again, he'd grown up Cuban and Irish, and between the two sides of the family, he'd heard stories about ghosts, pixies, *chupacabras, espíritus* and all kinds of otherworldly beings. Maybe because of that, he hadn't even been shaken when he'd seen Miguel's and Maria's ghosts.

Maybe that was why he'd been invited to join the Krewe along with Brett. But the Krewe only had offices in New York City and Alexandria, with teams dispatched all over the country as needed, and for years he'd wanted to fight the good fight in his native Miami. Still, it was hard thinking that he and Brett would no longer be partners; they'd worked together for several years and had become good friends. He'd always felt safe knowing that Brett had his back.

Of course, for now Brett would be coming and going. Lara wasn't giving up her job at the Sea Life Center, so they were going to be long-distance lovers for a while. And he knew that the Bureau could transfer him anywhere, but unless his bosses forced him to leave Miami, he just wasn't ready to move yet.

"I'll keep it in mind," Diego assured Brett. "Let's finish this, shall we?"

That morning they'd arrested a human trafficker named Amelio Parva and his partner, known only as Pancho, in the act of betraying and abandoning at sea a group of Cuban refugees who'd paid handsomely to be brought safely ashore. With the bad guys in custody, the rescued refugees had been taken to a detainment center, where Diego and Brett had just arrived so they could sign off on the paperwork.

"Here's hoping they all get asylum," Brett muttered as he parked. The people being held here weren't criminals, but even so, the facility was surrounded by barbed wire.

Once inside, though, it wasn't so much a prison as it was a hospital.

Diego finished signing, then handed the papers to Brett and wandered over to look through a window into a social room, where the newest refugees had been allowed to gather.

Diego noted a woman sitting in a rocking chair. She was probably about seventy, gray-haired, very thin, with sharp blue eyes. She noticed him, too, and stared at him hard.

She lifted a hand and beckoned him over. He wasn't sure how, but he knew she had something important to say to him.

Brett touched his shoulder. "Ready to go?" he asked.

"Hang on. I just want to talk to someone for a minute," Diego said.

"I'm not sure if we should —" Brett began.

A doctor exited the room just then, and Diego went over to him. "Hey, we were on the detail that found these people today. Mind if I go speak to one of them?" Diego asked.

"I don't see why not," the doctor said.

As Diego stepped into the room, everyone stopped what they were doing to look at him.

The old woman was still watching him,

and she lifted her hand to him again.

He walked over and hunkered down by her chair.

She smiled — a toothless smile that was still somehow beautiful. *"Gracias, gracias,"* she said, then picked up his hand and brought it to her cheek. "I will live out my days here," she said in heavily accented English, smiling, and glancing up at Brett, who had followed and was standing just behind Diego. "Thanks to you." Then she met Diego's eyes again, her own bright and piercing. "But you — you must be very careful. And you must go where you are called. You understand? You will know. You must go where you are called."

He rose, smiling, his mind spinning with thoughts. He wondered if she had been considered a *bruja,* a witch, back home, if young girls had come to her, wanting to know if they would marry the loves of their lives.

"Thank you, senora," he told her. *"Muchas gracias."*

She smiled sweetly. "You are a good man, but sometimes that isn't enough. Listen with your soul and you will survive."

"Thank you, senora," he repeated.

He joined Brett, ready to leave, but stopped when she spoke again.

This time her voice was odd — it was suddenly deep and husky, and she sounded like a man. Stranger still, there wasn't a hint of an accent as she spoke.

"I just want to protect her, too."

Diego spun around to look at the old woman. Her head was down, her eyes closed, and she appeared to be sleeping. No one else was anywhere nearby.

He shook off his unease, and they left the facility. Diego was glad that his mother's parents had come to the States when they had, aware that there was trouble ahead.

"She liked you," Brett teased.

Diego shrugged. "What's not to like?"

"You know, you *are* divorced, and Lara has a lot of friends," Brett said.

Diego stopped walking and laughed. "No. No, no, no. I don't need to be fixed up. I can find my own dates if I want to. I'm cool, okay?"

"Whatever you say," Brett said.

Dinner was delicious. Scarlet had chosen one of the town's many barbecue restaurants, where she'd run into a number of people she'd already met casually. Afterward she headed down to one of the bars where a local band played live every night.

It was on her way there that the one flaw in the evening happened.

As Scarlet walked down the sidewalk, dodging people — including a number of children who asked their parents to buy them "moose droppings," the local name for little balls of chocolate aimed at the tourists — she was approached by a man in his thirties wearing jeans and a striped cowboy shirt. She would have found him handsome and appealing if the weird way he'd come on to her hadn't been so unnerving.

"You need to be careful," he told her without preamble.

"Excuse me?" she said in shock.

"You shouldn't be running around alone," he said. "You have to be careful. There's something going on."

"I'm always careful, thank you," she said, trying to get past him and be polite at the same time. "And what's going on is that you're bothering me."

"Be careful," he persisted.

He gripped her arm, but she was so upset she didn't feel anything. She paused and stared at him, then realized people were staring at *her*.

"Listen —" Scarlet began.

"You're one of us. And they'll come after

you. They'll want *you* dead, too."

Really shaken now, she jerked her arm away. "Leave me alone," she said firmly. People were still staring at her, and that upset her further. She loathed making a scene. She left him behind and hurried down the street.

Once she was in the bar, she felt fine. She'd been there several times before, and the drummer in the house band, Eddie Keye, had even asked her out. She'd told him the truth, that she wasn't ready to date again yet. He'd accepted her refusal with a smile, and they'd become friends. She waved to him as she entered, then took a seat in the corner, where he joined her during the break between sets and she told him about her strange encounter.

When the band had finished for the night, Eddie walked her to her car. He assured her that he would deck the guy if they ran into him again. "Probably just a drunk," he said.

Scarlet shook her head. "He didn't seem drunk."

"A loony, then," he said reassuringly.

They'd reached her car by then, and she thanked him for escorting her, then hesitated. "It's just been a weird day," she said, and told him about the strange pictures on her camera.

"Did it come with a memory card? They might have been there when you bought it," he said. "Some practical joker's idea of funny. I say you should just chalk it up to the fact that the world is crazy and let it go."

It was good advice. "I'll do that," she promised.

"Drive safe, and call me when you're ready to hit the trail to romance again," he told her cheerfully.

"You're my number one guy," she assured him.

She waved to Eddie and started the car, wondering why she still felt so uncomfortable.

Scarlet had the feeling that someone was watching her. Not the man who had approached her before. Someone different. Someone who wouldn't come up to her but would stalk her — and then pounce.

She shook off the feeling, telling herself she was just feeling residual anxiety after the strange events of the day.

It was time for bed.

She drove carefully up the steep winding road to the ranch. She was still becoming accustomed to getting around here and was dreading her first winter.

She felt lighter heading back, convinced

that someone had messed with the camera, and that natural vibrations, whether in the earth or the museum itself, had toppled the mannequin. No big deal.

The night was beautiful and very dark. She drove slowly and was glad of it when a buck leaped onto the road and stopped directly in front of her. He simply stood there, caught in her headlights.

"Think maybe you could move now?" she said after a long moment.

When he didn't budge, she gave her horn a tap and was grateful when he bounded off into the surrounding woods.

She drove on, frowning as she saw what seemed to be a sea of light at the Conway Ranch.

There were eleven guests staying there, but she hadn't heard anything about a campfire planned for that night. As she drew closer, she realized that the glow seemed to come from a multitude of headlights.

Her heart leaped into her throat when she got close enough to see that five cop cars and an ambulance with lights ablaze were parked on the property. A cop standing in the driveway motioned her to a stop and gestured for her to roll down her window.

"Who are you and what are you doing here?" he asked.

"I'm Scarlet Barlow. I work at the museum and live above it. What's happened?" she asked anxiously. "Ben and Trisha. Are they okay?"

He nodded to her gravely. "Yes, the owners are all right."

"What's happened?" she persisted.

"May I have your ID, please?"

She handed it over. He looked from it to her, aiming his flashlight at her face and making her blink.

"Says here your name is McCullough."

"I'm divorced. I haven't changed my ID yet," she told him. "See? My license says Scarlet Barlow McCullough."

He was looking at her as if she was a hardened criminal. "They're definitely going to want to talk to you," he said.

"They?"

"The detectives."

"But —"

"You're the one with the camera. The one who took pictures of dead people. The pictures that mysteriously disappeared, right?" he asked, his voice hard-edged.

"Someone messed with my camera, yes, but I don't see why that calls for police response."

"Really? Not when two people have been murdered exactly the way your boss says

46

they were in the pictures you showed him? Park your car, please, then follow me. Lieutenant Gray is going to want to see you, pronto."

Scarlet had advanced degrees in history and archaeology; she had worked at the Metropolitan Museum of Art in New York and on an important dig in South Florida. She was bright, fun, cheerful, beautiful and eager for whatever life brought.

She did not tend to hysteria or tears.

Given all that, Diego wasn't sure how or why he knew instinctively when he answered the phone that she was going to be on the other end.

They were having a small farewell party for Brett at Sea Life, the dolphin facility where Lara Mayhew worked. Brett was flying to DC the next day for orientation. There was talk of him setting up a small Miami office for the Krewe, and if that happened Diego thought maybe he would take them up on their invitation, after all. Meanwhile, he had a party to enjoy.

The food had been catered and set up outside under a large tent. They'd visited the dolphins down at the lagoon earlier, and now everyone was just talking idly.

And yet, when his phone rang, Diego was

instantly alert, somehow sure it was going to be his ex-wife.

She'd moved to Colorado, and he hadn't let her see the ache in his heart when she'd told him she was going.

"Scarlet?" he said without even looking at the caller ID, stepping out into the darkness beneath a sea grape tree.

"Diego, yes, it's me."

"How are you? Are you all right?" he asked her anxiously.

"I'm . . . oh, Diego, I'm so sorry to bother you, but I'm in real trouble."

"What did you do?"

"Nothing!" She sounded indignant, even angry.

That was good, he thought. "Then what happened?"

"Two people were murdered, and they think . . . they think I was involved!"

"Why?"

"My camera. The views here are gorgeous, so I bought a good camera at the Miami airport before my flight out. It was working fine, but then today it took pictures of things that weren't there. Bodies. Dead bodies. And then they disappeared."

"The bodies?"

"The pictures!" she said. "The thing is, Ben saw them. Ben Kendall, my boss. He

48

didn't mean to get me in trouble, he was just so stunned when the bodies were found that he blurted it out about the pictures without thinking. They were killed right here at the ranch. They weren't guests, and so far no one knows who they are or why they were here. From what I saw on the camera and what the cops have said, the man was cut to shreds and shot, and the woman was just shot. And they think I did it! It's horrible. And now I'm at the police station, and all I could think to do was call you."

"They think you did it?" he asked, incredulous. Scarlet wasn't perfect, and she could certainly get good and angry. But murder? Never.

"Okay, let me get this straight. They're holding you on suspicion of murder because of pictures that were on your camera but that aren't there now?" Diego asked.

"Yes."

"Then they have nothing."

"Except Ben saw the pictures, too, and he told the police about them, so they think I erased them."

"They need to get the camera to a police tech and examine the memory card."

"They already have."

"And they're still holding you?"

"Yes!"

"I'll be there as soon as I can. I'll make some calls, get the right people involved. Just don't go snapping at anyone until I get there and can straighten things out."

"I don't snap."

"You do when your pride is hurt. But don't let them get to you, okay? Just be honest with them."

"Yes, of course."

"I'll be there," he promised.

"Thank you," she whispered.

And then she was gone.

He suddenly found himself thinking about the refugees they had rescued and the words the old woman had said to him.

But you — you must be very careful. And you must go where you are called. You understand? You will know. You must go where you are called.

He'd always been open to possibilities in life, but he'd never been superstitious or a believer in omens.

But now . . .

It was time to join the Krewe.

He headed back inside to find Brett, and he prayed that the Krewe really did operate as efficiently and swiftly as he'd heard.

Because with or without official benediction, he was heading west.

He found Brett talking to Matt Bosworth, a longtime Krewe agent, and pulled them aside.

"This Krewe thing — I want in. But first I need help."

"What is it?" Brett asked.

"I've got to get to Estes Park, Colorado, fast. As fast as possible. It's Scarlet. She's in trouble. They're holding her for murder."

Diego was amazed at the speed with which things happened after that. In short order their transport was set up for early the following morning, and he still had a few hours left to sleep. Luckily he'd taught himself how to sleep in any circumstances, even in the middle of a case.

But that night his sleep was disjointed and troubled. His dreams were of the old woman, and of Scarlet walking toward him through a fog.

A fog filled with the faces of the nameless dead.

The one place Scarlet had never expected to be in Estes Park was an interrogation room at the police station.

She understood that she wasn't under arrest, at least not yet. Officially, she had only been asked in for questioning. But the questioning, she quickly realized, was intended to trip her up and lead to her arrest.

Her camera was with the police techs, and she really did understand why they suspected her and didn't blame Ben for being so shocked that he hadn't been able to stop himself from talking about the pictures. She hadn't been allowed to speak with him, but she had seen him and Trisha, arm in arm, standing on the porch together, looking as if they'd been hit by a sledgehammer.

Meanwhile, she was reeling from the fact that two people had been found murdered right where the majestic elk had been standing earlier. Right where the bodies had been in the pictures.

And then there was that wacko in town who had warned her to be careful and had said she was "one of us," whatever that might mean.

In one day, her world had gone mad.

"Tell me again about your day, Mrs. McCullough," her interrogator said. Lieutenant Gray was somewhere between thirty-five and forty. He'd started out in a suit, but his jacket was gone now, his sleeves rolled up. His hair was military short, and his eyes were tired, his face haggard. His name fit him very well, she thought.

Though she had told him a dozen times

that she was divorced, he insisted on calling her Mrs. McCullough. Somehow it seemed especially painful to hear that name tonight.

They never would have treated her like this if Diego was there, she thought.

And it was true. He would have stopped them cold.

She had told Lieutenant Gray as much. He hadn't been impressed.

"The guy divorced you, huh?" he'd said at one point, his tone implying that whoever her husband had been, he'd been smart to separate from her.

She felt like a little kid, desperately hoping that someone bigger and tougher really would come to defend her.

And he would come, wouldn't he? She'd made him her first phone call, and miraculously, he'd answered. He'd certainly sounded as if he intended to get here as soon as possible.

By morning, she hoped.

"Mrs. McCullough?" Gray repeated. "Pay attention. Tell me about your day again."

"I woke up. I showered. I made tea. I had a bowl of cereal. I checked my email," Scarlet said. "I went downstairs and spent the morning cataloging a display case of Civil War weapons. I inspected each for its condition, which I noted in the records. I went through the old display cards to find out when each piece was received by the museum. At noon I went back upstairs to my apartment and ate a tuna fish sandwich. No, wait, it was closer to twelve thirty, I think. But the sandwich was definitely tuna," she said, trying very hard to maintain her temper. "At one o'clock I was back downstairs. I've been making notes on the different mannequins, their composition, the year they were donated to or commissioned by the museum or, before the museum's funding, by the current owner of the Conway Ranch during the years when it was only a private collection. I began working on that project soon after I got here, about two months ago."

"How late did you work?" he asked her.

"At four thirty I decided it was time to quit for the day. I went back upstairs and got my camera — I purchased it at the airport in Miami when I was coming out here. I have the receipt somewhere in the apartment. Wait — no," she added, furrowing her brows. "I think it was more like four forty-five. And I didn't go outside right away. I checked my email again first. Then I went out to take pictures. I saw a bull elk, who was practically posing for me. After that I went back to the ranch, where I talked to Ben Kendall. On the way I saw Angus Fillmore, Terry Ballantree and the Bartons down by the stables. Oh, and . . ."

"And?" he prompted.

"Horses," she said gravely. "There were horses at the stables."

He sat back. "I don't think you understand the trouble you're in," he said severely.

She shook her head. "Why? Over pictures that don't exist? That we thought we saw hours before the murders probably took place?"

She didn't know that for a fact, but it had to be true. There certainly hadn't been any bodies there when she'd taken the pictures.

He pointed a finger at her. "Ben Kendall saw those pictures. They existed — and you erased them as soon as you realized what you'd shown him."

"Do you want me to tell you about the rest of my day again?" she asked.

"Go on — but we might be where we need to be already."

"You have to be kidding."

"Do I look like I'm joking?"

"I went back to the museum. I went upstairs. I heard a thump. I called Ben, wondering if he'd given the key to someone so they could look around the museum. He said he hadn't. Then he came over and we

55

looked around together. We saw that the statue of Nathan Kendall had fallen over, so we picked it up. He talked about putting in an alarm system, then went back to the house. I got my things and went into town for dinner. I can give you a list of the places I went and the people I talked to."

He shoved a pad and pencil toward her. "I'll take it," he said grimly.

"I'll be happy to make you a list, but this is ridiculous. I spoke with my ex-husband, and I am not lying to you, he's a federal agent. He's on his way here, and he'll —"

She stopped abruptly. *And he'll show you who's boss!* she'd almost said. Now she wasn't just thinking like a scared child, she was sounding like one.

"He'll speak to your superiors and straighten everything out," she said.

Gray shrugged. "Ex-husband?" he said. "I'm sure he's just soaring his way right here."

She felt her cheeks burn.

He didn't know Diego. Diego would come.

There was a tap at the door. Lieutenant Gray scowled at her and went to answer it, leaving her alone in the interrogation room. She wondered if people were watching her from behind the glass, the way they did on TV.

She took the pad and began to write. A moment later, Lieutenant Gray, looking disgruntled, returned to the room.

"You can go," he told her.

"Just like that?" she asked surprised.

"I can lock you up for twenty-four hours if you'd rather."

She stood, anxious to leave. He opened the door for her.

As she passed him, she paused. "Why are you letting me go? It's not because you believe me."

"No," he admitted. "My captain said to let you out. They can't find anything on your camera to show those pictures were ever there. And," he added grudgingly, "you were seen in town. Specifically, people remembered seeing you on the street, talking to yourself."

"I was *not* talking to myself!" she protested.

Gray shrugged. "One of my own men actually saw you arguing with the air."

"That's ridiculous. I was stopped by a strange man and —"

Gray waved a hand, cutting her off. "You want me to hold you for twenty-four hours?"

"No!"

"Then leave. But I'll be watching you. Even if that ex of yours shows up."

"Thank you for a lovely evening," she told him, chin held high.

She felt as if everyone was watching her as she walked through the station and out to the street. When she reached the sidewalk, she realized she didn't have her car — she'd arrived in a police car.

Just as she thought about the best place to catch a cab, she saw that the Kendalls were there, Trisha standing still and watching as Ben paced. She was about to say something when Trisha saw her and came running over.

"Scarlet! This is so awful. Ben is beside himself. They've grilled him, too, but they didn't hold him like they did you."

Ben had reached them by that point. "Scarlet, I'm so sorry. When the cops told me about the murders, I — I wasn't thinking. All I could think of was the pictures, and I said . . . Oh, God, I'm so sorry."

"Both of you, please don't worry," she said. "It's over."

"I'm sure they know you could never do anything like that," Trisha said.

"They don't, but they do know I was in town at the time of the murders, and they couldn't find anything in the camera. They didn't give it back yet, but . . . it's over, it's okay."

It really wasn't over, she knew, but it was well past midnight and they were all ready to keel over. "What about the ranch?" she asked. "Who's looking after the guests?"

Ben waved a hand dismissively. "Linda has the house, and Angus is down at the stables. Six of the guests left, too upset by what happened to stay on. Only Mr. Ballantree, the Bartons and Gigi and Clark Levin are still here."

"What *did* happen?" Scarlet asked. "I mean . . . I know two people were killed but who and how and . . . ?" Her voice trailed off.

"Let's get to the car," Trisha suggested. She was the perfect wife for Ben, Scarlet thought. They were lovely people separately as well as great together. Trisha was ready to go along with whatever people wanted, but she was also quick to take charge when she needed to. Tall, lean and athletic, with short gray hair, she fit right in on the ranch.

Together they hurried down the street to the parking lot.

Trisha drove, and she glanced at Scarlet in the rearview mirror and said, "Ben saw them — the bodies, I mean — from a distance, but he couldn't tell what he was

59

seeing, just that something was there. He went to see what it was, and then he called the police on his cell. He waited there for them, and I kept people away."

"It was a mess," Ben said. "Blood everywhere. He was all cut up, and shot, too. The woman . . . she was just shot."

They were all silent after that, until they neared the ranch and Trisha said, "You're more than welcome to stay at the main house, you know, Scarlet."

"I'm fine, really. Only you and Ben have keys to the museum, and I'll be sure to lock up. I'm way too tired to pack up and move right now," Scarlet said. "But thank you."

There was silence for a minute in the car, and then Trisha said, "I hope you had a nice night in town. I mean, before all this happened."

"Nice and a little weird," Scarlet said.

"How so?" Ben asked.

"Just some guy pestering me on the street. But I ran into some friends, and one of them walked me to my car."

"Maybe something is going on with the planets," Trisha said, shaking her head.

Scarlet took a deep breath and then asked again, "Who were they — the couple who were killed?"

"We don't know. The police haven't

released that information yet, pending notification of next of kin," Trisha informed her.

"Young? Old?"

"I didn't — I didn't really look," Ben said. "I just turned the other way and called 911."

They were quiet again. They'd reached the ranch. None of them looked toward the woods as they parked and got out of the car.

Trisha slipped her arm around her husband's. "Let's see that Scarlet gets upstairs safely. We'll just walk through the museum and make sure no one's there."

"That would be great," Scarlet said. "Thanks."

Ben opened the door to the building. Trisha hit the lights. They walked through the museum. It was empty.

Empty, of course, except for the stationary residents standing on their pedestals, bearing silent witness to the night.

"Upstairs," Trisha said, and started walking up. Ben followed her.

Scarlet followed Ben, then paused at the foot of the stairs, staring at the mannequin of Nathan Kendall.

If the artist's rendering had been a true one, he'd been a handsome man. He'd been captured in time in his early thirties, the age he'd been when he'd died.

His eyes seemed to be wise and world-weary. They'd been painted blue.

For a moment she almost felt as if he would speak.

She forced herself to reach out and touch the statue.

Wood. It was made of wood.

"Scarlet?" Trisha called.

"Coming!"

"We're right next door," Trisha reminded Scarlet as she reached the top of the stairs. "And you really are more than welcome there."

"I know," Scarlet said. "Thank you. And thank you for waiting for me and driving me home." She hesitated. "I asked an old friend out here to help. My ex-husband, actually. He's with the FBI. Do you mind?"

"Mind?" Ben asked. "I think that's great."

"I'm guessing his partner will be coming with him. They should be here tomorrow, I hope. Sometime in the morning."

"Wonderful. We'll get some rooms ready for them," Trisha said. "For now, let's check out this whole place, just for safety's sake."

They went together from room to room, then wound up in the kitchen, staring at one another.

With everything seemingly safe and nothing more to be done that night, an exhausted Scarlet followed them downstairs and locked up behind them, then made her way back up to her apartment.

She couldn't help wondering, though, whether she really was going to be all right, or if maybe she should have agreed to sleep at the main house.

After all, two people had been brutally murdered just where the mountain rose to meet the Conway Ranch. She shouldn't be alone.

But she was exhausted, so exhausted that she didn't even take off her clothes as she pitched down on the bed.

It wasn't over, she thought. Not for her. Lieutenant Gray had said so.

But Diego was coming. He had said that he would, and he was always true to his word.

She thought she would never sleep, as her distraught mind kept going over the events of the day.

The pictures on her camera . . .

And then two people dead just like the people in the photos . . .

And then *she'd* been interrogated. The kid who had never stolen so much as a piece of gum.

To her amazement, her eyes finally closed

and her mind began to shut down. She was just so tired.

But her dreams were troubled . . .

Blood was everywhere in her mind's eye. She could see the dead, and they could see her. She felt their eyes, and the intensity of their regard sent chills up her spine . . .

Restless, she awoke. She walked into the kitchen and made herself a cup of chamomile tea. At the kitchen table, she sat sipping it, listening. The museum was quiet. The door below was locked.

Diego would be here soon.

She finished her tea, walked to the window and looked out. Everything was peaceful.

Bizarrely peaceful, given what had happened there in the woods.

And as she stood there, she felt once again that she was being watched.

She told herself that was foolish. "I am alone," she said into the empty air.

The feeling persisted, but she forced herself back to bed, leaving the door to her room ajar so that she could hear anything that went on in the museum.

Surprisingly, she fell asleep easily, and so deeply that she was untroubled by dreams.

The next thing she knew, she heard birds.

She smiled slightly, waking up. It was nice here, that sound of birds in the morning, with the feel of the sun, strong and warm at this time of year.

She opened her eyes, feeling as if everything would be all right.

Then she realized someone was standing at the foot of her bed, and a scream tore from her lips.

She stopped with a gasp when she saw who that someone was.

The decidedly not-alive statue of Nathan Kendall was staring down at her.

CHAPTER THREE

Diego wondered why he had ever turned down an invitation to join the Krewe of Hunters.

By 6:00 a.m. he was aboard a private plane with Brett Cody, along with Krewe agents — and lovers — Meg Murray and Matt Bosworth. They were flying out via a friend of Adam Harrison's, the man who had established and still ran the Krewe. Nothing they were doing was official yet — and might never be, Matt had reminded him. Until the local authorities asked for their help, they couldn't officially give it, but that didn't mean they couldn't run their own investigation.

That was one of the greatest assets of the Krewe. Their purpose was to investigate when there were strange and otherworldly elements to a crime, but they operated independently, beholden to no one and able to operate freely.

All Diego really knew was that he was incredibly grateful that he had been able to ask for assistance, and that it could so quickly and easily be granted.

"Adam will be coming out himself," Matt had told Diego earlier. "Estes Park is apparently one of his favorite places in the world. He's a major supporter of our national parks, and Rocky Mountain National Park is one of his favorites."

Diego was glad to have a seasoned agent like Matt on the case. Meg was still new — not even a year out of the academy — but she was a rising star, and since the Krewe had its own rules, their personal relationship was no barrier to the two of them working together.

All they'd had to do was make a few phone calls to set everything in motion. Special Agent Angela Hawkins — wife of Jackson Crow, their official field director — had made travel arrangements for them and found out everything the police knew so far regarding the murders at the Conway Ranch.

The dead couple was Candace and Larry Parker, who'd been visiting the area from their home in Denver. They had apparently headed out to Estes Park without hotel reservations for a lodge; one supposition was that they'd been hiking up to the Conway Ranch to see if there was a vacancy.

Based on bark found in abrasions on his back and blood found on a nearby tree, Larry Parker had been strung up and had his torso ripped repeatedly by a bowie knife or something similar, and then he'd been shot in the head. Candace had been shot in the gut and bled out in about twenty minutes, according to the medical examiner's estimate.

Bertram — aka Ben — Kendall had found the bodies at approximately 10:30 p.m. The medical examiner could narrow the time of death down to about an hour — sometime between eight and nine the night before, Monday, a beautiful, cool October evening.

There were more details about the insects and woodland creatures that had already gone to work before the bodies were found. Diego read the reports with a careful and practiced eye.

The police had questioned one Scarlet Barlow McCullough regarding reports of her having had in her possession a camera with pictures of a similar murder scene, pictures that were no longer on the memory card. The camera had been thoroughly examined by the police techs and no evidence of any such pictures had been found, nor could they find any indication that the camera might have been tampered with. Further, witnesses had been found to corroborate her claim that she had gone into town to eat and visit a local bar at the time of the murders. The guests and staff of the Conway Ranch had been questioned, as well. No one had seen the victims or anything suspicious, but they'd all been asked to remain in the area for the next twenty-four hours, though a number of the guests had elected to check out and rebook elsewhere.

The most interesting aspect of the case — one that might have tightened the noose around Scarlet's neck if not for her solid alibi — was that the bullets had come from a vintage Colt revolver.

Antique bullets and casings.

Like the ones in the museum where she worked.

Not that the museum was a model of security. It was part of a rustic mountaintop resort. The door locks could be picked by anyone with a modicum of skill. The only security on the property came from the cats in the stables, and they only kept the place secure against mice.

They touched down in Denver at 10:00 a.m. The drive out to Estes Park was about an hour, give or take, depending on traffic.

Diego knew that Scarlet had been released from police custody and was back at the ranch. He called her cell to let her know that they were on their way.

She didn't sound at all like herself. Her voice was raspy and anxious.

"Just hang in there, okay?" he told her. "Brett and a couple of agents from a special unit are with me, and we'll be there in an hour."

"Of course," she told him, then added, "Just hurry. Please."

As if he hadn't been concerned enough before, he thought.

He hadn't been to Colorado, and despite his eagerness to reach Scarlet and make sure she really was all right, he couldn't help noticing how beautiful the scenery was as they moved higher into the Rocky Mountains. They passed through charming small towns and what was obviously horse country, and saw ads for businesses dedicated to celebrating the Old West. Wild Bill Hickok had a museum dedicated to him, and the casinos all seemed to have modeled themselves on old mining towns.

But nothing could detract from the raw and even savage beauty of the land, soaring rock faces and crystalline waters that gleamed in the sunlight as they climbed toward Estes Park.

From the road, he could see the famous Stanley Hotel, gleaming in the sunlight.

Finally the road curved, they passed through a break in the trees and arrived at the Conway Ranch. Diego let out a breath he hadn't realized he'd been holding.

The main house was built of wood and handsomely varnished in its natural shade. To the left were the museum and stables, both nicely restored, as well. To the right, two more outbuildings — the smokehouse and the bunkhouse.

And surrounding everything was a dense forest that draped like a cloak over the mountain to the valley below.

Up the mountain he could see the bright yellow crime-scene tape, though the bodies were long gone. A lone officer sat in a patrol car in the parking lot, his head back and his fingers tapping on the steering wheel, presumably keeping time to whatever music the radio was playing.

Matt, who was driving, pulled up out front. Yes, everything here was magnificent, Diego thought, but the only nature he was interested in was the force of nature that was Scarlet.

■ ■ ■ ■

Of course Scarlet had screamed as if every hellhound from the dark unknown had come after her.

And of course no one heard her.

Something she would need to remember.

She'd leaped from the bed, staring at the thing in terror, all the while telling herself it was a mannequin, just a damned mannequin.

That meant someone alive and stealthy had carried it up the stairs and left it there to terrify her. But the doors had been locked, and only she, Ben and Trisha had keys.

After her initial shock of fear, her instinct had warned her that someone might still be in the building with her, lurking, waiting . . .

Well, they would know, after the way she had screamed, that she was now awake.

Were they waiting for her?

Next she thought of a weapon. She could grab a big knife from the kitchen. She wished she was a black belt, but she wasn't.

What she needed was a gun.

The place was full of guns, of course.

But they were all downstairs.

She did have one thing. Her spear gun.

She'd brought it with her when she moved, since she didn't own enough stuff to make renting a storage locker worthwhile. She'd gotten the spear gun in case of a visit from a too-inquisitive shark when she went diving, one of the things she loved about being a Floridian.

It was in her closet. Staring warily at the mannequin, as if half believing it could move on its own, she backed over to the closet and found the spear gun, then clicked the spear into the mechanism.

Ridiculous.

She lifted the gun toward the mannequin. "Don't you move — and I mean it," she said.

The effigy of Nathan Kendall just stared back at her.

She slipped from the room and into the kitchen, then down the hall to the living room and then on into the second bedroom. No one.

She dared to go downstairs. Inch by inch she swept the place — nothing had changed.

Nothing, of course, except that the pedestal near the stairs where Nathan Kendall usually stood was empty.

A key started to turn in the lock of the front door. She was standing there in flannel pajamas, a spear gun in her hand.

"Scarlet, coming in!" someone called. It was Ben.

In that moment she stood there as different scenarios flashed through her mind like wildfire.

Tell Ben what had happened? Accuse him or Trisha of having moved a mannequin upstairs in the middle of the night to give her a heart attack? Accuse them of giving someone else a key?

Someone was guilty of something, that much she knew.

Ben had found the bodies.

Could Ben have killed someone? Surely not.

Then she remembered her feeling of being watched during the night. Had someone really been out there observing her? Had that someone gotten in and brought the mannequin upstairs?

Was that someone Ben?

She had to keep her wits about her, had to keep silent. It was broad daylight now. Even if he was a killer, surely Ben wouldn't dare do violence right here in his own museum.

But if she told him what had happened . . .

She could wind up back at the police station with everyone thinking she was a lunatic, at the very least.

74

"Hang on!" she called. "Let me just throw on a robe."

She raced back up the stairs, threw on her robe, then struggled to carry Nathan into the living room, hoping she could keep Ben from noticing his absence from his usual spot.

She ran to the top of the stairs, amazed at what she had done. She had left her fingerprints all over the damn thing, and now she was going to pretend that it had never appeared at the foot of her bed.

"Scarlet?" Ben called as she heard the museum door open.

At that moment her cell phone rang. Diego.

An hour, just one hour, and he would be there!

She ran back down the stairs and through the museum, breathless as she came face-to-face with Ben.

He looked at her with surprise. "I woke you up. I'm so sorry. I forgot how late it was when we got in. I just came by to make sure you really are okay after yesterday."

"I'm fine. What about you and Trisha?"

He nodded. "We're going to be okay, though with the news rocketing around town and a cop car in front of the house, we won't be too busy for a while."

"Everything will be all right eventually, Ben, I promise. They'll catch the person who did this and prove it had nothing to do with the ranch, and everything will go back to normal. Just hang in there, okay?" she added quietly.

He grinned ruefully. "I was a stockbroker, remember? I'm used to life on the roller coaster. We'll be good. It's just that I love this place so much."

"And you *should* love it," Scarlet said. "Spend more time during the next few days riding the trails. Hike."

He brightened. "I can help you out here in the museum."

She opened her mouth, trying to figure out just how to answer him.

She didn't have to; the front door opened again and Trisha walked in. "Scarlet, you doing all right?" she asked.

Scarlet nodded. "I just got up."

"I can see that," Trisha said with a smile. "Want us to hang around down here while you go upstairs and shower?" She looked toward the stairs as she spoke, and her eyes widened. "Where's Nathan?" she asked, almost as if the mannequin was a living, breathing man who might have headed out for a morning walk.

"I have him upstairs," Scarlet said. "I'm

76

studying his construction. I think he was carved in the 1870s but I'm trying to ascertain who the artist might have been."

"You moved him upstairs?" Trisha asked.

"Yeah, I'm stronger than I look," Scarlet said lightly. "But, it's such a great figure, I want to know more about it."

"People whittled in these mountains all the time, so if you don't find a signature or anything, it won't be surprising. Back then, once the snow fell, there wasn't much to do except sit around the fire and whittle," Ben said.

"That's always true in my line of work," Scarlet said. "Sometimes we can find the answers, sometimes we can't. But yes, I'd feel more secure if I knew the two of you were here while I was getting ready. Thank you. Come on up. Nathan Kendall's in the living room, if you feel like visiting him."

She turned and fled up the stairs, wondering for a minute if she'd asked a pair of psychotic killers to stand guard while she showered.

No. The idea that Ben and Trisha could be killers was ridiculous.

More ridiculous than that a mannequin had moved on its own?

She winced and silently prayed that Diego would arrive soon.

77

Taking a deep breath, she told herself that she had to behave normally. Still, she locked the door to her room. Her mind was racing, filled with all the crazy things that had happened in less than twenty-four hours.

Ben and Trisha, the murders, the mannequin at the foot of the bed, her feeling of being watched, the pictures, the man who had stopped her in town . . .

She finally turned on the water.

But even in the shower, she kept peeking around the curtain, making sure that Nathan didn't walk in to surprise her when she stepped out.

She was more relieved than she liked to admit when he didn't make another appearance.

Clean and dressed, she entered the living room. Nathan Kendall was still right where she had put him, and Ben and Trisha were talking about his merits. Despite herself, she couldn't help feeling suspicious.

Trisha turned to her with a smile. "I took the liberty of putting coffee on," she said. "Or would you rather have tea?"

"I'm happy with either," Scarlet assured her. "And no liberty — you own this place."

"But we've given you the apartment as part of your employee package," Ben said.

"That means we're guests in here right now."

"Then I should be getting you coffee," Scarlet said. "And I hope you don't mind, but Diego, my ex, has three other agents with him. I can ask them to stay somewhere else if you'd rather."

"Four FBI agents to watch over us?" Trish asked. "I don't mind in the least. In fact, I'm thrilled."

"We have an almost empty bed-and-breakfast," Ben said drily. "Not a problem at all."

"They should be here soon. While we're waiting, I'll whip up omelets," Scarlet said. "I'm actually a pretty good cook," she promised.

She looked at her watch and realized that she didn't want to be alone in the museum.

And once Diego and his friends got here, did she tell him that either one or both of her employers might be a psychotic killer, or else a mannequin had moved all by itself? Even if he didn't think she was the killer, she really didn't want him thinking she was crazy.

That thought made her smile fade as she looked at Ben and Trisha.

"Any more news on the couple who were killed?" she asked.

"The police are still withholding identification pending notification of next of kin," Ben said. "But the town is buzzing with speculation. Scarlet," he said, clearly upset, "I saw them. I saw those pictures, and then I saw *them*. I have to admit, it's unnerving to think about something like that happening right here on the ranch."

"It can't have anything to do with us," Trisha whispered.

"No, of course not," Ben said. "But I'm a grown man and I have to say, I'm glad I keep a gun in the house, because I'm more than a little scared."

So am I, Scarlet thought.

But Diego was coming, and he would find a way to make everything right.

Now, looking at Ben's stricken expression, she decided she had to be crazy to think he and Trisha could have had anything to do with the deaths. And if they were after her, they could have killed her at any time.

Like the person who had moved the mannequin. That person could have killed her last night if he'd wanted to.

Unless the mannequin *had* moved on its own.

Okay, she told herself, that was enough of that. If she kept thinking along those lines *she* would start thinking she was crazy.

Diego and his friends would be there soon. All she had to do was hold on until then.

"I'll make breakfast," she said.

And then she fled to the kitchen to concentrate on creating omelets.

The minute Diego saw Scarlet come running out the door of the museum, eyes anxious and hopeful, he felt his muscles tighten, and an aching pulse began to pound through him. He wondered how things could have gone so wrong between the two of them when they'd loved each other so much.

Watching her run to him, blue eyes wide, chestnut hair streaming out behind her, he felt the same rush in his veins that he'd felt the first time he'd seen her. Her features were alive with intelligence, her movements the epitome of grace, even when fear, relief and a dozen other emotions were fighting for expression.

His love for her was as strong as ever, but she'd needed to leave him, and he'd never stood in the way of her happiness.

She'd gone through a miscarriage alone, while he had been on a case. In his defense, she'd never told him that she was pregnant. She'd been waiting for a special moment, a moment that had never happened, because he'd been so buried in his case. They'd tried to arrange a romantic evening, but somehow it had never happened.

And then it had been too late.

He noticed the attractive older couple who followed her out. He realized they must be Ben and Trisha Kendall.

Scarlet hurried toward the car, and he couldn't help noticing that her jeans and a blue sweater heightened the color of her eyes, which looked as clear and pristine as the sky.

He stepped out of the car, determined to be calm and professional, to keep his emotional distance and remember that she had only called him because she was in trouble.

She wasn't really in trouble anymore, he reminded himself; she'd been released. But the expression on her face told him that she was still upset about something, and he wondered what it could be.

To his astonishment, she threw herself into his arms.

For just a minute he allowed himself to pretend it was because she still loved him, and he reveled in the scent and feel of her. She smelled of the same shampoo she'd always loved, mixed with a light perfume.

She was warm and soft, and it was the most difficult thing in the world to tell his body that this embrace wasn't a prelude to more.

He held her tightly. She was trembling almost imperceptibly, but he could tell that she was scared, really scared, and Scarlet didn't scare easily. In her day she had crawled through Egyptian tombs, excavated Native American burial mounds and explored what many might consider to be the creepiest places on earth.

He held her, wishing he could somehow infuse her with some of his own strength.

Despite himself, he remembered, not just in his mind's eye but deep in his soul, the way they had somehow known instantly when they'd met that they were meant to be together. The way they had dated and fallen so quickly into one another's arms, and then into love. He remembered her laughter when she'd greeted him the night of his last birthday, wearing a bow tie, stiletto heels and nothing else. He would never forget the way she moved against him, with him, like a sweet, sensual heat wave.

But marriage was more than desire and even love, and they had somehow allowed it to fall apart.

Her call. But his fault, he knew. He'd been so blind. She had known that his work was important to him, of course, and she had never protested his long absences or said anything about the late hours as he let his career become all-consuming. He hadn't even realized that she'd slowly stopped talking to him because he never talked back, not about anything important. He didn't see what he was doing, how much he was gone . . . and that nights together, no matter how passionate, didn't make up for the things that went unsaid.

At last she pulled away and he felt her absence like a physical pain.

Brett cleared his throat and Scarlet turned to greet him. They had always gotten along well, and now she smiled, then gave him a big hug, as well.

"Thank you for coming," she said to Brett, and then she turned to the others, her eyes questioning.

Diego quickly introduced them. "Scarlet, these are Special Agents Matt Bosworth and Meg Murray. We met when they came down to Miami to work a case, and now Brett and I have transferred to their unit."

She thanked them both for coming, then turned to the older couple and said, "Ben and Trisha Kendall, owners of this fantastic place."

"Rattled owners, at the moment," Ben

said, shaking Diego's hand.

"This place is absolutely beautiful," Meg said.

"It is — or *was*," Trisha said.

"One thing we've learned," Matt said, "is that you can't let what happens somewhere affect your feelings about it. This place *is* beautiful, and I think I speak for all of us when I say we're not only glad to be here to help, but also to get a chance to enjoy the area."

"In fact, assuming you don't mind," Brett said to Ben and Trisha, "my fiancée is coming for the weekend."

"You're engaged? That's wonderful!" Scarlet said. "Is she FBI, too?"

"No, she handles media relations for the Sea Life Center," Brett told her.

Diego took control of the conversation then, taking refuge from his reawakened feelings in the details of the job. "Just so you know," he explained, "we're not here officially, though in a little while we're going to head down to the police station and see if Adam Harrison, the director of our unit, has managed to arrange an in for us." He turned to Ben and Trisha. "I don't know how many rooms you have available, but I think he plans on coming out, too."

"And we're all paying guests," Meg added.

"Not necessary," Ben said.

"Maybe not, but it only makes sense. Whenever we travel for a case, we have to stay somewhere," Diego said.

"Save the taxpayers' money," Ben told him, smiling as he put his arm around his wife's shoulders. "We're not the Vanderbilts but I invested wisely over the years. We run this place because we love it, not because we need the income."

"We'll let you and Adam hash that out when he gets here. Right now, we need to take a look at the crime scene, then check in at the police station and introduce ourselves," Brett said.

"You don't want to see the whole place first?" Trisha asked.

"I can't wait to look around," Meg said.

"And we will," Brett said. "When we're back."

Scarlet looked suddenly nervous. "All of you are leaving?" she asked.

"I'm staying," Diego told her.

She lowered her head quickly, but he got a glimpse of her expression first and could tell that she was tremendously relieved. Strange. Was she afraid of Ben and Trisha Kendall?

"We need to talk to the officer over there in his car, too," Matt said.

"They had people out there for hours — pretty much all through the night — after I called 911," Ben said.

"You never heard anything?" Diego asked. "You didn't hear the gunshots?"

"No, nothing," Ben said, as Trisha shook her head. "None of the guests did, either."

"Well, we'll take a look, see what we can see," Diego said. "Ben, you mind coming along? You can tell us what you found."

Trisha took Ben's hand, making it clear that if he was going, so was she. Scarlet, arms crossed over her chest, joined them without a word as they walked across the gravel parking lot toward the police cruiser.

The back of Diego's neck prickled. They were being watched.

He turned toward the stables and saw a grizzled cowboy standing in the doorway. The man waved to Diego.

Diego waved back, then looked over at the house. Upstairs, a curtain was pulled back. Someone was watching them from one of the bedrooms. He also thought he saw a face in a downstairs window, but whoever it was quickly stepped back, as if they realized they'd been seen.

Diego decided not to pretend. He waved to whoever was at the house, as well. No response.

The officer got out of the car as they approached and said, "Can I help you folks? No lookie-loos allowed up on the mountain, just in case that's what you're here for."

Matt stepped forward to produce his credentials. The officer looked at him and then at the others. "This is of interest to the FBI? Why?"

"Let's just say there's something about it that resonates for us and leave it at that," Matt said.

The officer nodded, studying them. "Don't go past the tape," he told him. "Not unless I get an official okay from my boss."

He got back into his car and Diego figured he was calling headquarters, alerting them that the FBI was interested in their crime scene.

Diego turned to Ben as they all started walking up the slope. "Tell us what happened, how you discovered the bodies."

"I had been at the stables — I'm a horse guy, spend as much time as I can there — and was walking toward the house when I saw lumps up by the trees, lumps that shouldn't have been there. It was too dark for me to tell what they were, so I walked over and . . ."

He paused and drew a shaky breath.

"He was a bloody mess. She was just . . .

bloody. It looked as if he had been . . . cut up before he was shot. I was shaking so badly I dropped my phone. I had to pick it up from the dirt to dial 911. I turned my back to them and just stared down at the house until the cops arrived. I think I was in shock when they finally got there. I couldn't help thinking the scene was just like the pictures Scarlet had shown me, and I said so to the cops, and I am still so damned sorry I did."

Diego looked at Scarlet. "Tell us about those pictures."

"I don't know how they got on my camera," she said, and there was a mix of frustration and fear in her voice. "I ran into Ben and wanted to show him the shots I'd gotten of an elk. And they were just there. Pictures of dead people."

"The same dead people you saw?" Diego asked Ben.

Ben frowned and then nodded gravely. "If it wasn't them, it was just like them. One showed the guy hung up in a tree, but the other one . . . It was both of them, same position, same huge amount of blood. I handed the camera back to Scarlet, asked her what the hell was going on. She saw the pictures and she was stunned. And then they were gone. Just gone. And the elk was back where he was supposed to be."

"I didn't take those pictures," Scarlet said firmly. "And I didn't erase them."

"The police took the camera," Ben said. "They didn't find any sign of those shots, and they let Scarlet go."

Scarlet looked at Ben and then at the agents. "The thing is . . . well, it's strange, even stranger than it seemed at the time. I was thinking about it while I was cooking breakfast, and those pictures were like the story of this place. It was built by one of Ben's ancestors, Nathan Kendall. He was attacked one night. Whoever did it dragged him up the mountain and tortured him with a knife, then shot him. And when his wife heard him screaming and went to help him, she was shot, too. They never did catch who did it. There were several theories, but no one was ever arrested, much less convicted."

She paused, shivering slightly as she looked straight at Diego. "It's as if history repeated itself. He was tortured, then shot . . . she was shot but at least not tortured. They died the same way and in the same place as Nathan and Jillian Kendall died nearly a hundred and fifty years ago."

CHAPTER FOUR

Scarlet was extremely grateful — and still a little incredulous — that Diego had not only come to help her, but that he had also come so quickly *and* with a contingent of fellow agents.

She knew Brett, of course. He and Diego had worked together for years — she'd often felt that Brett knew her husband better than she did. Of course, in their line of work learning to think almost in tandem was imperative.

She still thought the world of Brett. He had been a good friend to both of them during the divorce, even helping her pack up when it had been time to leave.

But she'd never heard of the other agents or this "special" unit Diego and Brett had joined. She still didn't know anything, if it came to that.

Didn't matter. It had to be one hell of a unit if they'd gotten here in less than twenty-four hours simply because she'd asked her ex-husband for help.

She'd heard — the whole country had heard — about the Miami zombie case, and she'd known that Diego and Brett had been assigned to it. She had to assume that Matt and Meg had worked it, too, and that it was somehow connected to whatever made their special unit, well, *special.* She'd thought several times about calling Diego, just to see how he was weathering the stress. The pressure on law enforcement must have been terrible. She knew how he took his cases — or, really, the people who were part of them — to heart. The temptation to pick up the phone had been almost overwhelming at times.

But then she'd reminded herself that maybe he'd moved on. Maybe he had a girlfriend. Diego was a natural flirt. He simply liked people in general, despite what he did for a living and the kinds of people he so frequently had to deal with. Women, especially, naturally liked him. It was those dark good looks and killer smile. They couldn't help themselves.

He had never betrayed her during their two years together, but they weren't married anymore. She hadn't just left him, she'd left the state.

He'd had the right to move on.

The thought that he might well have done so disturbed her more than she wanted to admit, and that, as much as anything else, had kept her from making the call. Being so far away, cradled by the mountains, had acted like a buffer zone. It was almost as if she was looking back at a story about two other people.

But after Brett, Matt and Meg had left for the police station, and Ben and Trisha had headed back to the main house to check on their five remaining guests, Scarlet discovered that she suddenly felt incredibly awkward with the man she had once known better than anyone else in the world.

Admittedly, she'd been drawn to Diego at the outset because of the way he looked. He was tall and fit, and there was something of the aristocrat about his features, as if he was descended from a line of Spanish kings. She could see him wearing a conquistador's helmet and posing for a gold coin.

He was also charming, and quick to make her laugh. They were opposites in many ways. He was daring and quick to make friends, to dive into a situation or experience. She had been decidedly shy, at least at first, always wanting to know what made things tick. At first it had been great. He had taught her to be spontaneous, as daring as he was. She had taught him to look beneath the surface of things. They'd both learned about compromise.

She had believed then and still did that the reason they'd stopped talking was that they were trying to be considerate of each other, to avoid upsetting each other. She'd told him that she didn't need an explanation when he needed to work all hours. And she didn't. But maybe that had made him think she didn't care about his job, so he tried too hard not to bring work home.

And then she'd lost the baby. A baby he hadn't even known existed.

She knew this was not the time to analyze where and why they'd gone wrong, or why she had felt the irresistible need to flee from their marriage and from him, to ask for the divorce.

And still he was there for her the minute she called.

Now the others were gone and it was just the two of them. He wanted to hear everything from her point of view, starting with the pictures that had mysteriously appeared on her camera and then going on to cover her experience at the police station and anything else that might be relevant. So now they were up in the apartment, at the little table in the kitchen. She'd brewed more coffee and was sitting opposite him, much as she'd sat opposite Lieutenant Gray the night before. She kept noticing his hands. His fingers were long, his nails clipped and clean. She'd always loved his hands; they looked like a pianist's hands. Actually, he did play, but only for pleasure. He claimed he was awful, but in fact he was anything but.

She looked away, avoiding his eyes. She'd been anxious to be alone with him so she could tell him about the mannequin. But now that the moment was here, she was afraid he was going to think she was an idiot. He dealt with true evil every day. How was she going to explain her terror of a mannequin in a way that didn't sound ridiculous?

Then again, how the hell had the damned thing wound up at the foot of her bed?

Apparently he could still read her better than anyone else could, because he immediately asked, "What is it? Please, Scarlet, two people have been murdered. Tell me what you didn't want to say in front of everyone else."

She couldn't say it. Too silly. Or maybe not. There was still the possibility that someone made of flesh and blood, and in possession of a key, had moved it to terrify her.

"A mannequin moved," she blurted out.

She'd expected skepticism — perhaps polite, nearly hidden skepticism, but skepticism nevertheless.

"Okay, I saw a bunch of mannequins down in the museum," he said. "But which one, and how did it move?"

She let out a long breath. "Nathan Kendall — and he's not downstairs. He's in my living room about fifteen feet away from us. Yesterday he fell over on his own." She hesitated, then went on. "And when I woke up this morning, he was standing at the foot of my bed."

To her amazement, he didn't look at her with sympathy, as if the thin mountain air was affecting her brain.

He simply asked, "Who has keys to this place, Scarlet? The first thing, always, is to look for the simplest and most likely possibility."

"To the best of my knowledge, only Ben, Trisha and myself. And I just can't believe that either one of them would try to scare me that way." She met his eyes as if begging him to understand. "Diego, I was never afraid to be here. I loved this place from the moment I arrived. But I swear to you, I'm not crazy. The statue was on its pedestal at the bottom of the stairs when I went to bed after we finally got back from the police station. Ben and Trisha went with me to make sure the museum and the apartment were safe. I went back down with them and locked the door once they left. I woke up in the middle of the night, but I had a cup of tea and went back to bed. I'd had the feeling the whole time that I was being watched, though. When I woke up in the morning, Nathan Kendall was standing at the foot of my bed. Do you think someone got in and put him there without me hearing a thing?"

"First, thank God you're all right. And second, maybe. That's certainly the logical explanation, and we always look for the logical explanation first."

"I don't know which is scarier — the concept that a mannequin moved on its own, or that someone was in here and put it at the foot of my bed to scare me to death. You know me, Diego — I don't get spooked easily. I've studied mummies and excavated grave sites — you name it. But that mannequin . . . and those pictures . . . Ben and I both saw them, but I have no idea how they got there and no idea how they disappeared."

"The cops have the camera now, right?"

"Yes."

He shrugged. "Maybe we'll be able to get our hands on it. I mean, I'm sure the cops here are great, but the Bureau has the best techs in the world, and from what I hear, the unit can get anything expedited."

"From what you hear?"

"They asked Brett to join and annexed me to the invitation. I just accepted yesterday. After you called."

"After I called? So you accepted because of me?" she asked.

"I wasn't sure I wanted to, but when you called . . ." he said.

"Oh, Diego, I didn't mean to ruin your life. I was just so scared when the cops brought me in that I didn't know what to do except call you."

"You hardly ruined my life, it's an elite unit. And I was already on the verge of joining — this just helped me make the decision. I wasn't sure about leaving Miami, but I figured what the hell, I'm not tied down in any way anymore, so it doesn't really matter where I'm assigned so long as I like what I'm doing."

She couldn't meet his eyes or he would be bound to read her relief at hearing he wasn't seeing anyone seriously enough to want to stick around, so she just stared at her cup.

All she said was, "But you love Miami."

"No, Scarlet, I'm not in love with a place. Love is something you reserve for people."

He rose, heading toward the living room. She flinched inwardly, then stood a moment later and followed him.

When she caught up to him, he was examining the statue of Nathan Kendall.

"Heavy, isn't it? Whoever carved this did an amazing job. The artist caught real character in his face. He looks like a man who's been through hell but come out with his soul intact," Diego said.

"It's a good likeness. I'm hoping to find out who the artist was." She looked hard at the mannequin herself.

It was wood, just painted wood carved into the likeness of a man and dressed in period clothing.

It suddenly occurred to her that someone could steal those clothes and wear them, and she shuddered.

"Okay, I don't want to scare you, because in the end this may have nothing to do with the ranch, but tell me about the people here," Diego said.

"Well, you met Ben and Trisha."

"The only other people who, as far as you know, have keys to the museum."

"I can't believe either of them would do

this. I've actually known them for years. I met them right after college, when I was working at the Metropolitan Museum of Art. Before I knew you, in fact. I trust them completely."

"I'm not saying you shouldn't. It's easy to get hold of a key and copy it. Who else works here?"

"Angus Fillmore runs the stable. You'd know him if you saw him. Old guy, looks like something out of an old Western movie."

"I think I saw him," Diego said. "Who else?"

"The head housekeeper, Linda Reagan. She's around thirty, I think, and beyond competent. She hires seasonal help when the place is busy, the rest of the time — like now — she and Ben and Trisha handle the cleanup and the meals. Ben and Trisha have a private suite on the second floor, and Linda has a small apartment in the attic. Angus lives over the stables. He leads most of the trail rides, though Ben loves to take out the late-afternoon ride himself, and there are a few locals who help out as needed."

"Guests here last night?" Diego asked.

"A flock who fled immediately, though not before the police talked to them. There are five who stayed. Terry Ballantree's a young guy, here on his own. He's excited because he's a descendant of Nathan Kendall, just like Ben and me. There are also two couples still here. Charles and Gwen Barton are newlyweds from Mississippi, and Gigi and Clark Levin are from Texas. They're retirees, and they come for two months at the end of summer, beginning of fall, every year."

Diego nodded. "I'd like to meet all of them." He paused, studying her. "What else?"

"What do you mean, what else?"

"There's something you haven't told me yet," he said. "I know you."

She shook her head, lowering her eyes. "There is one thing, but I can't see how it means anything. There was a strange guy who stopped me when I was in town and told me to be careful, that I was one of 'them' and also one of 'us.' "

"What did he look like?"

"Maybe thirty-five. Dressed like a cowboy."

"Are you sure he wasn't just trying to pick you up? You're a beautiful woman, you know."

Coming from someone else, it would have been a compliment. From Diego right now, it was a professional observation, but it was still nice to hear, and she smiled. "Thanks. But I don't think so. I actually know pick-up lines when I hear them, and that wasn't one. He was probably just some drunk rambling on about who knows what. Although I ought to thank him, because he's part of why Lieutenant Gray decided to let me go. They found a witness who saw me talking to him. Well, they saw *me* talking anyway. Their view must have been blocked, because they didn't see him. Anyway, after I got away from him I went to hear a friend's band, and he walked me to my car later."

"I'm glad he made sure you were safe," Diego said.

She would have liked it better if he'd sounded at least a little bit jealous.

It was her own fault that he wasn't, of course. She had left him, and he had moved on.

Why hadn't she?

"I wasn't really worried at that point. The guy didn't seem scary, just weird, and I didn't know then that anyone had been killed." She paused. "But actually," she said, frowning, "when Eddie walked me to my car, I forgot about this earlier, but I felt as if I was being watched then, too. But not by the guy from earlier. By someone . . . different. Someone evil. That sounds crazy, doesn't it? It was probably nothing, just my nerves being on edge because of the freaky thing with the photos. Then I got here and found out . . ." She stared him straight in the eyes. "Diego, how could those pictures have been on the camera?"

"How closely did you look at them?"

"Not very. I was too stunned. They were bloody, though. I remember that much."

"And you never saw the murdered couple?"

"No. Only Ben saw them. And the police, of course."

"I need to get my hands on that camera," Diego said, "but for now, I'd like to meet everyone else here. Want to start at the stables?"

"Sure."

It was noon; rides were scheduled for ten in the morning, and three and five in the afternoon. Every once in a while they planned a special night ride, but only for experienced riders.

Angus Fillmore was alone at the stables, sitting on a bale of hay and enjoying a sandwich. He liked Scarlet, and she was glad, because she loved the horses and liked spending time around them when she could.

"Angus, hey, I wanted you to meet my — a friend. Diego McCullough."

"Well, howdy," Angus said. He didn't rise, but he did try to wipe the grease off his hand before he offered it to Diego.

"How are you doing?" Diego asked him.

Angus shook his head. "Bastards! Coming up here to kill people. I'm pissed off, is how I feel." Then, as if realizing he should say something about the victims, he added, "Sorry, too, of course. Sorry as hell for that couple, whoever they were."

"Anyone riding today?" Scarlet asked him.

Angus shook his head. "Nope. Ben made me cancel. Guess he wants to wait 'til they've got the crime-scene tape off the place. I hope to hell they catch the bastard quick." He frowned, looking at Diego curiously. "Saw you arrive this morning with some official-looking people. You the law?"

"In a way," Diego told him. "We're FBI."

"FBI?" Angus said, surprised. "They're bringing in the big guns."

"They didn't bring us in. Not yet. We're here to support a friend," Diego said.

Angus looked at Scarlet, shaking his head. "Heard they took you in for questioning. Idiots."

That was one of the things she liked about Angus, she thought. He had strong opinions and wasn't at all opposed to voicing them.

"I'm pretty sure they figured that out,"

Diego said.

"Well, glad you're here. Maybe you'll catch who did it. Animals, they only kill to survive. Human beings, they kill because they're sick mothers. Anyway, good to meet you, and good to have you here. You ride?"

"I wouldn't want to get on a bull, but I'm okay on horseback," Diego told him.

Angus nodded, as if that was important. "Can't trust a man who won't ride a horse," he said. "Can't always trust the ones who do, but definitely can't trust the ones who won't."

"Good logic," Diego said with a smile. "We'll see you later, and somewhere along the line, I'd love to go riding."

"Good man — we'll do it." Angus said. "And I'll do the guiding. Ben's a great guy, but he doesn't know the trails like I do. Born and raised in these parts. I can show you what needs to be seen."

Diego thanked him, Scarlet waved, and they headed for the main house.

"What are those two buildings over there?" Diego asked as they walked, pointing.

"That's the smokehouse," she said. "It was left as is, but you could still smoke something there if you wanted to. The bunkhouse is set up so they can handle more guests than the main house can hold."

"Was it occupied last night?"

"I don't think so. You'd have to ask Ben or Trisha."

"I'll do that," he told her. "So, let's go meet the housekeeper and the remaining guests."

"Linda's probably around, but the guests may or may not be there," Scarlet said. "They could have gone hiking or into town or something."

As it turned out, everyone *was* at the house. They were all in the huge dining room that stretched the length of the left side of the house back to the kitchen, with a nice counter pass-through for whoever was cooking each morning — usually Trisha.

The giant moose head hung between the pass-through and the door to the kitchen. It was about eight feet up and seemed to rule over the room.

There was one long table, and breakfast was served family style, with big plates of fluffy eggs, bacon and sausage, and Danishes, bagels and breads of all kinds.

The weekends were a bit different, with made-to-order omelets on Saturdays, and pancakes or waffles on Sundays.

When they entered, everyone except Linda, who was probably working, was clustered at one end of the table. A large

106

coffee urn sat nearby, along with cream, sugar and a plate of cookies.

Everyone was in jeans, except for Gigi and Clark, who wore sweat suits, but judging by the lack of actual sweat, Scarlet suspected they had intended to take their morning constitutional but hadn't made it.

Like everyone else at the table, they looked tired and worried.

"Hello, there," Ben greeted Diego and Scarlet as they came in. "Join us — we're busy thinking about all the things we don't want to do because we're depressed."

"It's strange," Gigi said. "I mean, we didn't know the couple who were killed. We never even saw them, but . . ."

"But it feels personal, because it happened right here on the ranch," Gwen said.

"And we didn't even know," Ben said.

"We didn't hear a thing," Trisha agreed.

"What were they doing up here?" Clark mused.

"How did they get up here?" Terry asked. "The police didn't find a car."

"There are hiking trails all through the woods," Ben said.

Clark stood suddenly. "I'm sorry," he said to Diego, offering him a hand. "We haven't met. I'm Clark Levin, and this is my wife, Gigi."

The others stood, too, and introductions were made all round.

"Pull up a chair — be depressed with us," Trisha said.

"Thanks," Diego said, pulling out a chair for Scarlet before sitting down himself.

Always courteous, she thought. But then, she knew Julia Lopez McCullough, Diego's mother. And while she was the sweetest woman in the world, she had been an old-fashioned parent and had taught her son manners.

"Coffee?" Ben suggested.

"Sure, thanks," Diego said, filling cups for himself and Scarlet.

"So you're a G-man," Clark said to Diego.

"A what?" Gwen asked.

"Government man," Clark explained, grimacing. "I guess it's not an expression anyone uses much these days."

"What kind of a government man?" Charles asked.

"FBI," Diego told him.

"I feel safer and less depressed already," Gwen said brightening. "And your friends — are they G-men, too?"

"Except for Meg. She's a G-woman," Diego said.

"With so many of you here, we really *are* safe, aren't we?" Gigi said.

"I told you before that we're safe," Clark said. "It's just a terrible coincidence, that couple being killed here."

"The police are certainly investigating every angle," Diego said. "But I think you're safe here. At the moment you even have a police officer parked down at the end of the drive." He turned to Ben. "Just to be sure I have everything straight, was anyone staying in the bunkhouse the night of the murders, or was everyone here in the main house?"

"Everyone was here. Unless someone specifically requests the bunkhouse, we keep it empty unless we need the extra space."

"How was it that no one heard the shots?" Gwen asked.

"Most of us weren't here," Terry said. "I was in town at the moose store. I don't remember the name of the place, but it was great. They've got moose shirts, moose mugs, moose welcome mats and wind chimes and you name it," he said to Diego.

"But Trisha and I were right here in the house," Ben said. "And we didn't hear a thing."

"We were watching television, and we had it turned up because someone wasn't wearing his hearing aids," Trisha reminded him.

"Trisha!" Ben said, his face turning bright red.

Trisha waved a dismissive hand in the air. "It's a tiny little thing, but Ben is embarrassed. He's afraid people will think he's too old to be fun if he wears hearing aids."

"Oh, Ben," Gwen said. "My sister wears a hearing aid, and she's only thirty."

"Anyway," Trisha said, "we were watching some cop movie, and it was full of gunfire. We might have heard those shots and not even known it."

Linda Reagan entered the dining room from the kitchen just then, shaking her head and setting something in front of Ben.

"Thank you," he said, his cheeks coloring again.

"No problem," she told him. "I thought you might need them."

Linda was tall, about five-nine, with ash-blond hair she kept swept back in ponytail and green eyes. She was far more than the head housekeeper, Scarlet knew. Among other things she discreetly managed guests who wouldn't leave on time or caused problems in any way.

"What did you find?" Trisha asked.

Linda didn't answer right away.

"Oh, just tell them," Ben said.

"His hearing aids," Linda said.

Heads lowered around the table as people tried to hide their smiles.

"Laugh at me," Ben said. "It will be good for your souls. Linda, this is Diego McCullough. He's an FBI agent, and he and some of his friends are here for a few days. They're friends of Scarlet's."

"Nice to have you," Linda said, sitting down at the table. "Terrible what happened. Do you have any idea what's going on?" she asked Diego.

"I don't know anything yet. We just got here this morning. My fellow agents are in town right now, though, seeing if we can be of assistance."

"Is it like it is on television? Do they get all mad when you guys show up?" Gwen asked, sounding eager for it to be true.

"There are certainly some police who are territorial, but not many," Diego said with a shrug. "Usually, everyone just wants to catch the bad guy."

"I get that," Terry said, nodding. "I've heard there are, like, dozens of serial killers at large in the United States at any given time. It's scary, if you ask me."

"It *is* scary," Diego said, then turned to Linda. "You didn't hear anything last night, either?"

"I wasn't here," she said, and smiled. "I had a date. The police questioned all of us, though. Every one of us had to make a statement, even if we weren't here."

"He must be quite a guy," Trisha told her. "She's so picky," she added to the others.

"Hey, my time is precious. We should all be picky," Linda said.

"Maybe, but as stunning as you are, you deserve to be even pickier than the rest of us," Charles said.

Linda cast him a disapproving look. Scarlet had a feeling Linda was simply offended that he would compliment another woman over his brand-new bride.

Gwen apparently didn't appreciate his comment, either, and she must have kicked him under the table, because he suddenly grunted in pain.

Ben clearly picked up on what was happening and quickly changed the subject. "Well, I'm just glad all of you decided to stay on here. Trisha and I really appreciate your loyalty."

"It's kind of strange, actually," Gwen said.

"What's that?" Linda asked her.

"To be honest, Charles and I were torn about where to spend our honeymoon. The Stanley is just so famous, and it's known to be haunted, plus the Stephen King connection is so cool. Years ago," she said, reaching for her husband's hand, "I was in the area, and I heard about this place, so I read up on its history. It's really sad, the way Nathan Kendall and his wife were killed. And now this couple . . . it's like history repeating itself. It's tragic, but it's scary, too."

"And sick," Charles said.

Everyone fell silent at that point, until Diego turned to Gigi and Clark and asked, "Did you hear anything?"

"We were in Boulder, having dinner with friends — we weren't here," Clark said.

"And you two?" Diego asked Gwen and Charles.

"We were . . ." Gwen blushed and fell silent.

"Occupied," Charles said. They smiled at one another, still holding hands.

"I just didn't hear anything at all . . . except for Charles," Gwen said.

Scarlet could feel the general consensus around the table. Too much information.

"Then you got one of your migraines and took something for it, but you were still tossing and turning so much that I took a sleeping pill myself," Charles said, rolling his eyes and looking at Diego. "I think Armageddon could have come and we would have slept right through it."

"Migraines are tough," Linda said, looking sympathetically at Gwen. "My mother used to get them. We had to keep the house dark and silent, and we kept bringing her cold towels for her forehead. If you get one again while you're here, let me know. I'm a good migraine nurse."

"Thank you," Gwen said.

Diego drained his cup and said, "Thanks so much for the coffee and the company." He smiled as he stood. "This is the first time I've been anywhere around here, so Scarlet's going to show me around a bit."

"Nice to meet you," Linda said, and the others expressed similar sentiments.

"And nice to have you G-men — and a G-woman — around," Charles added.

"Thanks," Diego said, as Scarlet got up, too, and said her goodbyes.

His hand at her back, they walked out together. She was stunned to realize how much she'd missed that simple touch; Diego had a natural ability to simply touch her or put his arm around her in a way that was . . .

Not possessive, not exactly. He didn't push or pull. He had always just touched her gently, a way of saying they were together that made her feel warm and wanted.

She reminded herself again that she was the one who had chosen to leave. She'd left because it had seemed clear to her that his work had come first and always would, but in hindsight she could see that so much of what had gone wrong had been her fault. She'd wanted to respect his work. She'd never wanted to become the little wife sitting at home, worried and always asking for reassurance or more of his time. She had told him that she was fine, and she'd really thought it was true.

But in reality she hadn't been fine at all. In trying not to be weak she'd tried too hard to be strong and lost what mattered most: the trust and emotional intimacy of a loving marriage. She'd never told him when something was really important. She'd waited for the right moment to tell him about the baby, when she realized now that the right moment would have been anytime she'd excitedly blurted out her news.

But after losing the baby, she had simply been too hurt to see clearly and to know what to do. Escape — from both Miami and her marriage — had seemed the only way to erase the pain.

But he was here now, and she was glad of his reassuring presence, because frankly, she was flat-out scared.

Of a mannequin?

Or of a murderer?

"Curious," he said when they were outside.

"What's that?"

"Ben Kendall not wearing his hearing aids and watching some shoot-'em-up cop show at the time of the murders. And really, Gwen couldn't hear anything but Charles?"

"Do you really think someone at the house could be involved? Maybe the killer just used a silencer," Scarlet suggested.

"No silencer, that much I'm sure of," he said, deep in thought. "So a number of people checked out after it happened, right?"

She nodded. "I'm sure you can get a list of their names from Trisha."

"Good. Brett and the others can interview them. I doubt they were involved, and I don't blame them for leaving, but that doesn't mean they shouldn't be investigated anyway. But, for now, let's go see this museum of yours."

Scarlet unlocked the door and they went on in. She turned on the lights and stood by the door, watching as Diego walked from one end of the room to the other, stopping to study the different figures and look in the display cases.

"Quite a collection of guns," he said.

"It is," she agreed.

"We'll get a locksmith in here this afternoon," he said.

"Pardon?"

"A locksmith," he told her. "I don't know if a mannequin can move on its own or not, but no matter what, I think it will be a good idea to change the locks."

"Okay. But we'll have to tell Ben. Or ask him, really. He does own the place," Scarlet reminded him.

"Of course," he said.

He had just about finished his walk-through when there was a knock at the door. She turned around to open it, but Diego was at her side before she had a chance to.

"You don't just do that," he said, his tone harsh.

"It's broad daylight," she protested.

"What? You think people can only be killed in the dark?" he asked, stepping past her and opening the door himself.

She almost laughed when Brett and the other two agents entered.

Diego had always been careful, though. Maybe that was part of what had driven the wedge between them. She tended to look for the good in people, while Diego often seemed to expect the worst. It came from what he did, of course, what he saw day in and day out. And when it had come to really thinking about a family . . .

Right now she didn't want to think about that. She didn't want to hurt. She needed help, and she was very grateful that Diego was here to provide it.

She'd never doubted that he would, of course, and that said something right there.

"Anything?" Diego asked the new arrivals.

"Nothing new," Brett said.

"But Adam is coming in tonight," Meg said, "and he said that by tomorrow morning we'll be on the job officially. Adam always knows someone who knows someone else. He's an amazing man."

"Wow. Is that really how it works?" Scarlet asked.

"Sometimes," Meg told her. "You'll love Adam. Everyone does. In fact, that goes a long way toward explaining how he gets things done and why this unit is so successful."

Matt looked at Diego. "Have you explained to her who we are?"

"She knows we're FBI," Diego told him. "I haven't had a chance yet to explain about the Krewe."

"The Krewe?" Scarlet murmured, and looked questioningly at him.

"Brett and I have just joined a special unit within the Bureau," he explained. "It's called the Krewe of Hunters, and it deals with the unusual — things that defy logic, things that cross over into the paranormal, the otherworldly. Adam Harrison isn't only in charge of the Krewe, he's the man who managed to get it formed in the first place."

"Adam has an uncanny ability to find people with extrasensory perception and other abilities that help them deal with the kinds of paranormal threats we face," Matt said. "For at least a decade, he did it quietly, hiring them to work for him privately. He's also a major philanthropist and knows most of the major players in government as well as private industry. So a while back he made things official and formed the Krewe of Hunters. The unit keeps growing, inviting new members, because this is a big country, and the evil side of the supernatural just keeps going."

"I look forward to meeting him," Scarlet said.

"Meanwhile, what do you know about Nathan Kendall and the way he and his wife were murdered?" Matt asked her.

"Do you want the long or the short version?" Scarlet asked.

"We're here for the duration," Matt told her.

"Then let's head up the stairs. You can look at Nathan while we talk about him,"

Diego said.

"Oh?" Meg asked.

"Come on upstairs and you'll understand," Scarlet said.

She'd half expected that Nathan Kendall would have moved again and was relieved to find that he hadn't. Maybe he knew she was onto him and this was a good time to behave.

Diego moved the statue over by the window, then leaned against the wall next to it, while the others settled themselves around the room.

"Nathan Kendall was a fascinating person," Scarlet began. "He was born in Virginia and fought under Lee during the Civil War. When the war was over, a number of the men in his company turned to robbing banks and holding up stagecoaches. They only stole from those they considered to be carpetbaggers, out to take advantage of the South while she was on her knees. But when someone was killed during one of their robberies, Nathan wanted out. He headed west and wound up here. He bought this land from a man named Rollo Conway. Conway had been searching for gold with very little success and needed the money. Nathan must have liked the guy, though, since he kept his name for the ranch.

"At the time, there was a United States marshal living in the vicinity, a widower named Tom Vickers. Nathan fell in love with the man's daughter. The man didn't trust Nathan and forbade the marriage, but when the he was out of town, Nathan and Jillian were married anyway. Back then, of course, when a United States marshal was off working, it could be months or years before he got back home. By the time he returned, Nathan and Jillian weren't just married, they had a baby, Zachary. One night someone tricked Nathan into coming outside, strung him up on a tree and nearly disemboweled him, and when Jillian came running out to his rescue, she was shot and killed. At some point the killer — or killers — decided they were done torturing Nathan, and he was shot, too. Their bodies were found the next day by Rollo Conway, who had come up to see how they were doing.

"There were a number of suspects, including Marshal Vickers, who hadn't wanted the marriage, and a number of Nathan's past affiliates, the men he'd left behind after they killed a man. No one ever discovered the truth. Marshal Vickers, naturally, raised Zachary, who went on to have fourteen children of his own. Ben is one of his descendants, and so is Terry Ballantree, one of the current guests here at the ranch."

Just then Brett's cell phone rang, and it was clear from his side of the conversation that the FBI had come up with some new information.

"That was HQ," he said as soon as he hung up. "They found out what Candace and Larry Parker were doing here. They lived in Denver, but they'd never been to Estes Park. They decided to drive up on the spur of the moment and see if they could get a room here at the ranch, so they asked a neighbor to keep an eye on the house and hit the road. And I think you'll be very interested to know why." He waited until they were all looking at him, then said, "Because Larry had gone onto one of those ancestry sites and found out that he was a descendant of Nathan Kendall."

Scarlet felt a chill settle over her. "So Nathan and Jillian's great, great, whatever grandchild and his wife were killed in the exact same way that Nathan and Jillian were?" she asked, shock evident in her voice. "Why? Why would someone do that?"

"I don't know," Diego said. "That's what we have to figure out."

"We have to warn them," Scarlet said. "Ben and Trisha and Terry." She tried not to think about the fact that she was one of Nathan's descendants, too.

"I promise we'll talk to them," Brett said. "Right now there's still a cop out front." He paused and looked at her in a way that sent a shiver down her spine. "There's one more thing, and it concerns you."

"What is it?" she asked.

"When our guys found out about the connection between the Parkers and Nathan Kendall, they ran a computer search. There are about two hundred people living today who can trace their lineage back to Nathan and Jillian Kendall," Meg said.

"That's not surprising, with Zachary's fourteen children," Scarlet said. "What does that have to do with me?"

Brett held her gaze with his for a long moment, then said, "You're one of them."

CHAPTER FIVE

Scarlet smiled. "Yes, I know," she said.

Her smile deepened as she explained. "That's part of why I'm here. Ben found that out years ago, when we were both living in New York. That's why we met. He tracked me down when I was working for the Metropolitan Museum and told me." She smiled and said, "I studied my whole genealogy after he told me about the connection. Zachary fathered eight boys and six girls. Infant mortality was incredibly high back then, but every one of them survived to adulthood. Must be something in the water out here," she joked, then went on. "I've got it all memorized, dates and married names and everything, so at the risk of boring you . . . One of the girls, Annabeth, was born in 1890. In 1908, *she* gave birth to Valerie Banks. Valerie gave birth to Genevieve Osprey in 1930, and in 1949 Genevieve gave birth to Leanne David. Leanne married Anthony Barton, and in 1970 they had my father, Eric.

"My grandparents and my parents were all born in Florida, so it was quite a surprise to find out my ancestors had moved east when most people were moving west and I actually had roots in Colorado."

Yes, she'd known about the connection. It had always been interesting, a fun fact about her family.

But now, in light of the current murders . . .

Now she was worried. No, not just worried. She was flat-out *frightened.*

Diego saw the expression on her face as she finished speaking and wanted to stride across the room, pull her into his arms and tell her that she didn't need to worry, that everything was all right, that he would die before he let anything happen to her.

He resisted the temptation. This wasn't the time or the place for something so . . . well, melodramatic. She'd called him for help, scared, but that didn't change the pain that lay between them.

And just because he would die for her, that didn't mean that someone wouldn't step over his dead body to do her in anyway.

"Well, it's good that we all know about

your family connection now," Brett said to Scarlet. "I hate to scare you, but if it has something to do with the killer's motivation, better safe than sorry, you know?"

Scarlet shook her head. "I was just about to tell you, actually, once you mentioned the victims' connection. I don't mind telling you, I hope it's just a coincidence that the killer murdered them here on what's sort of the family property. Just how were they connected anyway?"

"Larry Parker traced himself back to Lindana Kendall, another one of Zachary's daughters," Brett said.

"We don't know if it means anything or not," Matt said, "so there's no need to worry yet. There's no way to know whether the killer knew that Larry had a family connection to the ranch, or even that he and Candace would be coming here from Denver. He might have chosen them totally at random. Wrong place, wrong time."

"Seriously," Scarlet said, "if someone was looking to kill a descendant of Nathan Kendall, it would be easy enough to find one. The newspaper made a big deal of it when Ben and Trisha bought the place."

"The most likely explanation is either that the Parkers pissed off someone in town, or that the killer chose them for some reason of his own," Brett said. "Either way, he got them up into the woods somehow, then killed them."

"We have to follow up on anything that looks like a lead, though," Meg said. "Most of the time we go through dozens of possibilities before getting to the truth."

"But we're not big believers in coincidence," Matt said quietly, "so this connection is something we definitely need to investigate."

"Okay," Scarlet said, barely breathing. "What now?"

"I was thinking food," Meg said. "We haven't eaten all day. We should head into town and find a place that looks good."

"Lunch?" Scarlet said. "Really?"

Diego smiled at that. "Relax, Scarlet. There's always a hidden agenda. People talk. Business owners, waiters and waitresses, bartenders, other customers."

"I'll grab my bag," she said.

"We're not screwing up your work schedule or anything, are we?" Meg asked.

Scarlet shook her head. "The museum's only open Thursday through Sunday. The rest of the time I catalog and research. My time is pretty much my own."

She sounded good, Diego thought. Definitely stronger than she had when they'd arrived.

"So where do you suggest we go?" Meg asked.

"There are so many great restaurants in town, it's hard to choose," Scarlet said. "Estes Park is kind of the gateway to Rocky Mountain National Park, so it offers pretty much anything you can think of when it comes to restaurants and shopping. What do you feel like eating?"

"Food," Matt answered for all of them. "I'll go down and get our things while you guys decide who's staying where, and then we'll get going. We should spread out."

"I'm taking the extra room here at the museum," Diego said.

"We'll head into the main house," Matt said, looking at Meg.

She nodded.

"I guess that leaves me in the main house, too," Brett said. "Though I'd like it better if you had some backup out here, Diego. And Adam can join us in the house when he gets here. There are plenty of rooms, right?"

"There are seven guest rooms, so you should be fine. There's also space in the bunkhouse, but I don't think you'll need it," Scarlet said.

"Brett, let's go help Matt with the bags," Meg said, rising.

128

A moment later Diego was alone with Scarlet, who was staring thoughtfully at the statue of Nathan Kendall. Then, as if she'd suddenly made a decision, she turned to Diego. "You can just sleep with me," she said. "That way Brett can take the extra room and we'll have backup here in the museum."

"Scarlet . . ." he murmured uncomfortably.

"What? We were married for two years," she said. "It's not as if . . ."

"As if I'm not going to want you?" he asked quietly.

"It's not as if that would matter," she said.

He wasn't sure what he was feeling — a fever of desire, for one thing. And yet he found himself smiling. "It wouldn't matter if we had sex?"

She flushed and met his eyes. "The sex was always great. And it wasn't that we didn't care." She turned away suddenly. "Oh, my God. I wasn't thinking. I mean, there might be someone else in your life now."

"There's no one else in my life," he said.

"Then?"

"The problem is that it *would* matter. It would matter to me."

"But would it be so horrible?" she asked.

"Are you actually asking me to sleep with you?"

"Yes, I'm asking you to sleep with me. Whether that means sleep or . . . more, that's up to you. I'm not going to force myself on you."

His heart seemed to surge into his throat. She had always been so beautiful, and her honesty, combined with the teasing light in her eyes, had always added to her enchantment. Now her eyes were serious, with only a hint of teasing.

"It hurt, Scarlet. The divorce, it hurt. I'm still not over it. So I don't think sharing a bed with you would be a good idea."

She winced, looking at the mannequin again. "Please," she said softly.

"Because you're afraid of a statue?"

She shook her head. "Because I'm just plain terrified. Of everything. I mean, I know I should be strong. And maybe I can be. I'm just not feeling it at the moment."

He was so stunned by her words that he was surprised he was able to move. He walked over to where she was sitting, went down on one knee and took her hand. He had to turn this situation into something a little lighter.

Say no, he told himself. *Tell her you'll sit outside her door all night, waiting and watch-*

ing. Just say no.

He couldn't do it. The single word was beyond him.

"So now you're begging me to sleep with you?"

"Yes, I guess so," she said.

"Okay, fine."

"Okay, fine — you'll do it?"

"If you're begging, yeah, I'll do it. A guy doesn't get that kind of an offer every day."

He could tell that she wanted to look away, but he didn't let her, catching her chin and forcing her to meet his eyes. "Just remember," he said a little harshly. "I'm not the one who wanted the divorce."

She nodded. "I know that," she told him softly. "But it was never because I didn't want you."

They didn't get a chance to go any deeper. They heard footsteps on the stairs, and Diego stood up quickly.

A minute later Brett walked in with Diego's bag. "Where do you want this?" he asked.

Diego kept his eyes steady on Scarlet's. He wasn't going to lie, not where his partner and the Krewe were concerned. "Scarlet's room," he said.

Brett didn't blink. "All right. I'll take the other room, then. Double the security for

Scarlet. The main house will have Meg, Matt and Adam, and we can call in reinforcements if necessary."

"Excuse me just a second," Scarlet said, rising and hurrying out of the room.

Brett didn't say a word as he walked away to put Diego's bag in Scarlet's room, leaving Diego alone with the statue of Nathan Kendall.

"I don't know your true story," he said, feeling a little foolish addressing a life-size carving, "but hopefully we'll discover what really happened to you and your wife, and maybe save some of your descendants. But for now . . ."

The painted blue eyes of the statue stared back at him, and Diego suddenly discovered that he was smiling.

"But for now, I guess I ought to be thanking you," he said.

He left the room to join the others. He realized he was feeling famished.

In many ways.

Downtown Estes Park was filled with tourists. No surprise. Autumn was a beautiful time to be in the mountains, with winter's potentially lethal ice and snow yet to come. Temperatures were a continuation of summer's comfortable days and cool evenings, and the leaves were just beginning to change, covering the slopes with vibrant color. The gold of the trees, the blue of the sky and the streams, and the majestic white of the mountain peaks rising higher and higher in the distance all combined to provide a truly breathtaking vista.

Scarlet was surprised but pleased that the others looked to her for information about the area, and she embraced the role of tour guide with enthusiasm. She pointed out all the things they could do if they had the time, visit the Estes Park Museum to learn about frontier life or head up to the Mac-Gregor Ranch Museum, a homestead from 1896 and the only remaining operating ranch in the area. She also heard more about Lara Mayhew, Meg's longtime friend and Brett's brand-new fiancée.

As they got closer to town Scarlet pointed through a break in the trees. "That's the historic Stanley Hotel. If you're a Stephen King fan, like me, you'll enjoy taking the tour that talks about how he conceived *The Shining* while he was staying there."

"I'd love to get over there. It's certainly beautiful and *shining* up there on that hill," Meg said.

"And if you have time before you leave, you really should drive Trail Ridge Road through Rocky Mountain National Park. People say it's the most scenic drive in the entire country," Scarlet said.

She was sharing the backseat with Diego on her left and Brett on her right. She noticed that Diego was looking out the window as they drove, almost as if he was trying not to look at her. The longer they drove, the more she felt as if her left side was burning up. What on earth had she been thinking, inviting him to share her bed? A sense of longing swept through her with an intensity she wasn't prepared for.

What had gone so wrong? Why had she been so determined to get away from a man she had loved with all her heart? She knew intellectually what had been in her mind, but now, sitting beside him, knowing that he'd dropped everything the minute she'd called . . . She was starting to think she was the biggest fool who'd ever lived.

She reminded herself that back then he hadn't been there when she'd really needed him. And she hadn't been able to forgive that.

She hadn't let him explain or even hold her after — something inside of her had simply closed off.

They reached the compact downtown area and found a spot in a municipal lot. From there, she told them, they could wander and choose a restaurant, and if they felt like shopping along the way, well, there were plenty of opportunities for that, too.

She pointed out her favorite stores as they walked. While T-shirts with moose, bears, raccoons and other creatures emblazoned on the front were available everywhere, she made a point of showing them the shop Terry had talked about, where everything was all moose all the time. High-end stores offered crystal and silver, while others were more family-oriented and featured mountain animals carved in wood. Hiking and camping gear, along with every item of clothing that could possibly feature the words *Estes Park,* were plentiful, as well. Scarlet had always loved downtown, not despite the fact that it was completely touristy but precisely because it was, in the best possible way.

They settled on a barbecue restaurant. Vertical beams carved into totem poles rose to the ceiling, and there were giant wooden bears at the entrance, along with detailed carvings of woodland creatures that ran along the bar and climbed the walls. A children's play area, stocked with stuffed animals, was set up against one wall.

There were advertisements for the upcoming Testicle Festival, so Scarlet had to explain what Rocky Mountain oysters were. She wasn't surprised when they all grimaced and opted not to try them.

After the drive and the walk to the restaurant, Scarlet suddenly realized she was feeling relaxed for the first time since she'd seen those hideous pictures — until she noticed that even in the middle of their own conversation, the others were listening intently to everything the people around them were saying.

She listened, too.

"I just don't understand the police," a man at a nearby table was saying to a woman she assumed was his wife. "Two people were murdered at the Conway Ranch, but they don't say who they were or how they were killed. They just leave us in the dark. Hell, we don't know whether to stay in town or get the hell out of here. I mean, were they a couple of prostitutes? A couple of gangbangers? That would mean we don't have to worry."

She put a finger to her lips, nodding in the direction of two children cuddling with a stuffed bear in the play area.

"They can't hear me," he said, but he lowered his voice anyway. "I heard they found remains up on one of the mountains, too. Just bones, so they must have been there for a while."

"Where did you hear that?" the woman asked.

"At the hotel. Some guy heard it from some other guy, who knew a ranger, and the ranger talked to someone who saw the bones."

"Oh, Oscar. That's just hearsay," his wife said.

Scarlet had been holding her menu, and now she realized that her fingers were white from the tightness of her grip.

"Could be just a rumor," Matt said softly, so no one could overhear.

"Or there could be more to it," Meg said.

Their waiter came up just then, putting an end to any further speculation. Scarlet remembered the young man from a previous visit, and he remembered her, too.

He smiled when he saw her, and thanked her for coming back and bringing friends. "What can I get you all? We're famous for our moose-ball hot chocolate. Don't worry," he added, when Meg shot him a skeptical look. "Our moose balls are marshmallows. I'm Dane, by the way, and feel free to ask me any questions about the menu."

They all ordered quickly, and Scarlet realized that yes, they wanted food, but they also wanted to keep moving.

Diego went for the hot chocolate. "Have to try it," he told her.

Everyone else agreed and ordered it, too.

"So what brings you all here?" Dane asked. "The park? The ghosts at The Stanley?"

"Came to see Scarlet," Diego said. "Is this home for you?"

"Born and bred," Dane said. "My uncle owns this place. We're going to open a second one, and I'm going to manage it, maybe open a small boutique hotel one of these days."

"You know the area well, then, huh?" Meg asked, smiling.

"Sure do," Dane said.

Meg lowered her voice. "The couple beside us were talking about human remains, bones, that were just found recently. Have you heard anything about that?"

He nodded gravely. "A friend of mine's a cop. They're bringing in a forensic anthropologist to examine them. They're trying to keep it quiet, though, what with the murders that just took place."

"I can understand that," Diego said. "What do you think? Should we be worried?"

Dane shook his head. "No, I don't think so. This is a really peaceful place." He smiled. "It's got a kind of hippie vibe. I doubt the killer is from around here. He probably followed that couple from wherever they lived. I'm sure the police will have it figured out in a day or two."

As soon as he left to put in their order, Meg was on the phone, asking someone to look into the third set of remains. Watching the interplay between the four of them, Scarlet realized that they had some kind of tacit agreement as to who did what.

"This *is* great hot chocolate," Meg said, when their drinks arrived. "The kid in me will never get over my love of marshmallows."

The food came quickly, and as soon as they finished eating, they asked for their bill, which Matt picked up, explaining that it was on the Bureau. The family from the table next to them left when they did.

As they walked back toward the car, Diego's phone rang. He looked curiously at the caller ID, then answered. His side of the conversation consisted mainly of "okay" repeated several times, then "goodbye."

Scarlet was more than a little curious as to who was on the other end, and judging by their expressions, so were the others.

"Adam Harrison," Diego told them as he pocketed his phone.

"Is he on his way?" Meg asked.

"He'll be here in the morning," Diego said. "But he's already set things in motion. The police have requested our help, and we're scheduled to talk to the ME after he finishes the autopsies in —" he looked at his watch "— about two hours."

"Great," Matt said. "We'll drop Scarlet back at the ranch, then head to the county morgue."

Scarlet didn't like the idea of them all leaving, but she didn't exactly want to join them at the morgue, either.

"I'll hang at the ranch with you," Meg said. "Want to teach me some local history while they're gone?"

"You're sure you don't need to be there, too?" Scarlet asked, hoping she was doing a good job of hiding her relief that she wouldn't be left alone.

Meg shook her head. "I've been to more than my share of autopsies," she said. "Between the three of them, they should be able to handle it. I'd like to find out more about Nathan and Jillian Kendall, and the investigation into their murders."

"Okay. Sounds like a plan."

When they reached the museum, however,

they were surprised to find that the local police were there, along with Ben, who was pacing back and forth in front of the building, looking anxious.

"Search warrant," he said. "They're taking the guns — all the guns! They're antiques, and they're handling them like . . . like water pistols!"

"Because the couple were killed with an antique gun," Diego explained to him. "I'll go talk to someone inside and make sure they're careful with them."

"Did you know about this?" Scarlet asked Brett.

"No, but I'm not surprised," he said. "He was killed on the ranch with an antique Colt in working order. It's only natural that they think someone might have used one from the museum, then put it right back."

Scarlet nodded and tried to smile reassuringly at Ben. "I have a full inventory of what we have. Will that help them any?" she asked.

"I'm sure it will," Brett told her.

He went with her into the museum, where she was pleased to see that the police were actually being extremely careful. She also saw Diego speaking seriously with a man in a suit.

Lieutenant Gray.

He still looked weary and put-upon. But he was nodding agreeably as he listened to Diego.

"It's going to be all right," Brett said. "Diego's good with the locals. He always gets them on our side. I'm sure they'll be out of here quickly, you'll see."

Just as he'd predicted, the guns were collected in good time, along with a copy of Scarlet's inventory, and the police left.

Gray narrowed his eyes as he looked at Scarlet, passing by her with a stiff nod.

"Jerk," she muttered as soon as he was out of earshot.

"Gotta admit, he doesn't seem like the warm-and-cuddly type," Brett said lightly.

"Good thing that guy didn't want to be a doctor," Diego said, joining them. "His bedside manner would suck. Shall we get going? I'd like to talk with the medical examiner before Lieutenant Gray finishes checking those guns into evidence and makes it out to the morgue."

"Sure — Scarlet and I can get started on some historical research," Meg said.

"Sounds good. We'll be back as soon as we can," Diego promised.

Once they were gone, Meg turned to Scarlet. "Okay, so what have we got?"

"Reams of records, though I'm not sure

how many of them will be pertinent. I have a favor to ask first, though," Scarlet said.

"Sure, what?" Meg asked her.

"Help me get Nathan Kendall back down here. I really don't like having him in the apartment."

"The mannequin?" Meg asked.

"Of course the mannequin," Scarlet said. "What else?"

Meg smiled. "Well, his spirit might be wandering around here, you know. And if so, you don't want to get rid of him. The mannequin, though — yes, let's bring it downstairs. I have to admit, he looks pretty strange hanging out by the flat-screen TV."

"The bullets are in the lab, but they're still being analyzed," Dr. Robert E. Fuller, the ME, told Diego, Matt and Brett. "But I can tell you the basics. Handmade in a mold for an antique gun. No question about it. Handmade."

Fuller was in his midthirties and looked as if he would be just as comfortable at a country club as he was in the morgue. Tall, fit and good-looking, he could have been an actor playing a medical examiner on TV.

But he also seemed to be competent and knowledgeable. He went over the results of both autopsies, showing them the tears in

Larry Parker's abdomen. "Looks like he was killed by someone who hunts and knows how to gut his prey," Fuller said. "The killer didn't remove any organs, though, just cut him open as if he was going to disembowel him."

Candace Parker had been shot once in the chest, a fatal wound. Her heart had been nicked, and she'd bled out quickly.

"In case you're wondering how I can be so sure about the bullets, I do frontier reenactments with some of the people from my club," Fuller explained.

"And they were both killed with the same gun?" Matt asked. "Sorry if that sounds like a strange question, but we never assume anything. Based on the evidence the police found at the scene, it seems unlikely, but there could have been two killers."

"No question is too strange. I just answer what I can," the ME told them. "Same kind of bullet in both cases, and like I said, I know the official forensic analyst has to do a report, but I can tell you right now that both bullets were made from a mold older than the hills and fired from an antique Colt. I have a few in my collection, and I'm betting it was one of the army Colts, pre–Civil War. I'd even go so far as to speculate that it might have been something like an

144

1849 Colt pocket percussion revolver. A lot of frontiersmen had personal molds. Not only that . . ." He paused and shrugged. "Sorry for getting carried away. I'm just the medical examiner. You guys are the investigators."

"We want your thoughts and opinions," Diego assured him. "You clearly know more than we do about antique weapons, and probably more than the police techs."

"Okay, well, like I told you, I'm a historical reenactor in my free time. Like everybody else around here, I know about Nathan Kendall. As strange as this may sound, it looks to me like someone killed the Parkers the same way Nathan Kendall and his wife were killed. Nathan was cut up before he was killed — tortured, really — like maybe the killer wanted something from him. And the woman . . . I think she was just in the way. Same thing with the Parkers."

Diego had been studying the body of Candace Parker as Fuller talked. She'd been an attractive woman in her early thirties. Now it was difficult to tell exactly where the bullet had penetrated, because the Y incision had been sewn up by the time they arrived. He noticed that her legs seemed to be scratched.

"Are these wounds recent?" Diego asked.

"Those, yes, they'll be in the report. They look like they happened as she was dragged through scrub or thorn bushes of some kind."

Fuller went on to point out marks at both the Parkers' wrists. "You can see where they were bound. Bound, and maybe dragged up the mountain."

"They haven't found their car yet," Matt said. "I'm guessing they were stopped and probably threatened at gunpoint. Most people, with a gun pointed at them, do what they're told. We all play for time."

Brett turned to Fuller and asked, "Have you heard anything about another set of remains found up in the mountains?"

Fuller seemed surprised. "Thought the local authorities were keeping that quiet. They're looking at bone and some tissue fragments. I'm not involved. They brought in a forensic anthropologist."

"Do you know who?" Brett asked.

"I don't, but I know who could tell you more," Fuller said.

"Let me guess — Lieutenant Gray?" Diego asked.

Fuller nodded. They thanked him and left the morgue, walking out into a beautiful sunset.

"Anyone need to stop anywhere before we get back to the ranch?" Matt asked.

"I think we need to get back," Diego said. "We should talk to Ben and Terry, for one thing."

Darkness was coming, and though he didn't know why, he was growing increasingly uneasy. He knew Meg was a good agent, but he also knew that even the most experienced agent, working alone, could run into trouble.

And there was something about night falling . . .

It was darker here than he'd expected, and the forests were filled with life, not all of it friendly.

"I definitely think we should get back," he said emphatically.

"Let's do it," Brett agreed.

CHAPTER SIX

"Nathan Kendall's story isn't unique — not among Southern soldiers who were displaced after the Civil War," Scarlet told Meg.

They were seated at her desk at the back of the museum, where she kept her files and had her computer set up. She didn't have an actual office, only this space between two display cabinets. To either side of the desk against the wall were bookshelves holding titles like *Know Your Colt, Smith & Wesson — the First Years* and *Get to Know Winchester!* Her work chair was comfortable, and there were two easy chairs in front of the desk, along with a few scattered straight-back chairs for those who wanted to pick up a book and browse for a few minutes.

Meg sat in one of the easy chairs, studying one of the historic diaries that was kept under lock and key, and wasn't available for public perusal.

Nathan had kept a series of diaries, an ongoing journal of his life, both during the war and after. Scarlet had read it and found it extremely moving. She and Ben had actually discussed publishing it. He wanted a university press to take it on, and she didn't disagree, though she knew getting the right person to acquire it and shepherd it through the process wouldn't be an easy task.

"I can only imagine what it must have been like — *felt like* — and how bitter the men must have been after fighting so long and losing," Meg said. "Losing their homes, then seeing people come down from the North, intent on making money off their misery, taking over their shops and farms and even the government." She sighed. "If John Wilkes Booth hadn't shot Lincoln, the aftermath of the war might not have been so bad. Then again, you probably had some toughs on both sides who were going to take advantage of the confusion to become criminals no matter what. Like at least one of these bandits Nathan Kendall rode with," she said, indicating the leather-bound journal she'd been reading.

"Do you think it will matter — as far as finding out who killed the Parkers, I mean — if we discover who killed Nathan and

Jillian Kendall?" Scarlet asked.

"Considering it seems pretty clear that the killer intentionally imitated the Kendalls' murders, it's certainly possible," Meg said. "Understanding the human mind is really the last frontier, and when it comes to killers, you're talking some of the most twisted logic you can think of. At the moment, this seems like a relevant avenue to explore. Amazing to think that this man was actually your ancestor."

Scarlet laughed softly. "It didn't really mean much to me when Ben first told me. I knew I was basically an all-American mutt but until I came out here, my ancestors were just people who lived, worked, had families and died. But now I realize they were all individuals and they seem so much more real to me. You're reading Nathan's journal of the war years, right?" Scarlet asked her.

"Yes, and it's so sad. I'm at the part where his friend Jeff Bay — one of the guys he wound up riding with during his outlaw days — found out that his wife died in childbirth."

"I've read it," Scarlet told her. "Heartbreaking."

Meg nodded. "Listen to this. 'I watched my friend crumple. He fell to the ground at first, no sound coming from him. Then he

150

let out a wail louder than the most plaintive call of a thousand wolves. Had the enemy been within reach, they would have heard and known where to find us. The day after, we began the terrible fight at Gettysburg, and at first I did not believe that Jeff would make it through, he walked so boldly into the fray. We pulled him from certain death time and time again. But the second day of battle was even more horrible. My friend became an unstoppable killer, as if he was mindless of all else. I am amazed that he alone did not win us that battle, for he was responsible for a field of graves that day.' ”

"Hang on," Scarlet murmured, looking over at Meg. "This is after he bought this property."

"Anything?"

"I don't know, but it's lovely," Scarlet said, and started reading aloud. " 'Today is the start of a new life for us. Of course, thank the Lord above, it is possible only because I have never been prosecuted for the terrible things I did. Billie didn't understand how I felt when I told him that I had to leave the company. He said that a good Yankee was a dead Yankee, and all the better dead now, since we'd missed killing him during the war. But I never did cotton to killing. I saw the eyes of those Northern boys, and I knew that they were just as scared of dying as I was. But I'd have to shoot anyway — just as they had to shoot — and somehow, by the grace of God, I came out of the war alive and whole. And now here I stand, about as close to Heaven as a man can get. I still cannot believe my good fortune that old Rollo sold this land to me for what I can afford to pay. But he wants to work some property a little south of here, hoping to find gold at last, and he needed the money for supplies. Rollo wants to get rich from gold. I just want to stay here forever and see the mountains, valleys and streams, every morning when I wake up. Those are the riches I want to live for now.' "

Meg shook her head. "I'm glad he found peace, at least for a little while, before he was killed. Listen to this," she said. " 'Sharpsburg today by Antietam Creek. The dead were falling on the dead, the injured were buried beneath blown-off limbs and bloody bodies. All those men dying, and somehow the screams of the horses sounded loudest in my head. Fighting next to Billie, there came a point when he rallied me. A fellow from our company fell next to me. I watched his eyes roll back, watched him die, and I froze where I stood. Billie kicked me to get me moving again. A Yank in front of me went down. Billie stood over him and put a bullet into his heart. He told me it was a mercy that he killed the fellow instead of leaving him there to die slow. But I saw the hatred in Billie's eyes. He wants them all dead. Said even his father and brothers should die for joining the Yankee cause and turning against their own.' "

"Billie sounds like one hateful man," Scarlet said.

"But honest about his hate," Meg said. "Not the kind to hide in the shadows."

"In other words, you think that if Billie had killed Nathan, he would just have shot him straight out, he wouldn't have tortured him first," Scarlet said.

"What about the father-in-law?" Meg asked.

"I found an entry from the day Nathan met Jillian. It's really sweet," Scarlet said, smiling and flipping pages. She read: " 'She touched my soul like the first sight of the snow on the mountains. And when she turned to me and smiled, I felt as if the purity of the air and the warmth of the high sun had entered my heart.' "

Meg smiled for a moment, but her voice was grim when she asked, "But what about the father?"

"Oh, him. There's this. 'US Marshal Vickers is a master of authority or, dare I say, an outright bully. Perhaps I have the man all wrong and he is simply a good and doting father, worried for Jillian because of what he knows — or may know — about me. He fought for the North — I fought for the South. He should know nothing of my outlaw days, and yet he looks at me as if he does. I have never lied to Jillian. She knows everything about my past, yet I do not think she would have told him. Whatever his reason may be, her father has forbidden us to see one another. But my love — my sweet Jillian! — has informed him that she is an adult and a free woman, and that she will make up her own mind in this regard. Thus far, however, we meet only in secret. One day, she assures me, her father will accept me. He loves her and she loves me, so eventually, she insists, he must love me, too. I hope she is correct in this, though I fear she is blinded by the love of a daughter for her only living parent.' "

"Would he have killed his own daughter?" Meg asked.

"I hate to think of a father killing his daughter," Scarlet said, shaking her head.

"There are fanatics who would rather see their children dead than 'defiled.' And the evidence seems to say that Jillian caught the killer in the act. Vickers might have killed her to save himself," Meg said.

"I still think it has to be someone else," Scarlet said.

"We need to keep reading his journals. The way he was killed . . . I think someone wanted something from him, and the answer could be in the journals."

"It could have been anyone, then, one of his old running mates or someone from the area."

Meg laughed. "Which wasn't well populated at the time, at least, so that makes our job easier."

"I know no one called them serial killers back then, but I've read that they existed. Or it could just have been someone with a grudge."

"Exactly," Meg said, and looked over toward the stairs and the statue of Nathan Kendall.

Scarlet looked over at the statue, too. She wasn't sure why, but ever since it had shown up by her bed, she'd found it frightening.

It was just a mannequin, she told herself. Of one of her own ancestors.

She turned her head, choosing *not* to look at it.

Because now, whenever she looked at Nathan Kendall, she felt as if he was looking back at her.

She tried not to let Meg see the unease in her eyes. And she was glad that — awkward as it would undoubtedly be — she'd asked Diego to sleep with her.

Yet, would it really be so awkward? She'd often wondered whether, despite what she'd done back then in response to the deep hurt and her wounded pride, life could change and they could somehow get back to the way they'd been. She'd thought about him so often on lonely nights, times when she couldn't even talk herself into going out and enjoying the company of friends, much less contemplate dating again. Diego had filled her mind then, just as he did now. She remembered the first time she'd seen him, the first time he'd touched her, how her flesh had come alive at the mere feel of his finger idly touching her hand across a table, desire sweeping through her like the sweetest fire.

There was a knock at the museum door, and Scarlet nearly jumped out of her chair. "Do you think the guys are back already?" she asked Meg.

"I don't know. Sit tight." Meg was already on her way to the door. She opened it a crack and peered out. It wasn't the guys.

It was Lieutenant Gray.

"Lieutenant Gray, hello," Meg said. "How can we help you?"

Gray seemed his usual hard-core, jaded self. "I understand it's now all about how *I* can help *you,*" he said curtly. "I understand the FBI has taken the lead on this case."

Scarlet saw Meg quickly lower her head, as if to hide whatever she might have been feeling at the lieutenant's displeasure.

Apparently Adam Harrison and the Krewe of Hunters really *did* get what they wanted.

"Well, then, thank you so much for making yourself available to us," Meg said, her gratitude apparently genuine. "We don't really see ourselves as taking the lead, though, We see all law enforcement as working together. Come on in — Scarlet and I have been reading through some old documents."

"Well, I've just been going through a few *new* documents — Mrs. McCullough's recent inventory of the museum's collection of weapons. And it seems that our list of pieces taken from the museum and her inventory don't match up." He looked past Meg to stare suspiciously at Scarlet. "One gun on your list isn't in our evidence locker."

"What's missing?" Scarlet asked.

"An 1849 Colt pocket percussion

revolver," Gray told them. "And, according to the lab reports, it just might be the weapon that killed Larry and Candace Parker."

Diego saw what was clearly an unmarked police vehicle in the Conway Ranch lot as they drove up.

"What the hell?" he muttered, feeling his tension grow.

He suspected the car belonged to Lieutenant Gray, and he knew Gray resented their presence. Worse, the man was still convinced that Scarlet was somehow complicit in what was going on.

"How much do you want to bet that's Lieutenant Gray's car?" he asked his fellow agents.

"Not a dime, but he could just be here to give us information," Brett said.

"Oh, yeah, 'cuz he's such a team player," Matt muttered.

"Well, let's go see, shall we?" Diego asked.

They went in without knocking, and to Diego it looked almost as if Scarlet had been waiting for them. And yet, when he strode in, looking at her questioningly, she almost smiled.

"Upstairs," she told him. "Lieutenant Gray — first name Ernie, by the way — is having a cup of coffee with us."

He looked at her in surprise.

She shrugged. "He seems to have made a complete turnaround. Meg's with him now. I just came down to turn on the outside light, in case it was dark by the time you got back."

"All right," he said skeptically. "I guess coffee sounds good. And we need to talk to the man anyway."

"He's also investigating the remains found up on the mountain," Brett said. "I wonder what changed his mind about us?"

"I think I can explain that," Scarlet said. "It turns out he's another of the many descendants of Nathan Kendall. Come on up," she told the three men. "We've got sandwiches for dinner, too. And Lieutenant Gray is on a roll, telling stories."

"Wait, wait," Diego said. "Gray came here to tell you that he's a descendant of Nathan Kendall?"

"No," she said, serious now. "He came to tell us that we're missing an 1849 Colt pocket percussion revolver. When they compared my inventory to the weapons the forensic team took, they discovered that one is missing."

Diego looked over at Brett and Matt.

So the couple *had* been killed with a

159

weapon from the museum?

"What is it?" Scarlet asked.

"Time to get a locksmith in — now," Diego said. He headed upstairs, uneasily aware that the statue of Nathan Kendall seemed to be watching him as he went. As the others followed, he wondered if any of them sensed something eerie about the mannequin, too.

In the kitchen, he greeted Lieutenant Gray, who really did seem to have done a complete one-eighty, judging by the way he and Meg were laughing about something. Gray had a sandwich in front of him. A large pot of coffee sat on the stove and there was a big plate of sandwiches on the counter.

Gray smiled and said a friendly hello, then added, "I gather you guys were just at the morgue."

Diego nodded. "And I'm glad we did. Did you know that your medical examiner is also a historical reenactor? He named that exact model as the possible murder weapon."

Gray nodded. "Yeah, I know. And he's right, according to the forensic lab. Handmade bullets out of an antique mold. The bullets weren't antique, though. They were made of new materials, melted lead and gunpowder. Someone was in the museum and stole the gun that killed Mr.

and Mrs. Parker," he said solemnly, then tried to lighten the mood with a joke. "Or maybe Nathan Kendall has come back to kill people for . . . I don't know, trespassing on his land or something. Hell, that statue downstairs looks pretty damn lifelike. Maybe it stole that gun and gets up to no good at night, when everyone else is asleep."

Diego saw Scarlet's eyes widen. "How sure are you that the gun that's missing from the museum is the gun that killed the Parkers?" he quickly asked Gray, hoping to focus people's attention away from Scarlet.

Gray looked at him curiously. "Let's see, an 1849 Colt pocket percussion revolver is missing, the same weapon the murderer used and not exactly your garden-variety gun. Hell yes, I think the murder weapon is the one that's missing from the museum."

"Do you have a suspect in mind?" Diego asked.

Gray shrugged, frustrated. "The department got and executed a search warrant for the Conway Ranch, but the gun wasn't anywhere to be found. It's at the bottom of a lake somewhere, I suspect. We've questioned everyone who was here at the time of the murders, but there's no evidence pointing to anyone at all."

"The museum has no security to speak of

and never has," Meg pointed out.

"A situation that's about to change," Diego interjected.

"Meanwhile," Meg said, shooting him a frustrated look, "there's nothing but a basic lock on the door. Before Ben hired Scarlet, no one was living upstairs, and in fact the apartment was still being renovated. Dozens of workers were in and out, and the door was left open half the time. Foolish on his part, if you ask me, given the value of his collection, but his choice."

"I'm sure you're right and the murder weapon came from the museum, but since there was ample opportunity for pretty much anyone to steal it, that also means pretty much anyone could have used it," Diego said. "I'd pretty much guarantee, though, that your killer is someone who knew in advance about both the museum's weapons collection and the Kendall family history, quite likely someone who'd already visited the museum at least once."

"Which is pretty much anyone who's ever stayed or worked here at the ranch, at least when it comes to knowing about the guns. The family connection is another matter," Gray said. "We're not fools, Agent McCullough. I have men going over lists of all the workers and past guests."

"It could also be someone who lives in the area and knows about the museum and the ranch's history," Matt said.

Gray nodded. "Which is pretty much everyone in town. And then there are all of us who are descended from Nathan Kendall." He nodded at Scarlet and grinned.

Diego wasn't sure why, it looked to him that there was something scary about that grin. "True, though I'm not sure why one of the man's descendants would want to kill any of the others. It's not as if there's an inheritance involved.

"Listen," Diego said, looking at Gray. "We need a security upgrade for this place. Can you give me the name of someone reliable who can put in better locks and arrange a security system? I'd like the locks changed by tonight."

"Why don't you let me take care of that?" Gray offered, and promptly pulled out his phone to make a call. When he hung up, he was smiling. "There's a guy on the way," he promised.

"Thank you," Diego said. Whatever had changed the guy's attitude for the better, he was glad of it. He leaned forward to talk to Lieutenant Gray. "I understand that you're handling the human remains found up on the mountain."

"Yes, a month or so ago. I mean, what's left of the body was found a month or so ago. It had been there awhile. It's strange when you find remains at the tundra level. Because they're above the tree line, there's a lot less cover to protect them, so sometimes they're nearly perfect, if the snow comes in time to cover them, but otherwise, it's a crapshoot. In this case, we don't know yet when he — we do know it's a man, by the way — was killed, whether it's been months or even years. Our department experts can't agree. Betsy Wiggin, the department head, is convinced he died this summer, so not even a year ago yet. A couple of the others say the fabric scraps found under the body suggest that the remains are a lot older. But Betsy thinks we're looking at the reenactor wearing authentic clothing. At this point we've got a forensic anthropologist working on it, and we'll wait and see what he says."

"You said it's a man, but do you know anything else?" Matt asked.

"Somewhere between thirty and forty, but that's it," Gray said.

"No one similar in the missing persons database?" Brett asked.

"No one so far, but once we figure out

when he died, maybe we can focus our search more effectively."

"Have you done a facial reconstruction yet?" Diego asked.

"No," Gray said. "Right now we're focusing on how he died — along with when, of course. There aren't any nicks on the bones that suggest a knife wound. No bullets were retrieved from the area. He could have gotten himself lost up there and just frozen to death. Or fallen. We're still working on it."

Diego made a point of not looking at any of the other agents. He knew the Bureau had the resources to figure that out — and quickly.

"We don't believe he was from around here," Gray told them. "There's definitely no one missing locally who's anywhere near the description."

Matt cleared his throat. "We have an agent in our unit who's a brilliant forensic artist. We can bring her in, if you want."

When Gray didn't say anything right away, Diego thought he was going to refuse their help, since the case didn't have any connection to the murders of Larry and Candace Parker.

But then the lieutenant surprised him by shrugging. "Sure. Quite frankly, we have no idea what we're dealing with, and I'd appreciate any help."

"I'll get on it," Matt said.

"On another note, what can you tell us about the guests who left the Conway Ranch after the Parkers' bodies were discovered?" Diego asked.

Lieutenant Ernie Gray almost smiled. "The interview reports have already been emailed to all four of you."

"Thank you," Meg said.

"I like to think we could have handled this," Gray said gruffly. "But, hey. A solved murder is a solved murder, right?"

Scarlet stood. "I think I heard someone at the door," she said, and started out of the room.

Diego rose quickly, blocking her.

She turned to him almost indignantly. "I was going to look before I opened the door."

"That should be the security guy," Gray said.

Diego went with her to open the door and discovered that Gray was right.

He was young, no more than twenty-five, but he was with the police, one Officer Benjamin by name, and he seemed to know his stuff. He'd not only brought state-of-the-art locks, but he'd also come with an alarm system and a motion detector. He had the system installed and showed them how it worked, and by the time he finished, the agents, who'd left ridiculously early that morning, were dragging.

Meg and Matt said good-night and headed over to the main house, promising that before they went to bed they would tell Ben and Terry to use a little extra caution, just in case the connection to Nathan Kendall had played a role in the recent murders. Brett told them that he was going to call Lara before he turned in for the night.

"I can't wait for her to get here this weekend. You're going to love her," he assured Scarlet.

"Of course I will. If you love her, so will I," she told him.

Words, Diego thought. They were all saying the right words, but what difference did it really make if Scarlet and Lara got along? They would all be leaving as soon as this case was solved.

Except for Scarlet. Scarlet would stay.

And *that,* he realized, didn't matter at all. He'd come here to keep her safe. No matter where they might be in life, or with whom, it wouldn't change a thing. He loved her, and nothing mattered more than keeping her safe.

Brett left them to close himself into the far bedroom for the night and make his call.

And once again, Diego and Scarlet were left alone.

"I need to get some sleep, too," he said.

"Of course. Your things are in the room," she said. She sounded nervous, but she met his eyes as she spoke.

He shook his head, smiling slightly. "We don't have to do anything, Scarlet."

"What if I want to do something?" she asked.

The color of her eyes was like a mix of the sea and sky on a summer's day; the wistfulness in her voice seemed to touch something as old as time in his soul. He fought not to fall prey to his emotions, to remember that once they'd had something unique, special beyond anything he'd ever dreamed of, but it still hadn't been enough to last for all time.

And yet he couldn't stop himself.

"I have a feeling I could be convinced," he told her lightly.

She smiled. "Well, then . . ."

She turned to head for her room. He caught hold of her shoulder, and swung her back around and into his arms. He kissed her, relishing the softness of her lips, her tongue . . . and a hunger that seemed to match his own.

He broke away, breathless. Her eyes

seemed dazzling now on his.

"Wow," she murmured, then turned serious. "Brett is down at the other end of the hall."

He grinned. "And you don't think Brett knows what we're doing?"

She flushed. "Some divorced people hate each other."

"I never hated you."

"I only hated you a little."

That hurt — because he knew why.

He started to pull away, but she held him back. "Only a little bit — and only for a little while," she whispered, sounding almost desperate. "And I know that . . . that I was at fault, too."

"You were never at fault," he told her.

"But I was," she said. "I wanted the knight in shining armor all the time, the man who was charming and teased and laughed, and could make everyone around him comfortable . . . who even made me jealous sometimes, but not really, because I knew I was the one you wanted. I didn't want to get between you and your work, because I knew it was a passion for you, but at the same time I resented it for coming between us."

"I shouldn't have let that happen," he said. He started to turn away.

She stopped him, pleading in her eyes. "Can we forget the past for tonight? No past, no future. Just tonight."

His only answer was to pull her back into his arms. His physical response to her was almost embarrassingly instantaneous.

She felt him against her and practically melted into him. Her fingers started playing with the buttons of his shirt.

"Brett's down the hall," he reminded her, echoing her words in one last attempt to retain his sanity.

"Yes, but he knows what we're doing," she said.

Then she smiled, turned and walked down the hall to her room.

He followed.

She closed the door and kicked off her shoes. Her T-shirt hit the floor in seconds, her bra following suit without a pause. She shimmied out of her jeans and panties while he watched, and then she stood naked before him, smiling.

He grinned, pulling his holster and gun from his waistband, then set them on the bedside table before practically tearing off his shirt.

There had been a time when she'd hated the gun, when she'd asked him to put it out of sight the minute he got home, a request he hadn't recognized for what it was: an attempt to forget about his job for a little while and have him all to herself.

She didn't ask that tonight.

The minute he ditched the rest of his clothes she moved into his arms, her heated skin practically setting his aflame. "Remember how to do this?" she teased.

"I remember everything," he told her seriously. "I remember that one of the things that drives you the craziest is when I stand behind you and run the tip of my tongue down your spine. Want me to show you?"

She started to say something, but he didn't give her the chance. He caught her lips, then lifted her and set her down on the bed. He kissed her long and deeply, and he never really broke away, he just trailed down to her throat and her breasts, and then her midriff and along the soft silky flesh of her inner thighs.

She writhed and moaned against him, her fingers on his shoulders, her body arching in a way that fed his hunger and desire nearly to the breaking point. He made love to her slowly, despite the burning need within him, taking her almost to the point of no return, then backing off and finding her lips again, teasing her flesh as he savored the feel of her, the pleasure of being with her again.

She cried out softly again and again, until suddenly she became the aggressor, shifting until she was on top of him, burning his skin with kisses and caresses, and then sliding onto him again until he rolled her under him again and drove them both to a violent climax. Finally, exhausted, sated, the sound of their heartbeats like a crescendo in the night, they rested.

As he held her, he remembered how they had promised each other forever . . . and how soon they'd broken that promise.

He was surprised when she spoke.

"Thank you," she said softly.

He turned to her. "No, thank *you*," he said, and smiled.

"I — I haven't, um, I haven't really even dated since . . ." Her voice trailed off, and she looked away.

Resting on an elbow, he watched her face in the pale light that seeped in through the window. "Neither have I."

"What? I don't believe you."

"One dinner," he told her.

"Was she nice?"

"Yes."

"Was she pretty?"

"Very."

"Then what happened?"

"She wasn't you," Diego said softly. Then he pulled her against him. "Let's get some sleep. I really did get up at the crack of dawn."

"Whatever you want," she said, which sent his mind running in a direction conducive to anything but sleep. But a moment later she said, "Thank you for coming here."

"Of course."

"You didn't have to."

"Yes, I did."

"That's who you are," she said softly.

He didn't answer. He didn't know what to say.

"Diego?"

"Yes?"

"That's an admirable quality, you know."

Her fingers closed around him, and to his chagrin, he was instantly aroused.

Apparently forgetting her promise to let him sleep, she slid atop him. "And so is this," she teased.

They made love again, and it was a very long time before he went to sleep.

CHAPTER SEVEN

The dreams that filled Scarlet's unconscious mind came with morning's light rather than the deepest darkness of the night.

It seemed to Scarlet that she was waking up, roused by the glow of dawn slipping into the room. The sun. But then the sun was suddenly surrounded by a haze, as if a mist had come from nowhere to dull its brilliance. And that notion was ridiculous, she knew, because mist didn't come in bright sunlight, it came on days when storms were darkening the skies. But logic didn't matter, because the mist was there, diffusing the glow of the sun. And then . . .

Someone was walking toward her through the mist.

No, there were two of them . . .

Two men walking toward her. One moved stiffly, like the living robots she'd seen entertaining tourists in Times Square. The other moved naturally, shaking his head as if in amusement at his companion's awkwardness.

They both looked to be in their thirties, wearing jeans, Western-style shirts and cowboy hats.

At first she wasn't afraid.

"We're just trying to help," the awkward one assured her, reaching the foot of the bed. It was the statue of Nathan Kendall, she realized.

"You're one of us," the other said. She wasn't sure who he was; she couldn't see him past Nathan.

"We're coming back," Nathan said.

"We're trying to help," the other said.

"Trying to save you," said Nathan . . .

That was when she awoke, bolting upright from the dream. She stared at the foot of her bed, terrified that the statue would be standing there again.

It wasn't, and she breathed deeply in relief.

Diego. Diego was here.

She stretched a hand out across the sheets. Diego *wasn't* here.

He'd always been an early riser, even when he'd stayed up late. He was probably just in the bathroom or in the kitchen making coffee. And Brett was there somewhere, too. She was safe.

She inhaled deeply and told herself that she'd simply had a weird dream.

All she had to do was let the dream drift away and she would be fine. She reminded herself that she'd had a pretty spectacular night. But now she needed to shower and face the day. At least now she wasn't alone.

She showered quickly, and realized from the wet towels and familiar razor by the sink that Diego had showered and shaved earlier. There was something comforting about seeing the evidence of his presence there.

She dressed quickly and headed to the kitchen.

There was an unfamiliar older man sitting at the table. His hair was snow white, neatly cut, and he was studying one of Nathan Kendall's journals.

For a moment, she froze, wondering about her sanity, her dreams and mannequins that moved.

She stood there gaping, wondering if the man was real or not.

He was.

And he proved it by standing up as soon as he noticed her and smiling.

"Scarlet, hello, I'm so sorry to have startled you. Brett let me in a little while ago. I'm Adam Harrison." He offered her his hand.

Relieved and feeling more than a little silly, she smiled and quickly walked forward to offer him her hand in return.

"It's very nice to meet you. I've heard all about you, of course. You were so kind to send everyone out here so quickly to help me."

"I was happy to do it. Come, why don't sit down and join me?"

"Just let me get some coffee," she said. She poured herself a cup and sat down beside him.

"Phantom photos — now that's something new," Adam said.

"I wasn't the only one who saw them," she said, and realized that she sounded defensive. "Ben — Ben Kendall, my boss — saw the pictures, too. They were there — and then they weren't."

"I don't doubt you for a minute. The camera will be on its way to our own people back East very soon. We'll find out what's going on."

"That's great, thank you," Scarlet said. Then she asked, "Do you know where Diego is?"

"I do. He and the others are with Lieutenant Gray. They're heading to the morgue to examine the remains that were discovered up on the mountain."

"Ah, okay," she said. She didn't know what else to say, so she asked, "Can I get you something to eat?"

"No, I ate on the plane, but feel free to get yourself something. Once you're done, I would love to see your museum. I understand it holds an extensive weapons collection."

"It does — except that it's not here at the moment. The police took all our weapons. Except —"

"Yes, I know. You're missing an 1849 Colt pocket percussion revolver," Adam said. "Most probably the murder weapon."

"Someone must have broken in here and stolen it," she said.

"They won't now," he assured her. "Not only do you have an alarm system, but we know exactly where all the keys are — with us."

"Didn't Ben ask for a key?" she asked. "He does own the property."

"We asked him not to for the time being," he told her. "Go on. Grab yourself some breakfast. While you eat, I'll bore you with the story of my life."

"I doubt any story about you could be boring."

He smiled at that. "It all depends on what you're willing to believe."

■ ■ ■ ■

The fact that anyone could actually tell anything about the remains that had been found up on the mountain was mind-boggling to Diego.

There was virtually nothing left.

They didn't see the medical examiner; they saw a woman named Tammy Vargo, who was a forensic anthropologist and bone specialist. She was a no-nonsense woman with iron-gray hair and sharp features, but she was happy to speak with them, pointing out everything she'd been able to discover about the dead man.

"There wasn't enough soft tissue left to determine cause of death — probably because he was left out in the open. As the ME probably told you, there are no nicks or scratches on the bones, so it's unlikely that he was stabbed. If he was shot, it was a through-and-through and, again, never even nicked a bone. He was in his midthirties, maybe six-two or six-three. He died sometime between two and six months ago, tops. I linked the fabric fragments to a designer brand available here in town and all across the country. He never had a cavity, so we won't get any help from dental records. No fingerprints, of course. No breaks in any of the bones — guy never even broke a toe. My guess is that he froze to death — the tundra level gets very cold — but as to why he was caught out there that way, I don't know. He could have been bound and left, but no evidence of rope or any other kind of cord or whatever turned up. I wish there was more I could tell but I can't. This appears to be the skeleton of a man who — until his demise — was incredibly healthy."

"Thank you anyway," Diego told her. "It's actually helpful to be able to rule things out."

Matt added, "We have a forensic artist coming to do a likeness. I hope you don't mind."

"They aren't my bones," she said. "Somebody somewhere is probably missing him. If an artist can help ID him and bring someone peace, I'm all for it."

As they were driving back to the ranch, Brett asked Diego, "Do you think that guy's death could be related to the Parkers' murders? People do climb mountains, and sometimes they die on them."

"I don't think we have enough information yet to say. But what's going on is strange, to say the least. My gut tells me the

Parkers *were* murdered because Larry was descended from Nathan Kendall. I think the killer had a key to the museum — whether legitimately or because he stole it — and not only stole the gun, but moved the statue of Nathan Kendall into Scarlet's room to scare her when she woke up." Diego saw their startled looks and remembered that they weren't privy to that information, so he quickly explained. "I also think the killer tried to set her up, somehow putting those pictures on her camera, though how he managed that and then managed to erase them, I don't know," he said.

"Well, we'll know about the camera soon enough; Adam had it sent to Will Chan, and if anyone can figure out how it was hacked, it's Will," Meg said with assurance.

"Who's the artist you mentioned? And when is he coming?" Brett asked.

"*She* is Jane Everett," Matt said. "She's from Texas, and she's been with the Krewe a few years now. She's the best I've ever seen. She'll be in and ready to work her magic by tonight."

"Let's hope whatever she comes up with will help us find out who he is," Brett said.

"If he'd been from here, someone would have reported him missing," Meg said.

Diego looked out the window as the conversation faded. That morning, before they'd left, he'd stopped by the statue of Nathan Kendall. He was going to jokingly thank it for spooking Scarlet and giving him the kind of night that he'd once taken almost for granted and then thought he would never experience again.

Yet he'd never said a word, because something about the mannequin had seemed . . . different.

He'd only just joined the Krewe, but he'd researched the unit and its members extensively when Matt and Meg had come down to Florida to help with his zombie case.

They all saw the dead, just as he and Brett had.

But the mannequin . . .

It was wood and paint.

Still, he could have sworn the damned thing had smiled at him as if saying, "Yeah, friend, I did you a big favor. Now take good care of what you have, okay?"

Thinking about the mannequin, the unidentified remains and the murders, he asked, "Where are Nathan and Jillian Kendall buried?"

"We can ask Scarlet — I'm certain she'll know," Meg said.

"I'd like to see their graves," Diego said.

"Not a bad idea," Matt said.

When they returned to the museum, Diego used his new key to open the door, then disarmed and reset the alarm. It was broad daylight, of course, but an alarm system was only ever as good as the way it was used, and he intended that they should use it.

The others headed up the stairs. He paused in front of the mannequin again.

Had something subtly changed about it? Or was it all in his mind?

He heard laughter drifting down from upstairs. Scarlet's laughter. It was wonderful to hear it again.

The mannequin stared back at him. Suddenly he found himself back in Miami, in that room at the detention center with the old woman.

I just want to protect her.

Once again, the words seemed to have come from the mannequin.

"Yeah?" he said softly. "Well, so do I. And I'm flesh and blood, and I'm not leaving until she's safe," he assured the mannequin. He felt a little like a fool. Ghosts were one thing. Lots of people made very credible claims to have seen and even communicated with them.

But talking to a mannequin? That was something else entirely.

Or was it?

"Diego?" Brett called from the top of the stairs.

He climbed up to join the others and found them gathered around the kitchen table, where an older man who had to be Adam Harrison seemed to be delighting Scarlet.

She looked over at him. "Brett was saying that you wanted to know where Nathan and Jillian were buried. They're up the little mountain peak behind the stables. There's a small historic cemetery up there. You can hike to it, which is a long trip, or you can ride."

"What are the chances of us all taking a ride?" he asked.

"They're good," she said. "No new guests have shown up, so the horses are just standing around the corral. And," she added, grinning, "Angus seems to like you."

"Adam, are you joining us?" Matt asked.

"I think I'll spend some time getting to know everyone here at the ranch," Adam said. He pulled a small notebook from his pocket; he was obviously old-school.

"Owners — Ben, real name Bertram, Kendall and his wife, Trisha. Head housekeeper, Linda Reagan. Angus Fillmore runs the stables. The remaining guests are Terry Ballantree, newlyweds Gwen and Charles Barton and retirees Gigi and Clark Levin. The Levins are regular visitors, coming every year. I'm thinking they could be quite helpful."

"The guests may be down in town," Meg said.

"If they are, they'll come back eventually. I can rock on the porch, talk to Ben and Trisha, or interview the housekeeper. There's plenty for me to do here," Adam assured her.

"Are there enough horses, Scarlet?" Diego asked.

"There are eight, so we'll be fine. Angus can take us. Ben doesn't let the horses out unless it's with Angus or himself," she said.

"All right." Diego looked around the room and grinned. They were all dressed casually enough to go riding, except for Adam, who was in a suit. Diego had a feeling Adam was always in a suit. It was a good thing he didn't plan to go riding with them.

Scarlet's eyes met his, and she quickly looked away. She didn't actually blush, but he knew she was thinking about last night. He smiled, lowering his own eyes.

It was good to be back with her. It made

185

the day better — no matter what it brought. And tonight . . .

He had no intention of thinking about tonight and all the nights to come. Not now. Time for that later, when this case was solved. When Scarlet was safe.

Scarlet had always loved the fact that she'd grown up with sun and water — and horses.

Her favorite of Conway Ranch's hack line was Blaze, a bay gelding with, naturally, a blaze on his forehead. He was a good sixteen hands high, had beautiful gaits and seemed to like just about everyone.

Of course, she wanted to think that he especially liked her.

Angus was happy for the chance to tack up the horses and go for a ride.

After he'd saddled the mounts he'd decided upon for each rider, he confided to Scarlet, "Thank the Lord you all want to go riding. I like it here, and no matter what Ben says or what his finances are, with nobody new coming to stay, I was getting worried he might lay me off 'til things pick up again. So you say where and we'll go."

"We want to ride up to the old cemetery," Scarlet said.

He studied her for a minute and then shrugged. "A little creepy, but okay."

As the Krewe and Scarlet mounted up, Angus said, "Don't worry, no one is on a kicker or a biter. And they know these trails better than me. Just sit back and enjoy. There will be a lot of single file up the mountain, so keep up. They'll want to snack along the way. It's not mean to stop them. In fact, it's better for their bellies if you do. They know they're not supposed to stop for a nibble, but they're going to test you, so be bosses. Gentle bosses, but bosses."

Angus led the way. Scarlet was behind him, and Diego rode close behind her on Zeus, another magnificent gelding, black as pitch except for his four white socks.

It was an hour up, but it was a surprisingly pleasant hour. Angus lifted a hand to stop them a few times when they reached a clearing, once to observe a herd of elk, who stopped grazing to look up at the riders. They passed a wild turkey and a number of pheasants as well and Angus gave a little speech about each animal they passed along the way.

The day was cool but not cold. The ride offered all the natural beauty that brought people from all over the country and the world to the Rocky Mountains.

Eventually they reached a high plateau. Angus stopped and dismounted, and told them all to do the same. "Tether your horses to the trees, though. Trust me, it's a long, lonely walk back down," he said.

Scarlet knew the cemetery, having been up to visit it several times.

Once upon a time there had been wrought-iron fencing surrounding the whole of the place, which covered a bit more than half an acre. The gate, decorated with ornate ironwork, was unnecessary at this point, since most of the fencing was long gone.

The sun slipped behind a cloud as they gathered in the cemetery. The chill in the air, the sudden onset of a mist that softened all the details of the scene, seemed perfect for such an excursion.

Scarlet wasn't sure why, but she walked straight over to a large obelisk.

It was new. Ben had arranged to have it installed just a year ago.

It had been erected near the original headstones for Nathan and Jillian. Scarlet knew that the stones themselves were special; many of the graves were marked only by wooden crosses, which were periodically replaced by a women's historical society. There were also three decrepit mausoleums on the property, and half a dozen concrete sarcophagi.

The remote location made such monuments a rarity, proof that only those with money could afford to bury their dead for eternity, or a few centuries anyway.

She walked over to the Kendalls' original gravestones and knelt down beside them. She'd seen them on her previous visits, and they hadn't changed. Had she expected them to?

Presumably Jillian's father, the United States marshal, had ordered the tombstones for his daughter and son-in-law. Maybe he had shown equal regard for Nathan because he was raising the man's son, or maybe he hadn't wanted to increase his neighbors' suspicions that he was behind the murders by slighting him. Except for the names and dates of birth, both tombstones read the same:

Young, beautiful, on the path to good, six feet under in boxes of wood. Let their souls soar to the greatest height, let their love rise up to the brightest light.

"Really lovely — especially since the father-in-law was a suspect in the murders," Meg said from behind her.

Scarlet shook her head. "I just can't believe the man could have killed his own daughter."

"Could have been one of his ex-comrades from the war and his marauding days," Meg mused.

"Or a madman from anywhere around here whose crimes are being replicated now," Matt said, looking higher.

Scarlet followed his gaze. They could see great peaks of the Rockies rising around them. Some had slopes where the trees were still a rich green, while others were turning, glowing with stunning fall colors.

But all the peaks were already covered in snow.

As she looked out, she saw something moving in her peripheral vision.

An elk? More pheasants?

A cloud moved; the sun rose higher.

For a moment the day was bright.

And in that light, leaning against a tree, Scarlet saw the man who had stopped her in town the night she had gone to dinner — before she'd known that anyone had been killed.

She stood quickly, staring at him. "Wait!" she cried, rushing toward the trees.

The sun shifted again. The man was gone.

"Scarlet, what is it?" Diego asked, instantly at her side.

"The guy who was bugging me the other night," she said indignantly. "He followed us up here! But, how the hell . . . ? Or maybe, he's the kind of ghoul who hangs around in cemeteries for fun."

Of course, she was hanging around in a cemetery herself.

Diego was already heading into the trees, closely followed by Matt and Brett.

Meg stayed behind with her and Angus.

Scarlet noticed that they never left her alone — not even in hot pursuit.

"What's going on?" Angus asked, baffled. "Ben owns this land, but he doesn't care if people come up here. People can still be buried here, if they want."

"I just saw someone who —" Scarlet broke off. "I met him in town the other night, and he was just creepy, that's all."

"The guys will just make sure he's not up to anything," Meg promised.

Angus snorted. "Free country."

"Angus, you don't think it's strange that someone who stopped me in the street and said some very weird things just happens to be up here now?" Scarlet asked.

"I think people come to the mountains because they like nature — and being left alone," Angus said.

"Then he should have left *me* alone," Scarlet said.

Diego, Matt and Brett were gone for a

long time, but when they came back they announced that they hadn't found the man or any sign of where he'd gone.

"Wonder where he went," Meg said.

"One trail up, one trail down," Angus said. "Couldn't'a gone anywhere else."

"I saw him," Scarlet said firmly.

"Well, he's gone now," Diego said, studying her. "Midthirties, you said, right?"

"Midthirties, maybe six feet, not fat and not thin, sandy-blond hair," Scarlet said.

Everyone except Angus looked at her strangely.

She wondered what was wrong with them. Did they think she was so stressed she was seeing things?

"Is there something I don't know?" she asked.

Meg shook her head. "No. Whoever was here, he's gone now. I guess we've seen everything there is to see here, so it's probably time to go back."

Diego put his arm around Scarlet's shoulders and started walking toward where the horses were tethered. She felt uneasy again. Was he being protective — or pitying?

The others had gotten ahead of them when he stopped walking suddenly. "That's a strange plaque — very modern."

The flat bronze plaque had been set in front of a relatively new wooden cross.

"Rollo Conway," he said. "So the guy who sold the land to Nathan Kendall is buried here, too?"

"Yes. He died years after Nathan and Jillian," Scarlet said. "But Jillian's dad — who lived to ninetysomething — allowed him to be buried here. I think this was pretty much the local cemetery back then, even though it was on ranch land. It was an old Native American burial site back before anyone owned land here. The site is actually on the national historic register. It will always be protected, no matter who owns the property."

"Anyone else buried here we should know about?" he asked her.

"Not that I'm aware of," she said. "Thing is, the old records aren't always complete. And up here, the ground shifts, markers rot away in the elements, people are reburied elsewhere." She smiled. "Unless we start digging people up and, I don't know, DNA-testing them, we can only do the best we can with the records available to us."

"What about Jillian's father? The United States marshal?" Diego asked. "Where was he buried."

She pointed across the cemetery to one of

the decaying mausoleums. "He was entombed, not buried."

"And Zachary Kendall?"

"He moved to Los Angeles in his later years and is buried there," Scarlet said. "When the marshal had the mausoleum built, he probably assumed Zachary and at least some of the children would share it with him. But life — and death — don't always work out as planned."

"Apparently not," Diego said.

"Come on, let's head back."

She followed him but stopped again before they reached the horses. "Diego, do you really believe me?"

"Of course."

"You don't even know what I'm asking you to believe me about."

"You never lied to me, so if you've said something, I believe you." He gave her an odd smile, almost wistful.

She looked away. His smile also reminded her of the previous night. It really had been spectacular.

It had taken her away from everything that was going on.

Now it was still daylight and she should have felt safe, but she kept thinking about the man she'd seen leaning against the tree.

She didn't know why he made her feel so

uneasy. The other night he'd mostly seemed obnoxious, even if a little bit weird.

Now, seeing him again way up here in the middle of nowhere, she found him downright creepy.

"I was talking about the fact that I really did see someone just now," she said. "But it's not just seeing that man again, it's the mannequin moving, the pictures on my camera. Am I crazy, or do you really believe me?"

He looked at her and nodded solemnly. "Every word," he assured her. "And so does every member of the Krewe."

"They're very trusting, for FBI," she said.

"They're very different for FBI," he said. "Come on, let's get going. Time to get back down the mountain so we can get back to the ranch before dark."

The late-afternoon sun seemed to dim even as he spoke. Scarlet looked up; the majestic blue of the sky had changed to mauve.

The sun slipped behind a cloud, turning its light an orange hue that darkened to an eerie crimson.

Yes, darkness was coming.

The strange red glow settled over the graveyard, the mausoleums and tombstones and simple wooden crosses, filling her with a sense of foreboding.

She wanted to throw herself against Diego and stay there in his arms forever, safe from the darkness.

The breeze lifted, the sun shifted, and she suddenly knew that she couldn't run away from the dark, she had to face it.

She walked past him toward the horses. He was a bastion of towering strength.

But better than that, he allowed her to find her own.

CHAPTER EIGHT

"I love Teddy Bear," Diego heard Meg say to Scarlet as they joined the others. "She's a great horse."

"She's a sweetheart," Scarlet agreed.

Diego turned away and walked back toward the graveyard, intrigued by the grand mausoleum Jillian Kendall's father had commissioned for himself. He stared at the tomb, and then back toward the bushes and forest area. He saw nothing, but he did notice the day had suddenly started to darken.

Colorado days were brilliant and beautiful. Nights could fall swiftly.

If someone had been lurking, that someone had disappeared.

Matt strode over and joined him. "I can't wait for Jane to get here tonight. If she's up for it, we can take her straight to the morgue so she can start creating a face for our John Doe. Even if he's not related to our case, maybe we can help solve another mystery."

"Sounds good," Diego said. "I can't help thinking that his death *is* related, though I could be way off base."

"If nothing else, it will be good if we can at least give the dead man a name," Matt said.

Diego was still staring at the mausoleum.

"You seeing something I'm not?" Matt asked him.

Diego turned to look at him. "Just an odd sensation. Like someone else is here. Think I'm sensing a ghost?"

"Maybe," Matt said. "The dead can speak volumes — when we let them."

Diego nodded and then shook his head slowly. "Well, if the marshal's here, he's not saying anything. Not to me, at least," he said. "Interesting man, though, from what we've learned. Maybe he wasn't the bad guy we've heard. Maybe he was just worried about his daughter. Nathan *was* a retired bank robber who was involved in a murder, after all."

"True, but a lot of men took a temporary wrong turn after the war, and the West tended to be pretty forgiving of such things," Matt said.

"Maybe, but someone sure hated Nathan, judging by the way that he was killed. I wonder if we'll ever be able to figure out the truth," Diego said. "And I wonder if that truth is important to our current case."

"I wouldn't be surprised. The case is lousy with people who've turned out to be descendants of Nathan Kendall. I wonder. Maybe everything goes back to something Kendall did — something that got him murdered and someone still wants revenge for today? There are a lot of possibilities, if that's the case." Matt was quiet for a moment. "I hate to say this, but I do think it involves Scarlet."

Diego's muscles tighten with a tension he couldn't dismiss. Thing was . . .

He agreed.

He looked around the graveyard again and asked Matt, "Did you see anything here? Feel anything? You're the old hand."

Matt laughed. "Not *that* old. You, Brett and I have all been with the Bureau for a long time, but not even I have been with the Krewe that long. But while I'm open to finding whatever else might be out there, I believe that our killer is flesh and blood. And someone right here in the area, close to us — and to Scarlet."

"Very close. We can't leave her alone for a minute, Matt. Not for a minute."

"We won't," Matt assured him.

"Never," Diego insisted.

No, we'll never leave her alone. So even if you bloody dead bastards want to reach her, you'll have to come through me.

Blaze whinnied when Scarlet approached him, which made her happy.

At least the horse really trusted her and seemed to like her.

But Diego had seemed sincere when he'd said the Krewe believed in her.

When they returned to the ranch they helped Angus remove saddles and brush down the horses for the night. Angus kept shaking his head, saying he appreciated the help, he just hoped he wasn't being helped out of a job.

Scarlet laughed and assured him that couldn't happen.

When they'd finished and were walking back toward the museum, Meg suddenly paused and looked across the valley to the hill where The Stanley Hotel sat. "I'd love to see The Stanley while I'm here," she said. "I loved *The Shining.*"

"You should take one of the tours," Scarlet said. "They talk all about the hotel's history as well as its ghosts and literary fame."

"Just out of curiosity," Brett said quietly, "but does anyone know why everybody would be standing on the porch staring at us?"

Scarlet looked over to the main house. Brett was right. Ben and Trisha, the Levins and Bartons, Terry, even Linda and Adam, were sitting there and staring. She'd noticed that morning that Adam was a great listener, and she was suddenly very curious to know what he'd found out while she and the others had been up at the cemetery.

She knew that at least some of the Krewe members believed that the killer was someone here at the ranch.

Terry waved enthusiastically. "Join us!" he called. "This may not be the South, but Trisha has whipped us up some amazing mint juleps."

"Not bad for a New Yorker, if I do say so myself," Trisha said cheerfully.

Diego laughed, walking toward the porch. "If I didn't hate mint I'd have one in a heartbeat, but I'm happy to join you anyway. How is everyone?" he asked.

"Tense, nervous," Linda said flatly.

"Speak for yourself," Terry said. "I'm not going to let some brutal jerk — who you people are going to catch any minute now — win by ruining my vacation. I'm breathing in my heritage. And," he added, "I'm trying to talk these guys into enjoying life with me. I'm taking a tour at The Stanley tonight, and I'm hoping to get them to come along."

"We were just talking about The Stanley," Meg said.

"Sit and tell us," Ben offered as he stood.

Diego shook his head. "That's okay. We've got to go clean up."

"You look fine to me," Linda assured him with a grin.

Diego grinned at her. "Well, thanks, ma'am. But trust me, I can smell me, and I smell like a horse. Not a bad thing if you *are* a horse, but . . ."

"Want to go to The Stanley tonight?" Terry asked.

"I have to meet a friend," Diego said. "Brett and Matt will be with me, but I'm sure Meg and Scarlet would love to go."

Scarlet looked over at him. There was a killer on the loose, and he thought she should go sightseeing? With one of the sort-of suspects? Even if she had Meg with her, it didn't sound like a great idea to her. And who was the friend he was meeting? Maybe the FBI artist Matt had mentioned?

"Adam, you know The Stanley, right?" Diego asked.

Adam nodded. "I was a guest there years ago. It's been changed since King made it famous, though."

"Wasn't the movie filmed there?" Terry asked.

"No, that was Oregon's Timberline Lodge," Adam said.

"I think we should go," Meg said to Scarlet. "It's a perfect opportunity."

"Okay," Scarlet murmured, giving in to the inevitable.

"Great!" Terry said.

"I suppose if we made a thing of it," Gwen said, "it would almost be like a party."

"We might be in," Gigi said. "We've been there before, of course, since we come up here every year. It would be fun to go with the rest of you, though. I mean, come on, we can't all sit around here morosely day after day."

"You'll definitely have fun if you come with us," Terry said.

"You'll have to count me out, I'm afraid," Clark said. "My back is acting up on me."

"In that case, I'll stay here, too," Gigi said. "Sorry to disappoint."

"Charles and I will go," Gwen said decisively.

"Sure. Why not," Charles agreed.

"And I wouldn't miss it for the world," Adam said.

"Scarlet, why don't you see if you can

make tour reservations there for tonight?" Diego said. "I'm sorry Matt and Brett and I won't be able to join you."

"What about you, Linda? Would you like to come with us?" Terry asked.

"God, no," Linda told him. "I'm as weary of the history of this area as it's possible to be. You'll all have much more fun without me." She waved and walked into the house.

"She does have attitude," Ben said to Trisha, but he was smiling.

"That's why we keep her, sweetheart," Trisha said, matching his smile.

"So . . . six of us?" Scarlet asked. "Don't get your hopes up — the ghost tours sell out fast." She headed inside.

When she returned a few minutes later she was smiling. "We lucked out. They had a cancellation. Let's be ready to leave in an hour, okay? It's only a short drive over, but the views are gorgeous, and you may all want to enjoy the lobby before we head down to the basement to start the tour."

"I'll head right up to get ready," Meg said.

She and Matt headed inside, and Brett waved a goodbye and started toward the museum.

Diego walked over to Scarlet. "You need to get changed, too. Come on."

As he led her away, she studied him curiously.

"What?" he asked.

"With everything that's going on, do you really think we should be sightseeing?" she asked.

"Sightseeing is exactly what you should be doing."

"I've seen the sights."

"Yes, but not with this mix of people. And it's intriguing to see who's going and who's staying."

"And why aren't you going?"

"I have to see a man about a horse," he said.

"Right." Her skepticism was plain.

"I have to see a woman about a face."

"What?"

"That artist who's also a Krewe member is flying in tonight," Diego explained. "If she can help us ID the remains found up on the mountain it could help."

"That's how you're investigating? By trying to identify a dead man who might not have anything to do with the murders? You're not going to grill a lot of people — the way the police grilled me?"

"I need to have a reason to grill them. You were taken in because of those pictures on your camera. We don't have a reason to

205

prioritize anyone over everybody else. But we will. Sooner or later the killer will make a mistake."

"What if the killer is long gone?" she asked.

He shook his head. He was serious, the light gone from his dark eyes as he looked at her. "Stay close to Meg. She's a crack shot, and she'll be armed. Adam will look out for you, too, but he leaves the action to the Krewe. Be careful and listen closely. You just don't know what insight you might gain tonight. Or what ghosts might speak," he said lightly.

When they reached the door, Brett opened it for them. "Nice to come home and feel certain no one else is here," he said lightly.

Scarlet had never so much as thought about it before all this started. Now she was grateful as hell to have the alarm system.

"Yes, it definitely is," she said.

And yet, she realized, she'd looked immediately at the statue of Nathan Kendall and her muscles tensed, as if she was certain he might have moved again.

He hadn't.

She relaxed, then felt silly for worrying in the first place.

"Let's get moving," Diego said huskily. "An hour passes quickly."

He looked at Brett, who looked back at him and nodded, and somehow she read the message that passed between them. Brett would stay in the apartment tonight, while everyone else was off doing things.

A sentinel.

"Have fun tonight," Brett said. He smiled, turned and headed for his bedroom at the end of the hallway.

Scarlet followed Diego into her room.

And she quickly learned why he'd wanted her to be aware that an hour passed quickly.

Jane Everett was a beautiful dark-haired woman in a business suit. Diego and Matt picked her up at the Denver airport at seven.

She greeted Matt with a hug and told Diego she was delighted to have another Krewe member. "So, are we heading straight to the remains?" she asked.

"If you don't mind," Diego said.

"Wait 'til you see what Jane is able to do," Matt told him. "You'll be amazed."

Jane smiled at Diego as Matt drove. "It's beautiful out here. I love the East, but I'm from Texas, and I do miss the West."

"Fill her in on what we know so far," Matt instructed him. "You're closest to the case."

As they drove, Diego told her about Scarlet's call, the strange photos on her camera and the way the statue had appeared in her bedroom. He related the history of the Conway Ranch and Nathan Kendall, and also explained that the man had nearly two hundred descendants, which might be a factor in the case.

"Adam told me that the Parker murders were essentially identical to Nathan and Jillian Kendall's deaths. But he also told me that no one's been able to determine how the man found up on the mountain died, whether it was violence or natural causes."

"That's true. But if we can find out who he is, maybe we can find out what he was doing up there and whether someone might have wanted him dead. Not to mention someone out there somewhere is looking for him," Diego said.

Jane was studying his face as he spoke. "You have a feeling it's all related, though, don't you? And that finding out who he is will help you solve the Parkers' murders."

"Yes, I do."

"I'll get right on it," she promised. "This has made the national news, you know."

"I know it's all anyone is talking about here," Matt said.

"I picked this up in the airport," Jane said, and pulled out a newspaper. A stock market downturn had taken the headline, but just below the fold was an article about the strange copycat murders in Colorado. The fact that the husband had been related to the husband in the original murder was mentioned, as well. So was the fact that the police seemed to have no suspects, and no clues.

"Well, the second bit's true," Diego said.

"Their car hasn't shown up yet, but the assumption is that the murderer found them in town and forced them up the mountain. There was nothing helpful at the scene, either — no hairs, no fibers, nothing."

"But we do have suspects," Diego said.

"Diego thinks there's a good chance it could be someone at the Conway Ranch," Matt said. "Guest, staff, even one of the owners."

"And you don't?" Jane asked.

"I'm not willing to narrow it down yet. I definitely think it has something to do with the past, though what, I'm not sure," Matt said.

"We're working it from every angle we can find," Diego told her. "They never solved the murders of Nathan and Jillian Kendall. I believe the killer now is counting on our inability to solve these murders, too."

"But why kill the Parkers? They didn't own the ranch. Does the killer have some

209

kind of grudge against the original owners, so he's going to run around the country and try to get rid of everyone who's descended from Nathan and Jillian? Surely that would be almost impossible. There's no inheritance, is there?"

Diego shook his head. "The family lost ownership years ago. Ben and Trisha Kendall bought the property."

"So it's not as if he's killing off all the possible heirs," Jane mused. "Well, I'm looking forward to working with this skull. Maybe . . ." She paused, looking at Matt.

"He's Krewe now," Matt said quietly.

"Maybe the skull will talk to me," she said.

Diego knew that should probably make him wonder about her sanity, but after what he'd seen on the zombie case, it made perfect sense.

"I'm all for the skull talking to you," Diego said. "I'm all for anything that will solve this case before anyone else gets killed."

There were more elegant hotels in the world and there were more historic places to visit, and there were certainly more ghosts at other venues, as well.

But Scarlet loved The Stanley; it offered history, beauty and charm, along with the splendor of the Rocky Mountains.

They'd visited room 217, where Stephen King had come up with *The Shining,* and rooms 401 and 428, which were reputed to be haunted. Their guide had cheerfully told them that yes, if you were flexible with dates, you could stay in any one of them.

They'd learned about the man who'd built the hotel, Freelan Oscar Stanley, the wealthy man who had, along with his brother, given the world the Stanley Steamer automobile. He had first come to the area in 1903 because he was suffering from tuberculosis. His wife, Flora, had wanted a home like the one she had left behind in Maine, and so The Stanley had come into existence. Flora herself still sometimes came in ghostly form to visit and play her beloved piano.

The hotel itself was beautiful, a grand white building built in the Colonial Georgian style, and their guide showed them through the lobby area and out to the majestic front porch before they headed to the next building on the tour, the theater.

Scarlet still didn't have her camera, and while she might have snapped some shots with her phone, she was too restless. The others all seemed to be enjoying themselves tremendously, though, and she was glad for them. She tried to envision what it would

211

be like if the murders remained unsolved and everyone had to keep on looking over their shoulders for a killer.

Ben and Trisha might decide that it was just too depressing, too stressful, staying on at the ranch, always wondering if the killer would come back, maybe for them.

She would have to move on herself, though where and to do what, she didn't know.

She lingered on the porch, feeling a little numb. That wouldn't happen. The one thing she knew for certain about Diego was that he never gave up. His cases didn't always end the way he wanted, but he always solved them.

Scarlet looked up and found Meg standing next to her. Adam was busy talking to their guide, probably discussing some piece of history. The other three were avidly flashing away.

Meg gave her a curious look, then flushed and looked away.

"What is it?" Scarlet asked.

"Nothing. None of my business," Meg said.

"Now you have to tell me whatever you were thinking, because not knowing is going to drive me crazy."

Meg took a deep breath and said, "Okay,

but remember, you asked. I haven't known Diego long, and I only just met you, but under circumstances like these, you get to know people quickly. So knowing what strong, smart interesting people you both are, and seeing how much you still care about each other, I can't figure out what happened between the two of you. You seem like the most perfect couple in the world."

"Far from perfect," Scarlet said, then paused for a long moment and finally said, "Work."

"Yours?"

"His," Scarlet said, letting out a sigh. "Ironic, huh, since I called him the minute I was in trouble."

"Not ironic — natural," Meg assured her.

"I guess," Scarlet said, shaking her head in puzzlement at her own behavior. "The thing is, I knew what I was getting into. We met, he flirted. We dated. It was whirlwind, but we were madly in love. We were married within months of our first meeting. It was bliss at first. I adore Brett, he's not just Diego's partner, he's my friend, so I never felt shut out. And Diego was genuinely interested in my job. I was working on a very old Native American site near downtown Miami. And when we had free time, we both loved horses, sun, the local beaches . . ."

"Sure sounds like a divorce in the making to me."

Scarlet hesitated, then went on. "Somehow, so slowly that I didn't even realize what was happening, things changed. First it was just a special dinner."

"He didn't show up?"

Scarlet nodded. "Then it was a banquet with my colleagues."

"Because he was working?"

Scarlet winced and looked down, and then met Meg's eyes again. "Then it was the miscarriage."

"Oh, I'm so sorry!" Meg said. "You were in the hospital, you'd lost a child — and he wasn't there?"

"To be fair," Scarlet said, "he didn't know I was pregnant. I kept looking for the perfect moment to tell him, but he was in the middle of a case and was never there. And then I wound up in the hospital. I called and called, but in the end . . . they released me before he ever returned my call. I just saw this bleak life where I'd always be alone, no matter what happened. When he did come home — upset because the case wasn't going well — I told him I was leaving, that I had to get away, go somewhere else. I was calm. He tried to make up, but I was just done."

"I'm so sorry," Meg said.

"He's a great guy. He's just too focused on what he does. I still love him. I probably always will."

"I think he'll always be in love with you, too," Meg said, and then looked at Scarlet questioningly.

"So what the hell am I doing now?" Scarlet said, her tone dry. "That *is* what you want to ask me, isn't it?"

What *was* she doing? It was crazy. But they'd been married, and it was only natural . . .

She hadn't wanted to be alone.

But that wasn't really why she'd insisted he sleep in her room.

And now they were like a pair of high school kids, eager and anxious, making love like rabbits just because they had an hour alone.

Even in the midst of this mess.

"None of my business," Meg assured her. "None of it was."

Scarlet never had a chance to respond, because she looked out to the broad lawn and saw the man.

The man who had stopped her in town. The man she had seen at the cemetery. He was standing behind a large family group and looking up at where she was standing on the porch.

"Meg!"

"What?"

"He's here!"

"Who's here?"

"The stalker — the man I saw in town and at the cemetery."

"Where?"

"There!" She pointed. "Right behind those people."

Meg walked firmly in the direction Scarlet indicated. Scarlet followed, ready to indignantly accost him.

But when they got to the spot where she had seen him, he was gone.

Meg stopped and asked, "Did you see where he went?"

"No," Scarlet said, frustrated.

"We'll find him once we're all corralled in the basement again," Meg said.

But they *didn't* see him there.

Meg told Adam what had happened, and Scarlet described the man to him.

Adam listened gravely, said he hadn't noticed him and then looked for him in the crowd, as well.

But he hadn't reappeared by the time the tour finished.

"I'm not crazy," Scarlet insisted to Meg.

"I really did see him." Then she fell silent, because the others were hurrying their way.

"I love this place," Gwen said. "I'm going to read every Stephen King book I can get my hands on."

"I'm reading up on the Stanley Steamer," Charles said. "That car in the lobby is something."

"Onward to the bar," Terry said. "I need a drink after all that walking around."

Scarlet was ready to protest; she just wanted to go back.

"Wonderful," Meg said. "I'm starving. I hope they're still serving."

"I wouldn't mind something to eat myself," Adam said.

So much for going straight back to the ranch, Scarlet thought. She knew she should have been hungry herself, but she wasn't interested in food. She just wanted to get back to the Conway Ranch and — she had to admit the truth — Diego. She forced a smile and said, "Don't worry. There's always the bar menu."

In the end they opted for the dining room. The food was always good there, and their waiter entertained them with more stories of the hotel while taking their orders.

Scarlet excused herself to use the ladies' room and headed into the bar. She was almost around the bar itself when she felt a light touch on her arm.

She swung around to find the man she was starting to think of as her stalker sitting on the last stool.

She almost screamed.

"If you would just listen to me," he said. "I'm trying to help you."

Swallowing her fear, she said firmly, "Leave me the hell alone."

The bartender swung around to look at her, as did everyone in the vicinity.

"I'm sorry," she said coolly. "But this man has been stalking me."

They stared at her, eyes widening.

She turned back to the bar stool.

There was no one there.

No one at all.

The closest person to her was an elderly gentleman in a wheelchair.

"Honey," he said, "I wish I had it in me to stalk you."

Scarlet winced. "I'm sorry," she said to him, nodding toward the empty stool. "I was talking to the man who was sitting there a moment ago."

Then she turned with what dignity she could manage and hurried toward the restroom.

CHAPTER NINE

"We searched as best we could," Meg said to Diego. "Adam and I went through the bar, the lobby, the grounds — you name it. We looked everywhere for the guy, and we couldn't find him."

They were standing alone in the ranch car park. Diego hadn't wanted to talk in the museum, where voices might carry. And he certainly didn't want to talk at the main house, where curious minds were everywhere.

But he was concerned and wanted Meg's private take on what had happened, so they'd come out here to talk freely.

When Scarlet had greeted him on her return, she had been calm — too calm — and yet distracted, as if her thoughts were somewhere else entirely even as she spoke to him. Oddly, he'd felt as if she was burning up with submerged anger at the same time.

Anxious to find out what was going on, he'd escaped with Meg, explaining that Jane had given him something for her, but he'd left it in the car.

It had sounded lame even to him, but Scarlet hadn't seemed to notice. She'd said little except that everyone had enjoyed the tour and she'd managed not to get frantic in front of anyone except Meg after she'd seen "the stalker," as she called him now, for the second time that night at the bar.

"Did you see him, too?" Diego asked Meg.

"No, I didn't, and neither did Adam. But if he was registered for a tour or if he's a guest, we'll find out," Meg assured him. "Do you think he could be the killer?"

"I just don't know. From what Scarlet has said, he just keeps warning her to be careful."

"Plenty of killers stalk their victims and warn them."

"I know that, but I don't think our killer does anything in public that would get him noticed. Wherever he found Candace and Larry — perhaps at a tourist attraction — I think he lured them away. Because no one witnessed anything. Their pictures have run in the paper. Several shop owners and a waitress remember seeing them. But no one saw anything happen to them. Someone who warns her and disappears . . . I don't know. The killer has to be someone who knows the area, though, and unless you're a big believer in coincidence, he knows local history, too."

"Nathan Kendall," Meg said.

"The ghost of Nathan Kendall?" Diego asked.

"You say that as if you find it hard to believe, and yet you agreed to join the Krewe."

"I'm open to anything, Meg. I know I saw the ghosts of Miguel and Maria Gomez after the Miami zombie case. And if anyone might want justice, it's Nathan Kendall. It's not that."

"What, then?"

"It can't be the ghost of Nathan Kendall. We've all seen the statue, and it's supposed to be a perfect likeness of the real man. If her stalker looked even remotely like Nathan Kendall, Scarlet would know that and say so. Someone did a good job of scaring the hell out of her with that statue."

"You don't think it moved on its own?" Meg asked, and he knew it was a serious question.

"I look at that thing sometimes and I could swear its expression changes. But no, I don't think it moved on its own."

"So you think someone got into the museum at night and, without being heard, wrestled that statue up the stairs and into her bedroom? Someone who intended to scare her?" Meg asked. "Someone who was alive and well?"

"I'm not sure about the 'well,' but otherwise, yes, that's exactly what I think. I think whoever did it may have been trying to make Scarlet look crazy. He could be behind the disappearing photos on her camera, too."

"So you think the real killer was trying to make it look as if *she* is the murderer?" Meg asked.

"Maybe. I'm hoping our techs can find out something from that camera of hers. Maybe it's just part of the killer's game — scare someone half to death and then . . ."

"And then what?" Meg asked. "Kill them?"

Diego nodded. "I mean, we have no idea if anything like this happened to the Parkers before they were murdered."

"We're not going to let him get close to her, Diego. One of us will stick to her like glue. She's going to be okay. She's stronger than you think. Stronger than *she* thinks."

"She was alone tonight," he pointed out.

"In a hotel full of people," she reminded

222

him. "Adam and I were right there."

"I know — we just have to be closer."

Meg was studying him oddly. As if she knew something she didn't want to talk about.

"You two are getting friendly," he said.

"I like Scarlet."

He lowered his head. "She told you about our breakup, didn't she?"

"It's not my business."

"Maybe, but I suspect your opinion of me took a hit."

"I'm no different from you," she admitted. "I've been as obsessed with work as the next person, trust me. I'd never judge you because sometimes your work comes first."

"I'd say maybe people like us aren't meant for eternal bliss," Diego said drily. "Except you found Matt."

"I got lucky. We found each other. Through work, actually. I know it's more difficult when you're not both in the same line of work, though."

"True. But whatever happened, it was my fault." He took a deep breath and met her eyes. "I can't let anything happen to Scarlet, Meg. I just can't. I'm definitely not the best person in the world, but I do know that my happiness depends on hers — and on keeping her alive."

Meg smiled sympathetically. "The missed dinners were your fault. The end, not so much. You didn't know." She was quick to change the subject. "Okay, so not Nathan Kendall's ghost, but maybe someone else's."

"Possibly," Diego said. He was open-minded but still uncertain.

"Matt, Adam and I . . . we all think she's seeing a dead man. And the thing is, she needs to let him get close, let him talk to her. I believe he's trying to help. Your mind is more than open, you know what I'm saying is likely true."

"Yeah," Diego said. "Likely. I think we should get back inside," he said, effectively ending the conversation.

She nodded, and they started walking up the path to the museum.

Diego turned to look back at the main house. There were lights on in several of the bedrooms upstairs. It was dim on the first floor; only the night-lights were still on. "Did Brett say if all the guests were in?"

"He did," Meg said. "Everyone was out at some point tonight — including Ben and Trisha. The two of them went out to eat and were gone about an hour or so. Terry, Gwen and Charles were with us, and Gigi and Clark went to town for a meal and a trip to the pharmacy. They came back about a half hour after Ben and Trisha. Linda Reagan was gone for about two hours, apparently on a date. She said he dropped her off afterward."

"Did you see him?" Diego asked.

"No. And Angus never left the stables," Meg told him.

The museum door opened, and Brett came out, frowning as he strode over to them.

"You need to get inside, Diego," he said, his tone as serious as his expression.

"What's happened?" Diego asked anxiously.

"Nothing," Brett said quickly. "I didn't mean to scare you. It's just that the police returned the collection of antique guns about an hour ago and . . . well, you need to see for yourself."

Diego arched a brow to Brett and hurried past him. Inside the museum, he found Matt standing with Scarlet, who was taking a gun from a display case. She looked at Diego defensively.

"Will you tell them that I know how to shoot?" she demanded.

"You know how to shoot," he said. "But —"

"But what?" she demanded. "You all carry guns."

"Scarlet, you don't like guns."

"I like historic guns just fine."

"Not to shoot!"

"At the moment, my likes and dislikes seem to be changing."

"Scarlet, whether you can shoot or not doesn't matter. We're not going to leave you alone, so you don't need a gun," Brett said quietly.

Meg and Brett had joined them by that point, and Scarlet looked around at the whole group. "Help me out here, guys. This is not a foolish thing I'm doing. Look, I'm not going to go crazy and shoot blindly," she said, arms crossed over her chest, chin high and defiant, and narrowed eyes as sharp as a hawk's. "But I'm not going to be a victim, either. This guy is following me. And I'm going to be prepared. I'm very grateful that you're all here, but you have a murderer to catch, and I don't want to be a burden. So what if I want to carry a gun? You all do."

"We all have permits," Diego reminded her.

"I won't carry it as a concealed weapon. I'll keep it ready here, so I'm able to use it if I have to, or if it seems there might be trouble, I'll carry it openly. The state only requires a permit for concealed carry," she said. She stared at him hard. "I'm good. I just want to have a gun available to me in case something none of us expect happens and I run into this guy alone. I'm not going to let myself be dragged through the forest and up the mountain."

They were all silent, not sure what to say.

"Look, here's the one I'm going to take," she said. "It's a modified Colt six-shooter from the 1880s. Ben said it's okay, and it's in good working order. That's why I chose it. I have bullets, and I won't even load it unless it's necessary, unless I'm alone or out in the forest or something. Okay?"

Diego knew they were all waiting for him to speak. The thing was, she did know what she was doing with a gun, especially an antique. Part of that was his doing — she'd been to the shooting range with him several times — and the other part of it was her love of history.

It was just that she'd always hated them.

"Okay," he said.

"Okay?" she questioned warily.

"Yes, take it. But you do have to get a concealed-carry permit. We're the FBI. We can't have you breaking any laws. All right?"

"Tomorrow. I'll get a permit tomorrow," she promised.

He nodded.

"Well, then, that's that," Scarlet said, smiling in satisfaction as she carefully collected the bullets for the Colt. "By the way, how's your friend?"

For a moment Diego had no idea what she was talking about. "My friend?"

"The woman you and Matt picked up at the airport tonight. Jane Everett. Is she here?"

"Not yet, though she will be. Right now she's at the morgue, working," Diego said. "We tried to talk her into waiting 'til morning, but she was eager to get started. She'll have a likeness for us by morning."

"Wow," Scarlet said. "I'm impressed." She started up the stairs, and the others followed. He could tell they were all still a little worried about Scarlet carrying a gun. But he'd spent days teaching her not only to shoot, but also all about gun safety, and if he hadn't trusted her to handle a weapon he would have objected to her having one.

"Would anyone like tea?" Scarlet asked when they got up to the kitchen. "Hot chocolate? Something stronger?"

No one spoke.

Scarlet stiffened. "What? You think I'm overreacting, don't you? That all this has driven me crazy, maybe even made me dangerous."

"No, no!" Meg protested.

"Scarlet, it's not that," Diego said.

"Then what?" she asked in confusion.

"We think you saw a dead man in town, and at the cemetery and The Stanley," Diego said flatly.

She stared at him then as if *he'd* lost *his* mind.

"Look, I know all about your 'zombie' case in Miami. This guy wasn't lurching around, half-decayed and talking about brains."

"That's not what Diego meant," Meg said quietly.

"What *are* you talking about, then?" Scarlet demanded.

"We think you're seeing a ghost," Diego said.

"Okay. Stop. I've spent half my adult life digging up old burial sites. My idea of the perfect vacation is exploring the pyramids at Giza, and the catacombs in Rome and Paris. I don't see ghosts!" She sat down in a huff.

"I never saw them myself — until they needed me," Brett said, taking the chair opposite her.

Meg sat down, too, looking at Scarlet with her eyes serious. "Scarlet, it began for me at a traumatic period during my childhood. It works that way for a lot of us. But sometimes it happens the way Brett said. Someone has the ability but it's dormant, for lack of a better word, until it's needed. Until a ghost needs our help."

Scarlet looked from Meg to Diego. "You're suggesting that a *ghost* is trying to talk to me. Do you also think a ghost killed those people? And that Nathan Kendall's ghost possessed that statue and walked up the stairs and into my bedroom?"

"Oh, no, not at all," Brett said. "That statue is far too heavy for a ghost to lift."

"Not any ghost I've ever encountered, and that's quite a few," Meg said.

Scarlet sat back. "You're crazy. You're all crazy. I've begged crazy people to come out here and help me."

"Scarlet," Diego said, "it's not crazy. It's true."

"So you really do think that a ghost stole an antique Colt from the museum, and killed Candace and Larry Parker?"

"No, not at all," Matt said. "I'm quite certain they were murdered by a living person."

"That's a relief. No, it's not. I mean, do you all really believe in ghosts?" Scarlet asked, looking from one of them to the next.

Her gaze stopped when she met Diego's eyes.

"Yes," he said flatly. "The thing is, I know you're afraid of this 'stalker.' And he may be alive and someone we need to watch for carefully. But he also may be someone who — alive or dead — can help us."

"You really are serious," she said, her voice barely a whisper. "And Adam — is this what he believes, too?"

"Adam created the Krewe precisely because he believes in possibilities exactly like this," Meg said.

"So basically, you think I want to arm myself against a ghost?" Scarlet said.

"Uh-huh," Meg said.

"Okay, I'll take that under consideration," Scarlet said. She smiled suddenly. "So . . . anyone up for something to drink?"

"I'm ready for bed, to tell you the truth," Meg said, looking at Matt, who smiled and held out his hand to her.

"Same here," Brett said. "Good night all."

"We'll make sure the alarm is set," Matt said, turning with Meg to head back down the stairs.

Diego was left alone in the kitchen with Scarlet. She looked at him skeptically, and he wondered if he had suddenly grown horns.

231

"What we're telling you is true," he said quietly.

She stood and walked into the bedroom. He hesitated for a moment, then turned out the kitchen light, checked the living room to make sure everything was in order and followed her. Her lights were out, and she was already in bed. He wondered if she had crawled in fully dressed.

"I can take the couch, if you want," he told her.

"Don't be ridiculous," she said.

"You're upset."

"Yep," she said.

But as he waited in the doorway, she suddenly got out from under the covers.

She wasn't fully dressed. In fact, she was totally naked.

The slight moon glow seeping in through the curtains highlighted the sleekness of her body like an opal mist. She walked over to the doorway and slipped an arm around his neck, then whispered huskily, "I hear that upset sex is incredibly hot."

He smiled, then found her lips with his. He indulged in a slow, simmering, hungry kiss before lifting his mouth from hers.

"I feel so used," he whispered.

"I'll use you well," she promised.

"Promises, promises," he said.

He lifted her and the feel of her naked body against him fed the searing need that ripped through his body. He set her on the comforter and started to undress. Suddenly she was kneeling in front of him, pulling at the buckle of his belt. Her lips and tongue teased at the flesh of his belly, and he quickly stripped off the rest of his clothes and took her in his arms again, rolling with her onto the bed. She found her way on top and proceeded to kiss and tongue her way across his chest, then moved her way downward.

She suddenly sat bolt upright, grasping for the covers.

"What?" he demanded.

"Diego, ghosts — they don't . . . Oh, my God! Are we being watched? By a ghost?"

His rigid body tightened a notch, yet somehow he couldn't stop himself from laughing. "From everything the others have told me, ghosts tend to be polite and discreet. They aren't voyeurs out to make secret sex tapes."

"Are you sure?" she demanded.

She was still straddling him, back erect, breasts firm, nipples aroused. She was like an Amazon warrior, proud and alert and ready to do battle.

"I'm positive."

He sat up and pulled her back into his arms.

They could both be the aggressor in sex, and she'd been doing a magnificent job, but he wasn't about to lose the moment.

He rolled her beneath him and caught her lips with his mouth, her hands with his, and he turned the tide, pressing kisses down her throat and her breasts, her abdomen and below, until she writhed and whispered his name.

And forgot about ghosts.

They made love until the wee hours.

Upset love proved to be incredibly hot indeed.

It was still early when Diego's phone vibrated under his pillow, where he'd put it before finally going to sleep. He glanced at the bedside clock and saw that it was only seven thirty.

"McCullough," he answered quickly, keeping his voice low.

"It's Jane. I'm sorry to be calling so early, but I received a call from your friend Lieutenant Gray last night. He asked if the police could have my rendering as soon as I had something. He wants to get it into the papers. I figured you and the rest of the Krewe would want first look."

"Yes, thank you. Where are you? Still at the morgue?"

"Just heading up to the ranch. Adam said I'll be staying in the main house."

"Yes, but come to the museum first. It's to the left of the parking lot, but there's a sign that says Conway Ranch Museum, so you won't have any trouble finding it."

"Thanks," she told him. "Be there soon."

He hung up and bolted out of bed, heading straight to the shower. Scarlet didn't stir. Only when he was dressed did he wake her.

She blinked and stared at him with groggy eyes.

"Jane is on her way with her rendering of the man killed up on the mountain. Feel free to go back to sleep if you want. One of us will stay with you. We won't leave you here alone, even if you do have a gun now."

"No, no, I'm up."

She jumped up and ducked beneath his arm, then grabbed her robe and ran for the shower. Diego headed out to the kitchen to brew coffee.

It was already done. Brett was up.

"Jane is on her way," Diego told him.

"Good. I'm anxious to see what she's come up with. If we can ID the guy, maybe we can find out if his death is related to the

Parkers'."

"I think I'll give Lieutenant Gray a call while we're waiting," Diego said.

"I talked to him last night when he returned the museum's gun collection. They've questioned the guests who left the ranch right after the murders. A banker from Pittsburgh, and his wife and daughter. A family from New York who had never been west of Chicago. Nothing suspicious about any of them, and none of them saw anything suspicious, either."

Diego nodded and made a call.

"Lieutenant Gray."

"It's Diego McCullough. Just wanted to check in with you and let you know our artist will have something for you soon. Anything new on your end? Besides none of the other ranch guests having anything useful to add."

Gray sounded frustrated. "Nothing. I've questioned half of Estes Park. No one saw the Parkers leave with anyone. No one has found their car. The forensic team has given me diddly-squat. You?"

"We're hoping the picture will help in linking the cases, or even help us prove there's no connection," Diego said.

"That's it? That's all the FBI has got?"

"At the moment. Thanks for returning the

236

museum's gun collection."

"Still no sign of the murder weapon, but the rest are all clean. Under the circumstances, I'm sure you understand why we're looking at anyone associated with the ranch."

"Same here."

"The murder weapon . . . who knows when it was stolen. *If* it was stolen."

"So your top suspects are the Kendalls — and my wife," Diego said.

"I thought she was your ex-wife, but . . . whatever. If she's guilty, then —"

"You know she was in town."

"Maybe she slipped back up the mountain."

"I think she parked in a municipal lot. You can probably document that," Diego said.

"Get me that picture as soon as you can," Gray said.

Diego hung up.

Brett had been watching him the whole time. "Since we know it's not Scarlet — Ben or Trisha? Or someone else here?"

"Ben did find the bodies, and everyone else seems to have an alibi for the time of the murders," Diego said. "Anyway, I'm going to head outside to meet Jane when she arrives."

"I'm going back on the computer — see if

we've missed anything on Ben and Trisha," Brett said. "I'll call HQ, too — tell them to dig deeper." He hesitated. "Ben did have access to the museum and the Colt that killed the Parkers."

"I'm surprised Gray hasn't arrested him already. He brought Scarlet in just for having pictures on her camera."

"Pictures Ben told him about," Brett reminded him.

"True," Diego said. "But do you really see him being capable of it? He's not a young man."

"It doesn't take a young man to pull a trigger."

"Yes, but Larry Parker was strung up a tree. That takes strength."

"Maybe Ben and Trisha are a pair of psychopathic killers," Brett said.

Diego let that thought settle, trying to envision the two of them slinking into town, somehow getting the Parkers alone, then dragging or forcing them up the hill. "He's living his dream in his ancestral home. Are you saying his dream was to re-create his ancestors' deaths?"

"As a motive, it's a little off," Brett agreed. "But we'll look into his — and Trisha's — past. If nothing else, it always helps to eliminate suspects."

"True," Diego agreed with a nod, then headed down the stairs to await Jane's arrival.

He stepped outside into a beautiful fall day. The sun was already up, and the air was crisp and clean.

The sight that greeted his eyes, the peaks of the snowcapped Rockies rising over the tree line, seemed so serene that it was hard to imagine the horror of bloodshed intruding.

But intrude it had.

As he stood in the sun, he heard car tires on the gravel drive. He stepped forward. Jane had arrived. She parked, and he headed over to greet her.

"Grab my portfolio, will you?" she asked as she got out of the car. "I sketched his face from a few different angles. I have no idea of eye or hair color, obviously, so I played with that a bit, too."

"You don't even look tired," he told her.

She flashed him a smile. "I am, but I'll sleep as soon as we're set with this." She grabbed her purse and her computer bag, and started toward the museum.

She paused, looking around as they entered the museum. She smiled, as if she had somehow come home.

"Wow. Authentic. I love a place like this,

small but real, and full of treasures. Those mannequins are incredible," she said, then frowned suddenly and approached the statue of Nathan Kendall. "Amazing workmanship," she said.

"That's Nathan Kendall, the man who founded this ranch," Diego said. "His father-in-law had it commissioned after the murders. He also commissioned one of his daughter, but she seems to have been lost over the years." He shrugged. "It's no wonder you like the West. I understand you worked in Texas at one point."

"Not to mention my husband, Agent Sloan Trent, is from Arizona," she said. "We met at an old theater in Lily, Arizona. They had a lot of old props like the collection here. I'm always fascinated by all the history out here." She smiled ruefully. "I'll gawk later. Where would you like me to set up my computer and lay out my pictures?"

"Up in the living room," Diego said. "I'll lead the way."

Upstairs, Jane greeted Brett with a smile. Scarlet hadn't appeared yet, so Diego led the way to the living room. While Jane set up her computer on the coffee table, Brett called Matt and told him and Meg to head over.

Diego sat next to Jane as she booted up

her computer and hit the buttons to bring up her rendering.

"This isn't a perfect science," she reminded him. "But we know he was Caucasian, about thirty-five, so I worked with the standards for tissue depth and so on, and then, as I said, created different combinations of eye and hair color."

Her computer had a high-def seventeen-inch screen. As she hit a key, an almost photographic likeness of a face popped up. "There he is," she said. "Our John Doe. Not a bad-looking guy. Here he is with dark hair and blue eyes. Next I have him as a brown-eyed blond." She clicked. Another sketch.

"Face look familiar to you?" Diego asked Brett.

Brett shook his head. "No wanted posters or missing persons reports that I've seen."

"This is him with a cowboy hat, sandy hair and hazel eyes," Jane said.

There was a loud gasp from the doorway.

Diego turned to see Scarlet standing there, eyes wide, face white against the rich chestnut color of her hair.

She was staring at the computer screen.

"Scarlet?" Diego said, frowning at her reaction.

She looked at him in horror. "It's him!"

"Who?"

"My stalker," she said. "It's my stalker."

"Are you sure?" Diego asked her.

"Beyond a doubt. That's him — that's the man who stopped me in town, the man who's been following me. I'm absolutely sure."

CHAPTER TEN

Jane had risen and was watching Scarlet, who was transfixed by the computer screen.

"My God," Scarlet breathed, and then she turned to Jane. "That's scary, it's so real," she whispered. She walked closer to the computer and then, as if her knees had buckled, practically fell backward onto the sofa. "It's crazy," she murmured. "But it must be true, because that's him. That's the man who keeps trying to talk to me."

She looked at Jane again and suddenly stood, reaching out a hand. "I'm Scarlet. I'm sorry. I didn't mean to be so rude."

Jane smiled, taking her hand. "Not rude at all. I'm so sorry that you were startled by my rendering."

"Rendering," Scarlet repeated. "Rendering, yes." She seemed to grow even whiter. "You did this from a skull?"

"Yes."

"He's dead."

"Yes."

"Definitely dead?"

"Oh, yes. Very definitely dead," Jane said gently.

Scarlet sank back onto the couch. Diego moved over next to her, taking her shoulders and drawing her around so that she had to look at him.

"Scarlet, are you all right?"

"Yes. I think. And you're right. A gun won't do me a bit of good, will it?"

"No."

"So you know who he is?" Jane asked her.

"No. Before he started stalking me, I'd never seen him before."

"Hey!" a man called from downstairs. "It's Matt. Meg and I are coming up."

"We're in the living room," Diego called down to him.

Once Meg and Matt arrived, everyone rushed to fill them in.

"I'm not at all surprised that's the man you've been seeing," Meg said. "He clearly has a reason for coming to you. I believe he really is trying to help you."

"Why me?" Scarlet demanded. "He should have gone to one of you. You're the ghost experts, not to mention you're the FBI."

They were silent for a long moment, and then Meg said, "There was a ghost in

Miami, Miguel Gomez, and he went to my friend Lara. Brett's fiancée. She wasn't a Krewe member — still isn't. She's in public relations. He believed she could help him, maybe because she was the one who found his remains."

"But I didn't find any remains!" Scarlet protested.

"In one way," Jane said carefully, "we're no different dead than when we're alive. We like certain people. We instinctively trust them. We gravitate toward them. Whoever this man is, he's coming to you for a reason."

"Great," Scarlet said. "In that case . . ."

She stood up and looked around the room. "Where are you? I'm ready now. Come talk to me. Tell me whatever it is you want me to know."

Nothing happened.

"Where is he now?" Scarlet demanded.

"Wherever he chooses to be. He doesn't know you've suddenly decided you want to be friends," Matt told her.

"I *don't* want to be friends," Scarlet protested. "I just want to know what the hell is going on."

"He may prove to be your best friend," Diego told her softly.

Scarlet looked at him and shook her head,

clearly longing to disbelieve.

"He'll come to you again," Meg assured her.

"Wonderful," Scarlet said.

"Actually," Brett said, sitting next to her, "it really is. Scarlet, it's going to be okay."

"Yeah, right. All I know is, if you guys leave me alone anywhere, even for a minute, I'll show you how good I am with a gun by shooting off your toes," she threatened.

"We won't leave you alone," Diego promised.

Silence fell.

Diego turned to Jane. "Okay, let's go ahead and get the picture Scarlet thinks looks most like her stalker to Lieutenant Gray. You can email it to Krewe HQ, too, so they can keep trying to figure out who the hell he is."

As he spoke, his phone rang.

It was Gray.

"We've got another body," he said grimly. "And this one is fresh."

Scarlet didn't know what she was going to do with herself. There wouldn't even be any visitors to talk to, because no sooner had Diego hung up than Ben had called to tell her he'd decided not to open the museum that week.

"Just feels too awkward," he'd told her.

Frankly, she hadn't even thought about opening, but then, her brain didn't seem to be working very well.

"So . . . another body," Scarlet said. She bit her lower lip lightly. "Man or woman?"

"Woman," Diego told her. He wasn't looking at her. He was looking over at Matt, and she realized they were doing that thing they did, silently dividing into teams so they could go to work. She wondered who would be staying here with her.

She wasn't sure who she wanted it to be. She decided that what she really wanted was to quit, leave the case to the professionals and maybe board a cruise ship to an exotic island.

That, of course, wasn't happening.

"The journals," she said, as if she'd just made a great discovery. "We can keep studying the journals."

"Exactly what I was thinking," Meg said.

"You know, it doesn't always have to be you who stays," Scarlet said to her. "We're not playing girls against boys here."

"Honestly, none of us were thinking of it that way," Meg assured her. "But you and I have already started on the journals, so it only makes sense for us to keep going. Besides, I've always enjoyed research. Adam said he has a bunch of paperwork to catch up on but he'll stop by if he finishes in time." She turned toward Jane. "You need to get some sleep, but when you wake up, you're free to join us."

"We need to get going," Matt said.

"Who found her?" Scarlet asked, worried. "Not Ben, right? And where was she found?"

She knew she wasn't going to like the answer when she saw the way Diego looked at Brett.

She groaned before he had a chance to speak. "Near here, right?" she asked.

"Just down the mountain from the ranch," Diego admitted. "Hikers found her in the woods."

"How was she killed?" Scarlet asked.

"Shot," Diego said. "That's all I know."

"A young woman?" she persisted.

"Scarlet, we have to go now," he said.

"Of course," she said, standing. "Jane, can I help you with anything? They have a room ready for you at the main house."

"I'm fine, thanks. I'll take my computer, but I'll leave my portfolio here for now. I'll show everyone my sketches later. I'll get my bag from the car on the way."

Matt and Brett went with her as she left the room, but Diego paused, looking at

248

Scarlet. "Are you all right?"

"I'm fine — honestly. I've just got a lot to think about, that's all," she assured him. "Go — do your job. Find out who's doing this."

He nodded, looking as if he wanted to touch her, hold her, reassure himself that she really was all right.

He had to go, but she could tell that he really was torn between staying with her and leaving to do what he had to do.

Finally he gave her one last look and left.

She turned to Meg and forced herself to smile brightly. "Coffee? I hear it goes well with research."

"Yeah, and a bagel and cereal or something. I missed the breakfast part of our bed-and-breakfast stay, and I work much better when I'm well fed."

"I can make omelets if you want. Pancakes, French toast — whatever."

"Something quick and easy," Meg said.

"Okay, bagels," Scarlet agreed, heading into the kitchen. "We can eat, then head downstairs. I read the journals when I first started here, but I wasn't looking for anything specific, and I did some skimming. It will be interesting to go back and try to really understand what was going on before he was killed." She reached into the bread box for the bagels and popped a couple into the toaster.

Meg poured coffee for them and asked, "What do you think happened to the statue of Jillian?"

Scarlet shrugged. "Who knows? Over the years, things have been lost, broken, even stolen. If Jillian's statue was even half as well done as Nathan's, someone might have decided it was worth real money and taken it. I asked Ben and he said he knew her father had it made, but he'd never seen it. It was already gone the first time he came out here years ago."

"I'm going to keep going with Nathan's Civil War diary. Maybe something in it will spark an idea with something you're reading."

The bagels popped.

"Coffee, bagels and the Civil War. Agent Murray, you do know how to lead an exciting life."

"Not to worry, Scarlet. I've come to love the quiet. Trust me. I don't mind leaving the dead to others."

Scarlet winced. She hadn't meant to sound callous.

Another woman was dead.

"Let's hope we can find something in those journals," she said.

"I won't be at all surprised," Meg said. "The dead speak in many ways."

Lieutenant Gray met them outside the crime-scene tape. "Just to warn you," he said, "some victims look almost as if they're asleep. Not this one. Caught her in the face — right in the face — as well as in the gut, just like he shot Candace Parker. We can't find any shells or cartridges, so he picked up after himself."

"My gut says she'll turn out to be local and that it's the same killer," Diego said. "The killer didn't know Candace Parker, so he didn't care whether we saw her face or not. I think not only did he know this woman, so he didn't want to see her face after she was dead, lots of people around here know her, so he didn't want her recognized right away, in case that led us right to him."

"What are you, one of those profiler guys? Gotta tell you, I don't put a lot of stock in that," Gray said.

The man really did look like a tired hound dog, Diego thought. It was hard to imagine that he and Scarlet were related, even as distantly as a hundred and fifty years ago.

"I'm not a profiler, but every agent studies psychology at the academy," Diego said.

"And I'm not saying I know everything about our killer, much less his victim. But I do think we'll discover that this woman is local."

He ducked under the crime-scene tape. The medical examiner was by the body, hunched down with his back to them and his kit at his side, swabbing blood.

Dried leaves crunched under Diego's feet as he approached, and the ME looked up. Diego was pleased to see it was Dr. Robert E. Fuller.

"Hey," Fuller said. "Gray told me you were coming. I couldn't tell how he felt about it. The man's mind seemed to be in something of a *gray* zone."

Diego smiled grimly at Fuller's dry humor. "I'm not surprised," he said. "What have we got here?"

"Female, as you know. I'd say twenty-five, maybe a little more. About five-six, weight about a hundred and thirty. There's a lot of blood, but the hair looks to be medium brown." He hesitated. "I can't tell you about the eyes, though," he said softly, "because they're gone. She was killed at point-blank range. She was dead before he shot her in the face, though. The kill shot was to her abdomen. Huge hole, though, so I think she bled out quickly. For her sake, I hope so anyway. Take a look at the wrists — she was tied and dragged up here. She was wearing jeans, otherwise I'm sure her legs would show scratches from that, but you can see the evidence on her clothes. And she's missing one shoe — a white sneaker."

Diego looked down toward where the road was, but he couldn't see it from there. He turned and looked up toward the Conway Ranch. He couldn't see the house or any of the buildings, because the trees and underbrush were so thick.

"Almost perfectly halfway between the road and the ranch," he said.

"No one could see what happened from either direction," Fuller said.

"No car left down on the road," Diego said, "which supports your theory that she was dragged through the woods."

"Yup," Fuller agreed.

"Time of death?" Diego asked.

"Sometime late last night or very early this morning," Fuller said. "I'd say between 11:00 p.m. and 2:00 a.m."

"Gray told us hikers found her. Do you know any details?"

"A young couple. The girl was so startled she fell and twisted her ankle. The boyfriend accompanied her to the hospital. They know you or one of the others will want to interview them."

He would, of course, Diego thought. But he didn't think they would be able to tell him much.

Their best lead would be getting her ID'd quickly, because the killer had known her. He was certain of it.

Maybe she had rejected him, so he'd wanted to hurt her the way she had hurt him. And he had to wonder . . . Was she yet another descendant of Nathan Kendall?

"Any idea what the murder weapon was?" Diego asked Fuller. "Antique?"

The ME was thoughtful for a minute. He looked past Diego to Gray, who was giving instructions to the crime-scene techs.

"Another Colt — a Walker model. It was the most powerful handgun out there until the invention of .357 Magnum," Fuller told him. "He shot and killed her here, then picked up after himself. There were three shots. Maybe she squirmed, but he missed anything vital first — there was one bullet that just got her in the arm. I've gotten it out already, it will go to the lab. The second ripped through her abdomen like a cannon, which tells us more about the gun, as well. The third destroyed her face. I don't have the second two bullets yet, but I do have the first, which is why I can be so confident of the weapon. It's rare, if that helps you any." He shrugged. "Sorry — I'm pretty sure of the gun, at any rate, because I've studied old weaponry. Hope that helps."

"It does. Thanks."

Diego looked out over the area. Matt and Brett were carefully following a trail of broken brush and flattened leaves, staying to the side so as not to taint any evidence. The terrain was steep, filled with jutting rocks, old twisted trees and thick brush.

He watched his step as he caught up to them as quickly as he could.

"There!" Matt called. He was ahead of Diego by about fifty yards. "I can see down to the road. He must have driven her there, parked, then dragged her up the hill."

"What have you got?" Gray shouted from above.

"The trail leads to the road."

"I'll send the techs over. Maybe the killer left something by where he parked," Gray called back to him.

Carefully avoiding the killer's trail, Diego half walked and half slid down the slope to the road. On the way he startled an elk. The animal stared at him for a moment, then bounded off.

"Fuller have anything useful yet?" Brett asked Diego as he caught up with Matt and

Brett by the road.

"Fuller thinks the gun used was another antique," Diego answered. "He's pretty confident, but he's not a hundred percent sure yet."

"And the guy is a fucking gazelle," Matt said. "That's tough terrain."

"A coordinated, history-loving, antique-gun buff. You'd think he would be easy to find," Brett said.

"At least we've got something to look for," Diego said. He hesitated, frowning. "I think we've got something else, too."

He moved over to a piece of brush by the flattened path, where something white was just visible.

He moved the leaves aside, then pulled gloves and an evidence bag from his pocket before he carefully reached for the once-white woman's sneaker.

Now it was white and red.

White.

And bloodstained.

" 'Brian Gleason, Jeff Bay and Billie Merton made their way here last week,' " Scarlet said, reading to Meg. " 'I'd expected them, because I'd received a letter not long after I bought this land. They were always on the run, of course, though, to my knowledge, no one knows that Jeff shot that man in cold blood during the robbery. In fact, on account of the masks we wore, it would be hard for anyone to swear that they'd seen us do any of the robbing or the killing. To be honest, I'd hoped never to set eyes on the three of them again, though they'll always be part of my heart and soul. You don't survive the kind of bloodshed we did without becoming kindred in some terrible way. Jeff is still bitter. Always says he should have been killed, not his wife and the son he never saw or held. Brian told me he keeps moving just 'cuz he has nowhere to go. His house burned down, and some Yankee carpetbagger is building a new place on the property. Billie says to fuck the North, the war and his family, even though they told him he could go home. Says he'd always be the enemy in their eyes, and, worse than that, a loser. I figured they'd just come by to talk some and then move on, but Billie had a fever. My Jillian, she's such an amazing woman. She had no concern with the war whatever, being in the West with her father for those terrible years. But she said a friend was a friend, and she was going to nurse Billie back to health. I don't think even my precious wife can help him, though. That fever just keeps on getting worse and worse. I think we're going to be planting Billie up on the mountaintop. Hope he'll find peace there at last.' " Scarlet stopped reading and looked at Meg.

"You think Billie is up there?" Meg asked her.

"I guess I have to keep reading," Scarlet said. She shivered slightly. The temperature in the room hadn't changed; it must have been the diary. "I'm going to run up and grab a sweater. Are you okay? Do you want me to get you anything?"

"I'm fine. I just feel like I'm being ripped up a bit. Reading this . . . Nathan cared about people, even those he didn't know. He's talking about a wounded Yankee he stumbled across. He was so struck by the fact that the soldier was so young that he dragged him back behind Confederate lines, then hoped the surgeons wouldn't inadvertently kill him. He writes that the Yankee medics were better equipped and better trained, and that if he was wounded, he hoped he was taken by the enemy."

"I know, it's such sad stuff," Scarlet said. "I'll be right back. I need to find out if Billie did die while he was here."

She hurried up the stairs to her bedroom. It was while she was rummaging in her drawer for a sweater that she suddenly felt as if ice crystals were racing up her back.

And she knew, even before she turned, that she would see him.

Her stalker.

The ghost.

Even as she turned, a warning was flashing through her head.

Scream. Run.

But she didn't.

She turned and stared at the man who had materialized by the window near the head of her bed. She thought that he'd been looking out, down at the stables or over to the next mountaintop, even feeling wistful, perhaps.

Maybe wishing that he could feel the cool mountain air on his skin, breathe in the delicious freshness and the scents of fall.

She stared at him in silence.

"Please," he said simply, looking back at her.

"You're dead, aren't you?" she whispered.

"Yeah, sucks, huh?"

"So why are you doing this to me?"

"You're a descendant. So was I."

"What?"

He let out an impatient sigh. "I came here after I was fooling around at one of those online ancestry sites. I traced myself back to Nathan Kendall and this place. You know what it's like when you're online. I'm from North Carolina, been hiking the Blue Ridge all my life. I couldn't wait to get out here, see Rocky Mountain National Park and the old homestead. I didn't even ask my girl or any of my friends to tag along. I wanted to experience it all by myself. Smart, huh?"

"Not very, from the looks of things," Scarlet said.

He shrugged at that. "A wiseass, huh? Great. I've been doing my best to reach you, and you just keep making me go poof. It's not easy, you know, getting someone to see you, much less managing to touch them. Mostly you're just kind of . . . there. No one sees you, no one talks to you. And if they *do* see you, they get scared and run away."

"Why don't you give me your name?" Scarlet asked.

"Dumb-ass cops. They don't even know that yet."

"It's not as if we have a lot to go on. We've only just gotten a good likeness of you to send around," she said. She realized she'd used the word *we*. Was she becoming one of them?

Or had she always been one with Diego?

"So?" she asked.

"So . . . what?"

"So what is your name?"

"Daniel. Daniel Kendall." He grinned. "Nice to meet you — cousin. A zillion times removed, of course."

"You, too. I guess. Having your name will make it easier for us to help you, at least," she said. "I'm assuming you want help, of course."

"I do. Unfortunately, I don't know who killed me."

"So you *were* killed," Scarlet said, saddened by the information. "But how can you not know who did it?" Scarlet demanded, her frustration showing.

"I didn't see his face."

"How were you killed?" she asked. "Do you know that?"

"Yeah, that I know. I was up in the tundra, striding along, amazed at how high up I was, amazed by how blue the sky was in the clear air, and then I felt a rush behind me. I turned, saw him coming, and the next thing I knew, I was on the ground, bleeding to death. Slowly. I didn't feel the knife. I did feel the dying."

"So the killer was wearing a ski mask?"

"No, it wasn't a ski mask. It was odd, like a bag over his head. Not paper. Something like a burlap sack."

"A burlap sack," Scarlet repeated. "And

neither one of you said anything. He just rushed you from behind, stabbed you — and left you?"

"Oh, he said something," Daniel told her.

"What?"

"He said, 'You're one.' "

"One what?" Scarlet asked.

"That's what I wondered," Daniel said. "But then I started drifting, I thought I'd become a snowflake or something, and I began to think he meant the number one. He sounded proud, as if he'd taken the first step on a fantastic adventure or something. Anyway, I'd planned to come here to the ranch the next day. See if there was a room, take a tour of the museum for sure. I'd seen your name and picture in the brochure and recognized it from the ancestry site. After he killed me, I wanted to warn you. I wanted to warn Ben, too, but he didn't see me. And while I was trying to warn you, that poor couple was being killed. And now he's just killed number four."

Scarlet stared at him blankly. "You're a ghost, and you're talking to me. Stalking me. And you can't even help catch your killer," she said.

"Nice appreciation for me trying to save your life."

She winced. All this was still so hard to believe.

At least she didn't have to wonder anymore if she was crazy or not, though crazy might have been easier. But Diego and the Krewe had suspected her stalker was a dead man.

And they'd been right.

"I'm sorry," she said sincerely. "I just, I wasn't . . . I never . . . I've spent half my life in graveyards and I've never felt so much as a cold spot, much less talked to a ghost before. Or even really believed that ghosts exist. Thank you for trying to warn me, and I mean that sincerely, but I can't help but wish you could identify your killer."

He lowered his head, smiling. "Apology accepted. I wouldn't have believed in ghosts, either, before I became one."

"Scarlet?"

Meg's voice came from the top of the stairs, and Scarlet could hear her footsteps coming up the hall.

Daniel's image began to disappear. He was almost gone when Meg stepped into the room.

But Scarlet could tell that she saw him immediately.

She stopped just inside the doorway, looking at what was almost thin air by then.

"Hello," she said. "I'm Meg. Meg Murray."

She sounded so natural that she could have been introducing herself to someone at a party.

Daniel's image solidified again. "Daniel. Daniel Kendall," he said. "Pleasure, Miss Murray."

"You're a Kendall," Meg murmured.

"Yes, he's been trying to warn me," Scarlet said.

Meg looked at Scarlet. "You're okay? You're not going to pass out or anything?"

"No, I'm not going to pass out," Scarlet said. "I'm fine. Absolutely fine."

Was she?

Meg turned her attention back to Daniel. "Do you know how you —"

"No, he doesn't know who killed him. That would be too easy," Scarlet said drily.

"You don't know?" Meg asked, shocked.

"He was wearing a bag or something over his head," Daniel said. "Like he took a potato sack and cut eye holes in it."

Scarlet gasped. "I can't believe I didn't think of it right away! Nathan Kendall wrote in his journal that he and his friends wore hoods when they robbed banks and stagecoaches and things." She looked at Meg. "The killer has read the diaries. And we know that his friends came here, so maybe that will help us figure out who killed Nathan, too."

"Hey!" Daniel protested. "Don't go all history buff on me. You need to find out who killed *me*. That's what's important, Scarlet. Because if you *don't* find out who killed me, he's eventually going to kill *you*."

CHAPTER ELEVEN

"Cassandra had only been here about a month," Mary Peterson said, sniffling, her eyes welling with tears again. "She came from Kansas City. Kansas City, *Kansas,*" she said with emphasis, as if that was really important. "Not Missouri. She grew up in different foster homes and finally tracked down one of her grandmothers — her mother's mother. She was in a nursing home, but she filled Cassandra's head with stories about the Rockies and how she was related to Nathan Kendall. She couldn't wait to come here, and she got a job right away at the Moose Pot Pie here in town. That's where we met. I work there, too. She was so pretty and so nice, and all the guys liked her. But she wasn't a flirt! She was a hard worker and a good roommate, and she planned to go back to school and get a good education. She had such a tough life . . . and now this."

Their victim was Cassandra Wells, and she was local.

Diego was sorry that he'd been right.

While they'd continued examining the crime scene, Lieutenant Gray had received a call from the station; a distraught young woman had called in because her roommate hadn't come home after work the night before.

And now Mary Peterson, best friend and roommate of the deceased, was at the police station, and Diego was questioning and consoling her at the same time. Normally, unless there were indications of foul play, an adult had to be missing for at least twenty-four hours before a report could be issued, but Lieutenant Gray had told his officers to take a report if a person had been gone for more than an hour or two.

Given the condition of the body, getting an ID might have proven difficult, but Cassandra had been bonded so she could handle money at the Moose Pot Pie, and the fingerprints matched.

"Did you notice anything or anyone special or suspicious in any way during the day?" Diego asked. "Was she dating someone?"

Mary shook her head dully. "No and no. Her education meant everything to her. She said she was getting old." More tears welled in Mary's eyes. "She was twenty-six."

"I'm so sorry," Diego said. "When did you last see her?"

"I was on the early shift. I left at five. Cassandra was scheduled to close, so she would have been there until eleven or twelve."

"Who else was working that shift?" he asked.

"Braxton and Stan," Mary said.

There was a pad on the table, and Diego gently pushed it toward her. "If you could give me their information, please?"

"Of course, anything," Mary said. "This just isn't fair. She was so excited to be living here. She felt like she'd come home. She said this was her place. She'd already been to the museum up at the Conway Ranch, and she'd met Ben and Trisha Kendall."

"She knew the owners?" he asked, a little too sharply.

"Of course. She adored the Conway Ranch." Mary suddenly lowered her voice, as if someone might overhear her. "I think they wanted to hire her. She said they'd talked about her coming on as manager."

"Great. Thank you, Mary. I'm curious — did she mention knowing anyone else who was descended from Nathan Kendall?"

She frowned. "No, I don't think so. I think maybe she'd been in contact with a few people online, but I don't know who, and I don't even know if they were from around here." She stopped, her eyes watering again. "What will I do? Her grandmother's dead, so she doesn't have any family. I work for minimum wage and tips, but I have to bury her. I can't let them just dump her in a hole without a headstone or anything."

Diego was glad he could help her with one thing, at least. "Don't worry," he said. "We can arrange for a funeral."

"Cops do that?" she asked incredulously.

"I'm not actually a cop."

"You're not a cop? And you're questioning me?"

"I'm FBI," he explained. "And I think Cassandra would be pleased to be buried in the old cemetery on the Kendall property. And . . ." He hesitated for a moment, wondering if he had the right to speak for a man he'd only recently met, then went on. "I have a friend who can help with whatever other arrangements need to be made. But you should know that the funeral can't take place right away. Not while we're still investigating."

He didn't think he should mention the word *autopsy* — not unless he wanted to see her start crying again.

He handed her his card. "Please, if you think of anything that could help, anyone who seemed especially interested in her, for instance, call me."

"Of course," she promised, then began to sniffle again.

He didn't try to tell her that it was going to be all right, because it wasn't. Her friend was dead. Nothing could ever fix that.

"Thank you," he said.

They both rose. She looked at him, wiping her eyes. "She would be glad to be buried in the family cemetery, I think. She was so excited to be a part of the Kendall legacy. She said that this was her permanent home. I guess now it is."

"Aha!" Scarlet cried.

She was back at her desk, reading further in one of Nathan's journals.

Meg, sitting across from her, was doing the same.

Daniel, who was clearly getting better at the art of visibility, was walking around, checking out all the artifacts in the museum.

Meg and Daniel both turned to look at her and said in tandem, "What?"

"We can cross one suspect off the list," Scarlet said.

"In my murder?" Daniel asked her.

She looked over at him and shook her head. "Daniel, you know that the police and the Krewe are working on that. I'm going at it from another angle, trying to find out who killed Nathan, on the theory that there's a connection between the deaths then and the deaths now."

"So you found out who *didn't* kill him. Wonderful," Daniel said.

"Process of elimination," Meg said.

"And what's this crew business? I thought the FBI was divided up into units?"

"Not that kind of crew," Meg said. "It's Krewe with a *K,* like the Mardi Gras krewes in New Orleans."

"I was in a Mardi Gras krewe once, back in college. My frat went down for it. One of the best times I ever had," Daniel said.

"Our Krewe is a special FBI unit formed by a man named Adam Harrison, who brought together a group of agents who, like me, can see ghosts like you. He needed them to work a haunted-house case in New Orleans, and the Krewe name just seemed right," Meg explained. "But much more important right now, Scarlet, what did you find?"

"Billie *did* die here about three weeks after he and the others arrived. They had a funeral and buried him in the cemetery up the mountain. There's no marker for him now, but that doesn't mean there wasn't one then. He probably had a cross that's long gone now, and the historical society must not know about him, so they never put up a new one."

"So that guy didn't kill Nathan. And that's important how?" Daniel asked.

"Process of elimination," Meg said again. "So what did you do for a living, Daniel?"

He grinned. "Tour guide. I took people hiking up in the Blue Ridge. I was pretty damned good, too." He paused. "Not good enough to hear a murderer sneak up behind me, though."

Instinctively, Scarlet stood and walked over to him — and then awkwardly realized that she couldn't put an arm around his shoulders.

"I'm so sorry," she said.

He nodded. "Yeah, so am I. I wish I'd met you while I was alive." There was something wistful in his eyes.

She smiled and realized that she probably would have liked him. "We'll find out what's going on," she promised.

"I read up on him, you know," Daniel said.

"Pardon?" Scarlet asked.

He pointed to the statue of Nathan

Kendall. "Our however-many greats grand-father. I know he became an outlaw after the war, but he had a moral compass and got out when he realized what was happening. And then he came out here and found a little piece of heaven. And love." He shook his head sadly, looking so real and solid that Scarlet could have sworn she could reach out and touch him. "It must have killed his soul, seeing Jillian killed, too."

"Yes, I'm sure it did," Scarlet said.

Suddenly Meg's phone rang. Scarlet almost jumped, then walked over to listen.

All she heard at first was "I see," followed by "How sad." A minute later Meg glanced at Scarlet with a grin. "Yes, we're fine, and we've taken a few steps forward here, too. You'll see when you get here."

She hung up, and her expression grew somber again. "The dead woman was named Cassandra Wells. She moved to the area not long ago because —"

"Because she's a descendant of Nathan Kendall," Daniel interrupted.

"You knew her?" Meg asked him.

"I can't say I knew her, really. But after I was killed, when I realized I wasn't going anywhere, I'd walk around town at night, eavesdropping. I thought if I just listened long enough, maybe I'd find out who killed me. One night I went and hung out in the Moose Pot Pie. She seemed like a good kid, nice to everyone, and whenever she had a break, she had her head in a book. I used to go back there, and I got to know a lot about her. I knew she'd come here because of Nathan Kendall, too. I knew we were distantly related. I knew she was trying hard to make something of her life. She didn't deserve to die that way." He looked over at Meg then. "You'd better get this guy. This has to stop before someone else gets killed."

"We will, Daniel. I swear it. My fellow Krewe members are out there now, interviewing everyone she worked with, her landlady, all her friends, to see if they saw anything suspicious or even just out-of-the-ordinary in some way. Her picture is going out over the media, and they're asking for help from anyone who might have seen her. Killers make mistakes, Daniel. No matter how good they think they are, they make mistakes."

"Scarlet," Daniel said, "you've met her."

"I have?" Scarlet asked.

He nodded gravely. "One night. I heard her talking to some guy about the great museum up at the Conway Ranch. She said one of the best things was the curator. Said you gave her a tour."

"How recently was this?"

"Sometime in the last few weeks, I think," he said.

She couldn't believe she had met the dead woman. A wave of sadness rippled through her.

"They'll catch him," she said passionately.

"Some killers get away," Daniel said.

"We won't let that happen," Meg vowed.

Daniel looked at Scarlet. She thought he seemed more upset about Cassandra's death than his own. "Whoever did this is a monster, Daniel, and the Krewe won't stop until they get him. They won't give up."

He studied her. "Your ex, you mean?"

"All of them," she said firmly.

How the hell did he know about her situation?

He really *did* eavesdrop.

He suddenly stepped forward and put his hands on her shoulders.

Just as she had that night in the bar, she felt his touch.

"You understand now, right? I was afraid it was going to be you. You were right here, working at the museum. I thought he'd go after you right away. You have to be so careful, really careful."

And then he faded away.

Scarlet turned to look at Meg.

Meg shrugged. "You get used to it," she said. "It takes tremendous energy for a ghost to make himself visible, not to mention to touch someone the way he touched you. He's used up all his energy for now."

"But he'll be back?"

Meg nodded.

Scarlet walked back to her desk. Was it going to matter if they found out the truth about Nathan's and Jillian's murders? That was so long ago.

And the man who'd killed Daniel had stepped up his game. Three people in a week, dead.

She walked over to the statue of Nathan Kendall. He didn't look anything like her or Daniel, yet she suddenly felt a fierce bond with the two of them.

Ghosts really did exist.

And mannequins didn't move on their own.

She suddenly realized that it was almost certainly the killer who'd been in the museum while she slept.

The killer had moved the statue.

And yet, he had left her alive.

Why?

Suddenly she wondered if the killer was saving her up to be some kind of horrific finale, the last of the Kendall descendants to die.

Braxton Hall was young, barely twenty-one. He'd been quarterback for his high school football team and had hoped to parlay that into a college scholarship and career. But a broken kneecap — the result of a skateboarding accident — had ruined that dream. Now he was attending a local junior college and working at the Moose Pot Pie.

Stan White was thirty, liked his job at the Moose Pot Pie — he'd told Diego at the onset that he intended to stay at the restaurant forever — and liked living close to Rocky Mountain National Park. He was also a great fan of recreational marijuana — a hindrance at the moment, since he just kept saying, "Oh man, not cool, not cool. Oh man, not cool."

Diego seldom interviewed suspects or witnesses together. But he didn't suspect either man of being guilty, and he hoped that something one said might trigger something important in the memory of the other.

Stan was slouched back in his chair, legs extended beneath the table. Braxton was sitting right up, hands slack in his lap, eyes red-rimmed.

"Cassandra was the best," Braxton said.

"The Moose Pot Pie seems like a pretty laid-back place, but isn't it unusual for restaurant workers to be bonded?" Diego asked him. "Did anyone mind?"

"If they minded, they could get a job somewhere else," Braxton said. "The owner is a great guy, but he was ripped off by a manager about five years ago, so he started insisting that his employees be bonded. But he's one of the best bosses out there. He doesn't breathe over your shoulder, and he left Cassandra in charge most of the time and didn't even come in. The guy's name is Vince Guttenberg, in case you want to talk to him."

"I know," Diego told him. "And one of my colleagues is talking to him now. So you two were both there with Cassandra 'til the end of shift last night, right?"

"Yup," Stan said.

"No, you cut out about a half hour early — your foot was hurting you," Braxton reminded him.

"Oh, yeah, that's right. Fell down my stairs last week and broke a little tiny bone in my foot," Stan said. "Hurts like a mother. That's why I've taken something for, you know, the pain."

"Stan, being stoned is legal here," Diego assured him. "It's okay. I just need your help trying to find out what happened to her. Was anyone hanging around in the street when you left, like maybe they were waiting for her to come out? Did either of you see anybody watching her last night? Did she talk to anyone in the past few days who seemed angry or upset?"

"I don't think so," Stan said, as Braxton shook his head.

"What happened when you closed up?" he asked, turning to Braxton.

"We locked the door at ten fifteen, when the last customers left. We don't seat anyone after ten, but we don't force 'em to leave if they're already inside. So we got the last people out. I cleaned tables, while Cassandra balanced the day's receipts and took the last charge card tips out of the register."

"And then?"

"Then we left together."

"And where did you go?" Diego asked.

"We started to walk to our cars together. But there was a band playing at the Twisted Antler that Cassandra liked — local guys — so she decided to stop in for a while before going home."

"Did you see her go into the bar?" Diego asked.

"No, we were by the city parking lot. There were still people out — it's really safe there. I headed to my car. She walked down the street." He looked down and then at Diego. "I wonder what would have happened if I hadn't. I wonder if she'd be alive — or if I'd be dead, too."

Scarlet was amazed to realize that she enjoyed Daniel's company, even if he was a ghost.

She and Meg kept reading the journals, while Daniel, who had reappeared after about twenty minutes, actually became helpful, wandering through the museum and periodically commenting on one piece or another, which had the unexpected effect of making Scarlet remember some bit of information stored at the back of her mind, and that would lead her to explore some new angle, either in the journal or online. At one point Daniel read aloud from the century-old note that described a Civil War-era surgeon's bag. " 'Last used by Dr. Avery Simpson, after a mining accident. Dr. Avery was called in to treat miner Brady Glee, possibly an alias of notorious outlaw Brian Gleason, but Glee unfortunately expired despite the surgeon's efforts.' " He stopped reading. "Did you know about this?"

"Of course," Scarlet said. "I know every artifact in here. But I've researched the pos-

280

sibility that the dead man might have been Brian Gleason and haven't found any support for it. Of course, I also can't find any reference to Gleason's death anywhere."

"Doesn't that make it more likely that Glee was Gleason and did die in that mining accident?" Meg asked.

"Yes, I guess you're right. It's just that in academia we try to find supporting sources before considering information verified," Scarlet said.

Daniel laughed softly. "This isn't academia, Scarlet."

Scarlet set down the journal she'd been reading, picked up her laptop and started keying in her notes.

"All right, let's see how the dates connect. Nathan bought the property from Rollo Conway in late 1868. His old buddies arrived in 1869, soon after he'd married Jillian. Billie Merton died in November of 1869. The mine accident was in the fall of 1870." She looked up. "And Nathan and Jillian were also killed in the fall of 1870."

"Before or after the accident?" Daniel asked. "Because if the mine accident was before Nathan and Jillian were murdered, and if Brady Glee *was* Brian Gleason, then he was dead before the murders, too, so he couldn't have been guilty, either."

281

"I don't have a date for the accident," Scarlet said. "I'll have to research that."

"Does the mine still exist?" Meg asked.

"No, it was sealed up around 1910," Scarlet said. "They mined for gold there, though not all that successfully. They panned in the streams around here, too. Rollo Conway tried that, but he never found much. That's why he sold this property to Nathan Kendall — he wanted to try his luck south of Estes Park."

"And yet he came back here and he's buried up at the cemetery," Daniel said.

"He was an interesting man," Scarlet said. She searched through the stack of journals on her desk and found the one she was looking for. "Here's Nathan's description of him. 'Rollo is what you expect to see, rugged and fit and old — yet how old, I really don't know. He has dark eyes that contrast with his snow-white hair and long beard. He could easily be mistaken for a preacher of some kind. Rollo, though, he claims that the ladies love him. Maybe they do — he's as fit as a fiddle, as mean as a boar when he chooses, and he talks the good talk. A rider coming through one day told me he knew old Rollo from back East. Supposedly he still sends money back to a woman and child there, though there was never any talk of him being married. He's mad as a hornet about selling this property. He'd kick the whole damned mountain if he could, so he told me.' "

"Sounds like the epitome of the old frontier type," Daniel said. "I guess you do get mean when you're always fighting off Indians and bears and whatever."

"I don't think he fought any Indians," Scarlet said.

"Still, can you imagine?" Daniel asked. "A lot of this area is so pristine and beautiful. But a moose — even a pissed-off elk — can kill a man. And don't forget the bears. Not to mention there wasn't any real law. Think how dark it is out here at night now, how the forest seems to stretch forever. Those guys had to be pretty hardy. There was no road out here or anything. Stanley was responsible for the first decent road to Estes Park."

"Have you researched Rollo Conway?" Meg asked Scarlet.

"I have what information there is. He didn't fight for the North or the South in the Civil War. He was already out here when the fighting began. He was originally from Massachusetts. There are records of him having property here and a bit south. I don't believe he ever found the gold he was looking for."

"What about the woman back East?" Daniel asked.

"I've never found any record of her. That doesn't mean that she didn't exist, of course. They didn't keep great records back then to begin with, and lots of what they did have was lost over the years."

"Back to the important stuff," Daniel said. "If it wasn't Billie Merton or Brian Gleason who killed Nathan and Jillian — and yes, I know we still can't say for sure about Gleason — then if it wasn't some stranger, that leaves the last of Nathan's outlaw pals, Jeff Bay, or his father-in-law, cold as ice in any book."

"Or Rollo Conway," Scarlet mused. "But if it was Rollo, why? He needed money, so he wanted to sell the property and Nathan bought it. Nathan did him a favor."

"Maybe he resented Nathan for having the money to buy it when he didn't really want to sell it," Daniel suggested.

"The way Nathan was killed, I can't help but think that someone wanted something from him. But what?" Scarlet asked.

"Scenario one, it was the father-in-law," Daniel said. "He was torturing Nathan to get him to tell the truth about his past, so he could prove to his daughter that Nathan was worthless trash. Jillian comes running out of the house to see what's going on, and he whirls around, startled, and — *bang!* She's dead."

"Scenario two," Meg said. "Jeff Bay. Brian and Bill are dead. But back in the day they stole something valuable, and Jeff thinks Nathan still has it. He tortures Nathan, Jillian walks in on the scene — *bang!* She's dead."

"Scenario three," Scarlet said. "Rollo Conway. But why? Killing Nathan won't get his land back. If Rollo did it, there had to be a reason, but I have no idea what it could have been."

"Are all the journals here?" Meg asked. "The man was certainly prolific."

"There are a lot of them, but I've always thought we were missing one. There's a gap between the last one and the one before it. He makes references in the last one to a disturbing visit, but he never says from who it was, and there's nothing in the previous one that qualifies. Now, of course, I'm thinking it was the killer."

They were all startled — even Daniel, who was dead! — by a sudden *whoosh* followed by a jolting *thud.*

Scarlet's heart leaped to her throat. Meg was on her feet in a split second, her Glock out of its holster and trained across the room.

There was silence.

Then Scarlet realized what had happened.

It was the statue. The damned statue of Nathan Kendall.

It had fallen off its pedestal to the floor.

"To the best of my knowledge, everyone was accounted for after our trip to The Stanley. But I can't swear to that," Brett said.

Cassandra Wells's picture was now all over the media, with the message that the police were seeking witnesses who might have seen her or anything suspicious the night before. Some broadcasters were suggesting that the Parkers' murders had been perpetrated by the same killer, though the police themselves were keeping quiet on that score.

Diego himself had gone on camera to say that he didn't wish to create a panic, but that all three victims could trace their lineage back to Nathan Kendall, though, since Zachary had fathered so many children, the relationship might be coincidence.

One station had interviewed the owner of Moose Pot Pie, who appeared to be genuinely devastated. Vince Guttenberg had been in Denver the night before, at a nephew's birthday party, and he had stayed over at his sister's house. He had returned to discover that his best employee had been murdered. He wasn't a suspect, and he wasn't even any help as a witness. He couldn't think of anyone who had shown Cassandra any animosity or even any undue interest.

They were still at the police station in a conference room with Lieutenant Ernest Gray, when a call from Adam came through on Diego's phone. Adam asked him where he was and who he was with, then suggested he put the call on speaker.

"We have a tentative ID on the victim from the mountain," Adam said without preamble. "HQ received a call from the Asheville, North Carolina, PD. A Daniel Kendall has been missing since he headed out on vacation, solo, a couple months earlier. He planned on taking a month, but when he didn't return, his girlfriend grew concerned and filed a missing persons report. It was difficult to do any kind of a real search, because he hadn't told her where he was going, other than 'out West.' That was followed by a call from a man named Leo Piper in Lyons, Colorado. He owns a hotel there and recognized the picture as a former guest who'd planned on hiking the Rockies and doing some genealogical research."

"Thanks, Adam. Kendall, huh? I'm assuming Daniel was a descendant of Nathan Kendall, too?" Diego asked.

"Yes, exactly," Adam responded. "Jane and I are about to go over to the museum and check on Scarlet and Meg. Then we'll head out to Lyons to see what Mr. Leo Piper can tell us."

"Damn," Gray said.

"Pardon?" Adam asked.

"I'm a descendant, too," Gray said.

"Perhaps you should excuse yourself from this investigation," Adam suggested.

Gray laughed. "And hightail it out of town 'til the coast is clear?" he asked. "No, no. Couldn't live with myself if I did that. I'm in for the long haul. I want to bring this bastard in. I don't care about the collar. I'm fine if one of you nabs him, I just want to be there when someone stops his ass."

Diego smiled. He liked Gray's new attitude.

Adam said his goodbyes and rang off. Gray excused himself to see if there had been any results from all the media attention and the posters he'd had his men plaster all across town.

Someone had to have seen someone or

something somewhere at some time.

"I think we need to hang out at a bar tonight," Diego told Matt and Brett. "The Twisted Antler. That's where Cassandra was supposedly heading last night. Gray already checked with the owner and the manager — neither remembers seeing her, and if she bought anything, she paid cash. But the manager said they have a lot of regulars, plus the staff, of course. Oh, and the band. We can divide and conquer, talk to as many people as we can."

Matt stood. "Let's get back to the ranch, and touch base with Meg and Scarlet. I'll give Adam a call and let him know."

He didn't have to call Adam, because just then Jane called Diego.

"Are you on your way back?" she asked.

"Yes, but why? Is something wrong?" he asked anxiously.

"No, but if you weren't headed here, I was going to tell you that you should be. We'll wait for you at the museum, then head down to Lyons once you get here."

"You're sure there's nothing wrong?" he asked.

"No, nothing. We have a visitor, that's all. Someone you're going to want to meet."

Before he could ask for details, she hung up.

CHAPTER TWELVE

The living room was already crowded when Matt, Brett and Diego arrived; Adam and Jane were there with Meg and Scarlet, and there was another man standing with his back to them as they entered.

Scarlet jumped up to greet Diego, her smile wide and welcoming. Then the unknown man turned around, and even before Scarlet reached him, Diego froze.

The man appeared to be flesh and blood. But, he wasn't. He couldn't be.

"Daniel Kendall," Diego said.

"Yes!" Scarlet said, sounding ridiculously happy for a woman who was hosting a dead man. "Yes, this is Daniel, who's been trying to reach me. Daniel, Agents Diego McCullough, Matt Bosworth and Brett Cody. Guys, meet Daniel Kendall."

"I'd shake if I could," the apparition told them, grinning.

"Nice to meet you," Matt said. "And also

sorry to meet you."

Diego looked over at Adam, then back to Daniel, and sighed. "I don't suppose you know who killed you, huh? Because if you did, you would have told Meg and Scarlet, and we'd be arresting him now."

"Believe me, you can't wish I knew who he was any more than I do." He shimmered for a moment, then solidified. "Sorry. I vanish now and then, so please bear with me. I'll be back as soon as I can."

"I can't really see you anyway," Adam said. "I can hear you loud and clear, though. I don't have that extra sense my Krewe do, though over time I've grown able to see my son," he said softly, then turned to Scarlet. "But you . . ."

"I see him as clearly as a mountaintop on a sunny day," she said, obviously pleased. Then she took Diego's hand and led him into the room, urging him into one of the big upholstered chairs.

He wasn't that good at seeing ghosts yet, either, Diego thought. He didn't want to say that to Scarlet, though.

But his abilities were firing on all cylinders tonight, though, because there he was, the dead man Jane had drawn, acting as if he was just hanging with friends on a lazy day.

"Any news on Cassandra?" Daniel asked.

"I knew her, though she didn't know me, if you see what I mean."

"I do. And we know where she was until just before her death," Diego said. "What can you tell us?"

Daniel went through the same story he'd told Scarlet and Meg earlier. His concern for Cassandra — a woman he'd never met, whom he'd only known as a ghost — was clear.

I would have liked this guy, Diego thought.

When Daniel had finished with his explanation, Meg went on to talk about the discoveries they'd made in the journals.

"Interesting," Matt said.

"Do you think we'll ever be able to figure out the truth about something that happened so long ago? We can't even question the suspects, much less find any forensic evidence," Scarlet said.

"Maybe we couldn't take someone into a court of law and prove their guilt," Diego said, "but that doesn't matter. We can still put clues together and come up with a truth that we believe, and that truth is what we need to help us solve the present case."

"I'll help any way I can," Daniel announced, then wavered. Seconds later, he was gone, leaving a frustrated "Sorry" hanging in the air.

For a moment everyone else was quiet.

"He's really gone?" Adam asked.

"Yes," Scarlet said.

"I guess it doesn't make much sense for us to go to Lyons anymore," Adam said. "When Daniel gets back he can tell us everything he did right up to the time when he was killed."

"In that case, we can all go to the bar tonight," Diego said.

"We're going to a bar?" Scarlet asked.

"Cassandra told a coworker she was going to listen to a band, but it looks as if she either never made it or wasn't there long before the killer got to her," Diego explained. "We want to talk to the regulars and staff to see if anyone saw anything. A place called the Twisted Antler."

"The Twisted Antler?" Scarlet repeated.

"Yes, you know the place?"

She nodded. "I have a friend who plays drums with the house band there. Eddie Keye. Nice guy. He might have seen her if she was there last night."

"Do you think someone managed to pick her up in the bar, then take her for a ride, drag her halfway up a mountain and then kill her?" Adam asked.

"It's possible. The killer surprised Daniel from behind," Meg said, "but we don't know how he's approached his more recent victims."

"He was wearing a burlap bag over his head when he attacked Daniel," Scarlet said.

"Obviously he can't do that if he picks up his victims in public," Meg added. "But here's the strange thing. Nathan Kendall and his cohorts — Jeff Bay, Brian Gleason and Billie Merton — wore similar 'masks' when they were robbing banks after the Civil War."

"I've got to think it's all connected," Diego said. "Meanwhile, food. Let's get into town and hit the Twisted Antler."

Scarlet noticed that Adam and Jane were walking along the sidewalk ahead of her and Diego, with Brett, Matt and Meg bringing up the rear. And while it all seemed very casual and natural, she was pretty sure that the others were consciously making sure that she was surrounded at all times.

It was rather nice to feel so protected.

When they reached the Twisted Antler, the band was just setting up. Eddie saw her and lifted a hand, smiling.

"I'll introduce you," Scarlet said.

"You go ahead," Adam told the others. "I want to introduce myself to the manager and let him or her know we're here."

As he left to speak with the hostess, Scarlet led the others over to where Eddie and his group were setting up.

"Hey," Eddie said as they approached, looking curiously at her entourage. He offered his hand even before Scarlet got a chance to introduce everyone.

"Nice to meet you," Eddie said. He pointed to his bandmates, who paused to nod and wave as they were introduced: Jack Isle on bass, Lee Bell on lead guitar and Hanley Warner on keyboard.

"Friends from back East?" Eddie asked. His tone was casual, but she could tell that he was assessing the group and in particular wondering how Adam — who was not only older, but also still wearing his signature suit — fit in.

"Diego is my ex-husband," Scarlet explained. "He's a federal agent. Adam —" she nodded in his direction "— heads his division, and Matt, Brett, Jane and Meg are also FBI. They're working the murders up at the Conway Ranch."

"Yeah, I was worried, wondering how you were doing. Bad stuff happening here," Eddie said. "I was going to take a ride up there, tell you maybe you should go back to Florida for a while." He grinned, looking from her to Diego. "But I see you're in good hands. Are you guys out to get to know Estes Park tonight or working the case?"

"Both," Diego said. "We know the most recent victim, Cassandra Wells, liked coming here, so we figured if anyone had seen anything, it might be you guys, or the staff and regulars here. Did *you* know her, by any chance?"

Eddie nodded. "Casually, from the restaurant and here. She seemed like a nice kid, kind of serious but nice. She didn't deserve what happened to her."

"Was she in here last night?"

"I didn't see her," Eddie said, "but then, I don't see everyone." He pointed back to his bandmates. "Hanley thought he saw her come in, then stand in the back. But she was gone when the set was over. He called that number from the TV and left a message, but no one's come in to talk to him yet. Hey, Hanley?"

The keyboardist stepped over as soon as Eddie called. Scarlet knew him casually, the same way she knew all of them, except for Eddie. She knew him better since they'd gone for coffee a few times.

Hanley kept his head shaved — crazy for cold weather, Eddie liked to tease him — but he'd gone mostly bald by the time he turned thirty, so he'd decided to embrace the bald look and buy himself a big old hoop earring. In truth, like Eddie, he was just a nice guy who loved his music.

"Hanley, you thought you saw Cassandra last night, didn't you?" Eddie asked him.

Hanley nodded. "Yeah." He pointed to the back of the room, where there was a ledge with a few bar stools to the left of the door, providing a better view of the stage than the bar itself did.

"She was just standing there, leaning against that support beam off to the left," Hanley said. "It looked like she was talking to someone, but they were behind the beam."

"Okay, now we know she at least made it inside," Diego said.

"I hope you catch the guy," Hanley said. "I wish you could pretend this was still the Old West and shoot the bastard's kneecaps out, then torture him to death."

"Hey, don't be shy, Hanley, tell them what you really think," Eddie said drily, and then looked at the others again. "I gotta say, screw that humane punishment thing. I feel the same. At least Colorado has the death penalty. I hope you get the guy and that he gets it."

Adam had joined them just in time to hear the last. He introduced himself and shook hands with the band, then said, "My agents — and the police — will get him. What happens next will be up to a jury."

"Unless he shoots at you, and then you get to shoot back, right?" Hanley asked. "Sorry, I was crazy about her. We were just friends, but not 'cuz I didn't want more. But she wasn't into dating, not until she got herself through school."

"We're allowed to defend ourselves, yes," Matt said.

"Well, I hope he shoots at you, then," Hanley said. "I mean, I don't want him to hit any of you or anything, but . . ."

"We understand," Brett said.

"Are you guys going to stay around awhile?" Eddie asked. "If you are, we can try to point out some of the regulars when they show up, along with anybody I noticed in here last night. Maybe they'll know who Cassandra was talking to or if she left with someone."

"That would be great," Diego said. "Thank you."

"I think your table is ready," Eddie said, pointing to where the hostess was standing and looking their way.

The others thanked him and headed over to take their table, but Scarlet waited and thanked Eddie again herself.

"The ex, huh?" he said, a rueful smile on his lips.

She nodded.

"But you're not ready to let go, are you?" he asked.

"He came to help," she said, ignoring his question.

"I just hope he's smart enough to know what he has," Eddie told her.

"I . . ."

"You've always been honest. You don't owe me an explanation."

"I don't really even have one," Scarlet said. "We're divorced, but he came to help me anyway, and yes . . . I do still care about him. And I hope you and I are still friends."

"We are. I just hope they really can catch this killer."

Scarlet nodded and hurried to join the others at the table.

Their waitress was there, trying to convince them that Rocky Mountain oysters were a can't-miss hit with visitors.

"I know what they are, and no thanks," Brett said. "I've never wanted eel in my sushi, either, even if an eel is just a snakey kind of fish."

Everyone else opted out, too. At Scarlet's suggestion they all went with beefalo steaks, which she explained were a little sweeter than regular beef, but very good.

Scarlet noticed a tall lanky man standing with his back to her by the same support beam where Cassandra had been standing the night before. She started to say something, but before she could, she saw a waitress move right through him, then pause and shiver before moving on.

The man turned and saw Scarlet, and grinned.

It was Daniel Kendall.

"We have a spy on our side," she commented.

"I thought Daniel might join us," Adam said, without turning to look.

"Good," Diego said. "All help appreciated.

Their food arrived just as Eddie spoke into the mike by his drum set and introduced himself and the band, Snow. They began to play. Hanley sang lead on their first number.

The band was good, and from the way the Krewe members applauded, Scarlet thought that they looked like any group of friends out for a casual night.

She wondered if they could ever really let go of what they did for a living and simply enjoy themselves, or if seeing the dead made wariness a way of life. Maybe it wasn't so bad even if it did. They seemed to have perfected the art of having fun while staying vigilant.

In the middle of the second song Scarlet saw Eddie nod toward a man near the front of the stage without missing a drumbeat.

Diego must have been watching Eddie closely, because she saw him nod in return, get up and head toward the man Eddie had indicated.

When the man turned, she saw that it was one of their Conway Ranch newlyweds, Charles Barton, and Gwen was sitting next to him.

"I thought everyone stayed in last night after we came back from The Stanley," Adam murmured to Brett.

"They didn't leave by the front door," Brett said. "And the back door is kept locked. Guests are only given the key to the front. I checked."

"I didn't see a back door," Jane said.

"It's behind the pantry, which is behind the kitchen, and that's behind the dining room," Scarlet explained.

"I didn't see or hear a car leave, either," Brett said.

"So they walked into town?" Meg said.

"I'm sure Diego is asking them, but I think I'll go join the conversation," Meg said. "Come on, Scarlet. Go with me."

They stood and headed through the crowd to where Diego was speaking with Gwen and Charles, arriving in time to hear him ask, "So you saw her?"

"Yes," Gwen said, giving a little shiver. "We saw her picture on the news earlier and realized we'd seen her in here last night. I don't think she ordered anything, she was just standing by the back. We were going to tell you about it, but then we didn't see you all day."

Scarlet stepped right into the conversation. "Hi, guys, just curious — how did you get here last night?"

Gwen quickly turned to her husband, a look of guilt on her face. "We told Ben we were in for the night when we saw him locking the front door, but then we were both wide-awake, and we saw an article about these guys in the guidebook in the room, so we decided to check them out."

Charles spoke up. "When we were dating, she used to sneak out the back to meet me, and we thought it would be fun to do that together. Trisha gave us a tour of the place when we got there, so we knew where the back door is and slipped out that way."

"And walked down the mountain to town?" Meg asked politely.

"Oh, no. But we didn't want to drive," Gwen said, "because we both wanted to drink, so we called Tim and Bess Weatherly, a local couple we met and wanted to get together with anyway. They picked us up just down the road. Walk? This far?" She laughed. "No way on earth. And we used the front door when they brought us back."

When Brett must have stopped watching and finally gone to bed, Scarlet thought.

"Where are Tim and Bess tonight?" Diego asked.

"Bess works tonight. She's a waitress at the twenty-four-hour omelet place," Charles said. He frowned suddenly, looking at Diego. "You don't think that we . . . Oh, no, no, no!"

"What?" Gwen looked confused.

"He's suspicious of us!" Charles said. He glared at Diego.

"We're not suspicious of you. We just want to talk to everyone who was here last night," Diego assured them. "We're trying to find out where Cassandra Wells went when she left here and whether she was still here when she met her killer."

"Like I said, she was just standing at the back, but she wasn't there very long," Gwen said. "Although I did see her talking to someone."

303

"What did he look like?" Diego asked.

"It wasn't a he," Gwen said. "It was a she."

"A woman?"

"Yeah. She was — hmm, not sure. She might have been tall, or she might have been wearing heels. And I didn't see her face, because she was turned away from me. She had long hair, though."

"Was she still here after Cassandra left?" Scarlet asked.

"I don't know," Gwen said. "I was watching the band."

"Do you think your friends might have noticed the woman who was talking to Cassandra?" Diego asked.

"I don't know," Gwen said. "You could go ask Bess, and Tim will be picking her up when her shift is finished. Neither one of them is related to Nathan Kendall as far as they know, but they called today to say they're not taking any chances and neither should we."

"Thank you," Diego said. "Enjoy the band." He glanced at Scarlet. "And they're friends of Scarlet's, by the way, if you want a CD or an autograph or something."

Scarlet looked at him curiously. He'd almost sounded jealous. She knew he wasn't, though.

Did she want him to be?

No, jealousy and possessiveness had never been a part of what they were and hadn't been why they'd fallen apart. She'd always trusted him completely as far as being faithful to her went. She'd never hounded him about where he'd been.

She'd just stopped talking to him.

"They're friends of yours?" Gwen asked. "Cool. I bought their CD last night."

The band chose that moment to break, saying they would be back in a few minutes, and headed down the back hall to the stage door.

Scarlet excused herself, saying, "Hold on — I'll ask them to come over and chat for a minute."

Eddie was just stepping through the door into the alley when she made it to the hall. He didn't smoke, but some of the band members did, so they tended to go outside and hang together during breaks.

She opened the door to find the alley filled with a thick fog.

"Eddie?" she called, moving forward. There was a Dumpster just steps from the back door, and Scarlet paused, noticing something lying on the ground in front of it.

A body, with nothing but blood and pulp where the face should have been.

She screamed.

Within seconds Eddie was there, and Diego and Meg came bursting out the back door a moment later, followed by Gwen and Charles and a spill of strangers.

Shaking, Scarlet pointed at the Dumpster. But the fog had lifted.

And there was nothing on the ground.

Scarlet stared blankly at the empty spot while the image of what she'd seen still burned before her eyes.

The Krewe members would understand.

Or would they?

She hadn't seen a ghost, she'd seen the ravaged body of a young woman who'd been attacked by an evil killer.

Despite her terror, she knew she had to reason her way out of the situation or risk having everyone think she'd lost her mind. "Over there — I saw someone. They ran down the alley, I think."

"Which way?" Diego asked her.

She met his eyes and could tell that he knew she'd made up the story to cover for something else, and also that he would cover for her.

"I'll go," Matt said. "Brett, you with me?"

Brett nodded, and they left.

Diego and Eddie both started toward her.

She quickly lifted her hands. "I'm okay. I

306

was just so startled. He scared me."

"I didn't see anyone when I came out," Eddie said, as the rest of the band came up behind him. "Bastard must have been slinking around behind the Dumpster."

"You guys have to be careful, too," she said. Even to her own ears, her voice sounded thin.

"This is Colorado," Hanley said. "I pack a legal gun, and I was in the marines, so I know what I'm doing. I can watch out for us."

Diego backed away to stand with Adam and the rest of the Krewe, checking out the crowd. The manager, a heavyset man of about fifty, urged people to go back inside. "Calm down, everyone, and let's head back in. It was probably just a homeless man, but not to worry. We have federal agents in the house tonight, and they're on it."

He walked over to talk to Scarlet. She'd been at the Twisted Antler often enough that they knew each other by sight.

"You all right?" he asked her.

"Fine. I'm sorry I scared everyone half to death."

"Can't be too careful, not with what's been going on lately," he said, then flashed a smile at Adam. "Nice to have you guys around. I think it will be good for business."

"Let's get everyone back inside," Adam suggested. "Eddie, if the band could start playing again right away, that would be a big help."

"Not a problem," Eddie said, and gestured to the rest of the group to follow him in.

Only when everyone but the Krewe was gone did Diego slip an arm around Scarlet's shoulders and ask, "What did you really see?"

"A woman," she said. "Lying there in a pool of blood with nothing left of her face. I don't know why, but I think it was Cassandra."

"What the hell were you doing coming out here anyway?" Diego demanded.

"What?" Scarlet asked, startled. "I — I wanted to ask Eddie and the guys to talk to Gwen and Charles."

"I don't care. Don't do anything like that again, Scarlet. I meant it when I said one of us will be with you at all times, but you have to make that possible for us!"

His tone was hard. She knew he'd been frightened for her, so she tried not to let her temper snap, without much success.

"Sorry," she said tightly. "Next time I imagine I see a butchered corpse, I'll try not to scream."

"I know how awful it is to see things like

that," Jane said to her. "I'm sorry you had to go through that."

"But it could end up helping us," Meg said.

"I don't see how," Scarlet said.

"We never know what may end up meaning something in the end," Adam said gently. "That's the challenge of what we do."

"I can feel her," a shaky male voice said suddenly.

Scarlet jumped at the sound, and Diego's arm tightened around her shoulders.

She whirled around to see that the speaker was Daniel Kendall, though he didn't appear as solid as he had earlier. She could see through him to the green Dumpster.

"I feel her presence," he said. "I think she needs help. She's trying to reach us."

"Can't she speak to you?" Scarlet asked. "You know, because you're both . . . ghosts?"

He lifted his shoulders in a shrug. "I don't know. I just feel something of her, you know — like when a woman has passed by you and you can still smell her perfume in the air." He looked at her. "It's something about you, Scarlet. I knew I had to reach you, maybe Cassandra feels the same way. I don't know why. Maybe she's afraid for you, too."

"Daniel," Adam said, "you may be onto

something. But for now, we need to head back in before people start worrying that something bad really did happen out here."

They said goodbye to the ghost, walked back in and headed to their table. Scarlet had worried that she might have ruined the evening for everyone. Instead, she had apparently turned a roomful of strangers into best friends.

They were all talking about what had happened. Then a young red-haired woman hurried over to Adam. "Sir, I think I saw the dead woman last night — I mean, she wasn't dead then, but . . . you know. She was talking with a man. Maybe he was the same man your friend saw out in the alley," she said, nodding toward Scarlet.

"Can you describe him?" Adam asked.

"Thirty, thirty-five," the redhead said. "Nice-looking, friendly smile."

Jane said, "If you can describe him a little more fully, I can sketch him."

"Really?" the redhead asked.

"Really," Jane said.

"I'm Miriam, by the way. Miriam Colby."

They introduced themselves, and Jane pulled the pad she was never without from her shoulder bag.

Brett and Matt returned while Jane was working. Scarlet saw them go over to the manager and shake their heads, clearly telling him they hadn't been able to find anyone. Which, since she hadn't seen anyone in the first place, was only to be expected.

They came back to the table, where Miriam was sitting in Matt's seat, watching Jane draw and, under Jane's prompting, giving her details on the guy's appearance.

"His nose was like *patrician,* I think. You know, perfectly straight, just the right size for his face."

"Like that?" Jane asked, sketching.

"Just like that," Miriam agreed. "The eyebrows should be a little more arched. And thicker."

"Okay, I'll adjust," Jane said, erasing and resketching.

Scarlet looked over Miriam's shoulder and gasped. She stared up at Diego and the others, and she could see that they, too, had seen the resemblance.

Jane had drawn an excellent likeness of Terry Ballantree.

Chapter Thirteen

When they returned to the Conway Ranch that night, they all headed straight into the main house despite the hour. Diego said that Ben and Trisha would just have to deal with the commotion and the fact that they might be waking up a guest.

Gwen and Charles had followed them back, feeling spooked after Gwen had come over to the table to chat, arriving just in time to see Jane's sketch.

"That looks like Terry!" she'd exclaimed. "But, we didn't see Terry here last night."

"Doesn't mean he wasn't here," Charles said.

From that point on, Charles and Gwen had stuck close to the Krewe.

Diego had to admit, he hadn't really figured Terry Ballantree for a murderer — but then, it was hard to think of anyone at the Conway Ranch in that light, even though logic led him to believe the killer was indeed connected to the ranch in some way. The timing of Daniel's death seemed to argue against Terry or the Bartons being guilty of murder, and yet, he just couldn't be sure that something hadn't gone on that they didn't know about.

Of course, the fact that Terry had spoken with Cassandra didn't mean that he had murdered her. But Lieutenant Gray hadn't called to say the man had come forward to say he had been with the victim. Then again, he reminded himself, he'd talked to several people tonight who'd seen Cassandra at the bar, and for various reasons none of them had talked to the police yet, either.

He ran through everyone connected to the ranch and was forced to admit that none of them fit the profile of a cold-blooded killer. Of course history was filled with sadistic killers who had appeared to the general public, even to their friends and family, to be just as sane and good-hearted as the next man.

He couldn't help it. He still felt it had to be someone close, someone associated with the ranch.

If the murder weapon really was the gun that had gone missing from the museum — and that seemed overwhelmingly likely — then that meant the killer knew about the gun collection and how minimal the security had been.

But Terry Ballantree?

Why not?

And if not Terry, who?

Ben and Trisha, who had tied their lives to the ranch?

Gigi and Clark, who spent time here every year?

Angus, who loved his horses and wanted to keep his job, or Linda Reagan, who ran the household with ease?

Gwen and Charles, who seemed to have no substantial connection to the ranch?

Or Terry Ballantree, yet another descendant of Nathan Kendall?

Trisha was the first to hear them come in, and she wandered out into the upstairs hallway in a long flannel robe, immediately followed by Ben, who had his shotgun behind his back.

"What's going on?" Ben asked, shaking his head as he walked down the stairs.

"Sorry to wake you up," Diego said, "but we need to talk to Terry."

"Maybe I should put on some tea," Trisha said.

"No need," Adam said, just as another door opened and Clark Levin poked his head out, with Gigi standing just behind him.

"What in tarnation?" he demanded. "Can't you people be quiet coming in?"

"Sorry to wake you, but —" Adam said.

"Someone else murdered?" Clark demanded.

"No, sir," Diego told him. "You're welcome to go back to bed."

"What? First you wake me, and now you tell me to go back to bed?"

"Stay up if you like," Diego said. "Ben, could you tell me which room is Terry's?"

"I'll show you," Jane offered, hurrying past him. "He's next to me."

She didn't even have to knock. Terry's door opened as she reached it. He looked disheveled, as if he'd just woken up and was still half-asleep.

"What? What's going on?" he asked her anxiously.

By then Linda Reagan had come down from her attic accommodations. She, too, was in a robe and looked worried. "What's going on?" she asked.

"Sorry to wake everyone," Adam said. "We just want to talk to Terry."

"At this time of night?" Linda asked. "Why?"

Diego ignored her and said without

preamble, "Terry, why didn't you call the police or talk to us about the fact that you talked to Cassandra Wells last night?"

"What?" Terry asked.

"Cassandra Wells. You were talking to her last night at the Twisted Antler," Diego said.

"That was Cassandra Wells? The pretty girl I was talking to?" Terry said, clearly shocked, his eyes wide. He sank down on the ground. "Oh, my God!"

Jane reached down a hand to help him back up, and Terry grasped her hand like a lifeline as he climbed to his feet.

He might have been faking his surprise, Diego thought, but if so, he was doing a damned good job of it.

"And how the hell did you leave the house?" Brett asked him, irritated. Diego lowered his head for minute, hiding a grim smile. His partner was angry that he'd been taken, he knew.

"Back door. I was down in the kitchen sneaking a snack — sorry." He shot a guilty glance at Ben and Trisha. "And then I got the urge to have a drink and listen to some music. Since I was already in the kitchen, it just seemed easier to go out the back."

"We also slipped out the back," Gwen admitted. "We were at the Twisted Antler, too."

"Why the hell would you people slip out that way? This is a B and B, not a prison!" Ben said.

Terry didn't even seem to hear him. He looked over at Diego. "I swear to you, I didn't know that was her. I haven't seen the TV all day. She was there and she was pretty, so I flirted a little. I gave her a horrible line — asked her if she went there often. She said she liked the music. I asked her if she wanted to make some music with me, and she said she was in school, but maybe she'd see me around sometime. That was it, I swear."

"We didn't see you there," Charles said.

"And I didn't see you two, either!" Terry snapped. His eyes narrowed and he turned to skewer Diego with an angry look. "Wait a minute? They were there, too, and you're questioning *me*?"

"We didn't talk to Cassandra Wells, you did," Gwen said.

It was going to get nasty, Diego thought, and he interrupted quickly.

"We're just trying to find out if anyone saw Cassandra after she left the Twisted Antler," he said quickly, and then asked Terry, "By the way, how did you get there? You didn't drive?"

"What? I walked. It's barely a mile, and

it's all downhill."

"And how did you get back?"

"A guy dropped me off at the turnaround about fifty yards down the drive," Terry said. "Then I used my key and came in the front door as quietly as I could."

"You won't mind giving us his name?" Adam asked.

"Bennie Lipton. He's staying at a place called the Snowdrop Inn," Terry said.

"Thanks," Diego said.

"Well, then, I suppose we should let everyone get back to sleep," Adam said easily. "We're very sorry for disturbing everyone, but we're trying to solve a series of murders before anyone else gets killed, and that means time is of the essence." He turned to Ben. "Would you mind coming with me to see that all the doors are locked?"

"No problem," Ben said, and the two of them headed down the stairs together.

"I'm embarrassed to admit this," Gwen said, "but I'm feeling very nervous. What if the killer decides to break in?"

"We can take turns sitting up and keeping watch," Meg told Matt cheerfully.

"Are you sure?" Gwen asked. "Because I have to admit, I'll feel a lot better if you do."

"I'm quite sure — as are we all," Meg said.

"Jane and I can take first shift," Brett offered, turning to Matt. "Then you and Meg can take over."

"Scarlet and I will head over to her apartment," Diego said. "We'll see you all in the morning. Scarlet?" he said, turning to her.

She smiled and raised a hand to the others. "Good night," she said.

"Curious," Diego said as they walked to her place.

"What is?" she asked.

"That Terry and the Bartons were at the same not-that-big bar and didn't see each other. Then again, I've been places and heard from friends the next day that they were there, too, and we never saw each other. If you're not looking for someone, it's easy to miss them." He stopped walking and made a point of studying the outbuildings, the parking lot and the stables.

"What about Angus?" he asked, looking at the stables. "What does he do when he's not out on a ride?"

"He eats up at the house sometimes, and I've had him over for sandwiches. But he has a little kitchenette in his apartment, so he goes in to town and shops periodically. He loves it up here on the mountain, though. Says he can tolerate people long enough for a trail ride, but he loves it when they leave. I like Angus. We've always gotten on well, maybe because we both love the horses. Why? No one saw him at the Twisted Antler, and a bar full of people and loud music is pretty much the last place I'd expect to find him."

"Maybe. But Angus is part and parcel of the Conway Ranch," he said. "And I wonder what he sees from up there above the stables? I think it might be worth talking to him tomorrow morning to find out if he saw anyone coming or going last night. It's odd, don't you think, that Terry *and* the Bartons decided to sneak out the back door on the same night to go to the same place but never saw one another."

They headed to the museum. Diego keyed in the alarm code as soon as he opened the door, turning on the lights downstairs.

The museum sat in silence; all was still.

He took her hand, put his finger to his lips to caution her and they walked along the rows of display cases and past the many mannequins, checking out the entire museum.

"You think someone is in here?" she whispered.

"No. But I don't like to think there's no one, then find out there is."

Finally satisfied, he reset the alarm, then

led the way upstairs.

Once again, he wasn't happy until he went room to room, assuring himself that they were alone.

"It's all good," he told her at last.

She looked at him and smiled, "Yes. Because you're here."

She headed to the bedroom. He smiled slowly and followed.

There were so many things they could say to one another, he thought, but maybe it was good that they didn't. Maybe it was best just to hold tight to this time — and to each other.

A flicker of unease stirred in him.

The victims had all been Nathan Kendall's descendants.

Like Scarlet.

He *had* to get her through this.

Or talking about the future would be irrelevant.

He followed her into the bedroom. She was already beneath the covers. He knew she was be naked, waiting.

He carefully set his Glock on the bedside table within easy reach.

And then he joined her.

He was grateful for the feel of her.

For the sound of her heartbeat, of her breathing.

And the brush of her lips on his naked flesh.

Diego had gone into superprotective mode.

He woke up first. Scarlet felt him rise, heard him walk through the upstairs, undoubtedly checking for anything suspicious, and then head down to the museum. She took a quick shower, feeling completely safe.

She wasn't sure what the Krewe had planned for the day, but she knew what she would like to do for part of it if time allowed, and that was head for a shooting range. She was capable with a gun, but Diego had been right: she'd never liked them. Too many people who were far too irresponsible owned them, which was a shame for those who *were* responsible. She'd understood why Ben kept his shotgun ready; they were on a mountaintop, and there were animals in the woods that could kill a person.

And now . . .

Now she had no intention of being vulnerable, a victim. She intended to be prepared, and if that meant becoming not just competent but adept with a gun, so be it.

After ascertaining that the museum was empty, Diego came upstairs to find her

322

showered, dressed and ready for the day. He looked as her with an odd smile for a moment — as if regretting that she hadn't spent a little longer in the shower so the night, too, could last a little longer — but then he told her that everything was fine, so he was hopping in the shower himself.

She told him she would get some coffee going.

"Lara is coming in today — Brett's fiancée," he told her. "You and she have something in common. The ghosts in the zombie case picked her to talk to just like Daniel picked you."

"Why Lara? Why me?" she asked him. "I was never law enforcement, I never believed in ghosts. I never even played with Ouija boards when I was a kid. Why am I suddenly ghost central?"

He grinned. "Daniel just likes you and wants you to be safe." His smile faded, and he set his hands on her shoulders. "That's basically it, Scarlet. The dead need our help. And we can certainly use theirs."

He left her to shower and dress, so she walked into the kitchen and started the coffee. Suddenly she became aware that something — someone — was in the room with her.

She steeled herself before turning to look

at the kitchen doorway.

She knew the young woman who stood there, though she wouldn't have remembered her name if she hadn't been all over the TV.

It was Cassandra Wells, and Scarlet did remember how bright and friendly and full of questions she'd been when she'd come to take the museum tour.

Scarlet was grateful that Cassandra didn't look the way she had the night before, a body soaked in blood with an exploded face.

Instead she was in jeans and a sweater, hair held back from her face by a headband, features pale, almost fully substantial, though Scarlet could just see through to the hallway behind her.

Scarlet was proud that she didn't feel the slightest inclination to scream, to fall apart.

Cassandra had chosen her, just as Daniel had, and she found herself feeling glad of that and hoping desperately that she could help.

"Hello," Scarlet said.

Cassandra let out a little sigh of relief. "You can see me?"

Her voice was weak, as if she was speaking from miles away.

"Yes," Scarlet said.

"You know me?" the young woman asked.

Scarlet nodded. "I remember when you came to the museum. You asked the best questions, and I could tell how interested you were in everything."

"I was," Cassandra said, ghostly tears misting her eyes. "You know what happened to me, don't you?"

"We do, and we want to help," Scarlet assured her.

And then Daniel appeared out of nowhere, standing right by the kitchen table. He met Cassandra's eyes and said, "I'm Daniel."

"You're dead, too, aren't you?" Cassandra asked softly.

"Yes," he whispered.

"Did we ever meet?" Cassandra asked him.

He shook his head. "I know you from . . . watching."

She almost smiled. "Haunting, you mean?"

"I guess."

Scarlet stared in amazement. They seemed to have forgotten that she existed.

"If I'd known you were in danger, I would have found a way to save you," he whispered.

"Thank you," Cassandra said.

Scarlet felt as if she'd walked into a bizarre case of speed dating. She cleared her throat.

"Cassandra, I'm sorry to interrupt, but time is of the essence here, and I'm hoping you can you help us. We need to know what happened the night you were killed. You were in the Twisted Antler. You talked to a man who's staying here at the ranch, Terry Ballantree. You also talked to a woman. I need to know who else you saw," she said. "I need to know who killed you."

Cassandra shook her head. "I should have stayed at the Twisted Antler," she said quietly.

"What happened?" Scarlet asked.

"I listened to the music for a while, but I was tired and needed to get home. I was walking down the street, heading for the lot where I'd left my car. I heard a noise from an alley as I passed. I turned to look and saw a guy wearing a bag — like canvas or burlap or something — over his head. And that was it. He dragged me into the alley. There were still people around, but I never managed to scream." She stopped speaking for a minute. "He threw me into a car and drove up the mountain, then dragged me into the woods and . . . and shot me. The gun — it's as if I can still hear it ringing in my ears." She paused again, laughed, and then cried. "I don't have ears anymore, though, do I? I'm not real. I'm air, a figment of your imagination. I'm . . . I'm dead."

Scarlet felt the ridiculous temptation to put her arms around Cassandra, to hold her close and comfort her.

She couldn't, of course.

But apparently Daniel could.

For a moment Scarlet wasn't sure where one ghostly image began and the other one ended. But she kept silent, her heart in her throat. Cassandra was sobbing. Daniel was soothing her.

At that moment Diego came into the kitchen. He obviously saw the ghostly pair in the doorway, because he slipped carefully past them, just as if they were real.

"I take it that's Cassandra," he said to Scarlet.

"Yes, she's here," Daniel said. "What about the couple who were killed the first night I tried to warn Scarlet?"

"The Parkers? What about them?" Diego asked him.

"Have you seen them?" Daniel asked.

"No," Diego said. "No, they haven't . . . returned."

Daniel looked questioningly at Scarlet, and she shook her head.

"They might know more than Cassandra and I do," Daniel said. "Larry Parker was sliced up just like Nathan Kendall was. And maybe they got a look at the killer's face, not just his mask."

"The mask was simple but so creepy," Cassandra said. "I remembered thinking, what the hell? It was just a bag with eye holes ripped out, but it was terrifying."

"Creepy or not, it makes it impossible for anyone to identify him," Diego said, pouring himself a cup of coffee.

"Why don't you try to find them?" Daniel asked.

"Daniel, you know yourself — the two of you came to Scarlet," Diego said. "We can't search for them the way we do the living. We just have to hope they'll come to us."

"Where are they? Their bodies, I mean," Daniel asked Diego.

He'd been about to take a sip of his coffee. The cup never made it to his lips. "The morgue," he said quietly.

"Where my body is," Cassandra said.

Daniel looked right at Scarlet. "You could go there and see if they —"

"No," Diego said quickly. "She doesn't need to go to the morgue. You know yourself, there's no good reason whatever for a spirit to hang out at the morgue. Candace and Larry won't be there."

"They could be. I was there for a little

while," Cassandra said, and began to cry.

Once again, Daniel stepped in to comfort her, taking her in his arms.

Scarlet looked at Diego. She didn't want to go to the morgue, but if it would help, she was willing.

"What about a séance?" Daniel asked.

"A séance?" Diego asked. "Daniel, you and Cassandra found Scarlet on your own. There was no mumbo jumbo involved, no candles and no ridiculousness."

"Said by a man to a pair of ghosts," Daniel said, laughing.

They heard the sound of a key in the lock, followed by the alarm beeping briefly downstairs. A moment later Brett called up to them, "Hey, guys, Lara's here!"

Cassandra faded away in a flash.

Daniel followed her, albeit more slowly, his arm still around her, his expression bereft, as if he was losing her.

Brett came up the stairs with Lara, a pretty five-foot-seven-inch blonde who clearly knew Diego well, judging by the warm hug she gave him the minute she entered the room. Then she stood back, anxious to meet Scarlet. They were introduced just as the rest of the Krewe came up the stairs.

Lara Mayhew was warm and sincere, and

obviously deeply in love with Brett. Scarlet could tell she made Brett happy.

But as soon as the pleasantries were exchanged, Matt said to Scarlet and Diego, "What's going on here? You two look as if you've been hit in the head with a brick."

"Our ghosts were here," Diego said.

"Ghosts — plural?" Meg asked.

"Daniel and Cassandra Wells," Scarlet said.

"Ah," Jane said quietly. "So it did mean something, you seeing her last night."

"Yup. Newly found ghost magnet here," Scarlet said lightly. "Daniel suggested I should go to the morgue and try to talk to the Parkers."

"He also suggested a séance," Diego said, as if Daniel had suggested that they all grow horns.

"Have you ever been to a morgue?" Meg asked Scarlet.

"No," Scarlet said.

"Spirits seldom linger there," Matt said.

"It's an ugly place to be, with what's left of your physical self lying on a stainless steel table," Brett said.

"But . . . a séance," Diego said. "I mean, we're above that, aren't we?" he asked hopefully, then answered himself with a groan.

"No, we're not against anything that might work."

Jane said, "Intriguing idea, actually — a séance. Why not?"

Diego looked over at her. "I assume you mean we should involve our suspects?"

"Involve our suspects?" Scarlet asked.

"Invite them to join us, see how they react," Diego told her.

"I don't think you'll ever get Angus to a séance," Scarlet said flatly.

"Probably not. But Angus wasn't at the Twisted Antler and he didn't discover any of the bodies, so I think we can back-burner him as a suspect," Adam said. "I actually think that's not a bad idea. We'll arrange it for tonight. I'll speak with Ben and Trisha."

"What if they refuse?" Scarlet asked. "And even if they agree, this will be one unwieldy séance. There are eight of us, then Ben and Trisha, Terry, Linda and Gwen and Charles. And what about the Levins? That's a party, not a séance."

"Meg and I were planning on following the Parkers' trail tonight," Matt said. "Take the highway in from Denver and stop at the places where they might have stopped, see if anyone remembers seeing them or seeing anyone or anything strange. I know their pictures have been out in the media, but sometimes you get better results with the personal touch."

"We're also going to try to figure out where the killer might have stashed their car," Meg said.

"And since Angus won't be coming, someone needs to keep an eye on the stables," Brett said. "Lara and I will stay here and keep an eye on the museum at the same time. And the back door to the main house," he added irritably.

"Well, Adam and I will be here," Jane said, smiling. "I know how to conduct a séance. Not that I think it matters whether we're séance experts or not, because if something is going to happen, it's going to involve Scarlet."

"Do you really believe we can convince the dead to come talk to us?"

"Who knows," Jane said. "But whatever happens, it will be interesting to see how the others react, don't you think?"

"If the killer's really one of them and he believes the dead are about to literally unmask him, things could become dangerous."

Jane looked at Scarlet. "Séance or morgue? Your call."

Scarlet was quiet for a long moment. She didn't like either option. "Let's start with a séance," she said at last.

"Great," Diego said. "So now, all we have to do is wait for darkness to fall, the moon to rise and the candles to flicker. I can't believe that's how we're trying to solve this case," he said. "But who knows? Maybe our ghosts will arrive and our killer will believe."

Chapter Fourteen

As Scarlet had suspected he would, Angus opted out of taking part in the séance.

His exact words were more definitive. "No. No how, no way, not now, not ever, and you must be kidding."

Scarlet, accompanied by Jane, had gone down to the stables to talk to him. She told him it was fine if he chose not to join them — they were just trying to see who might be interested. But despite that reassurance, the mere suggestion of a séance set him off.

"You want a séance?" he asked. "Oooooh, spooky. Why not do some really weird shit? Let's ride up to the cemetery at midnight so we can perform a Native American ritual and wake up *all* the spirits?"

Angus stared suspiciously at Jane, as if he held her personally responsible for all this, since she was the newest arrival.

Jane refused to be offended. "Maybe we'll do that, too," she told him cheerfully.

Scarlet watched Angus's reaction with amusement. He was an old grouch, but even he wasn't immune to Jane's charm. "We're just trying anything we can think of, Angus, because these murders are so awful and we need all the help we can get. It's fine if you don't want to be part of the séance, but will you be around tonight? In case we need you?"

"For what? You think the horses are going to start speaking in tongues?" Angus asked.

Jane smiled. "Not that, but you never know with horses. You know yourself — they're intuitive. If something bad is going on, they'll sense it and react. But no, that's not what Scarlet meant. It's just that you're smart, strong, and you know this ranch better than anyone. If anything is off, you'll notice, and it would be good to know you're out here, just in case there *is* any trouble. *Human* trouble. There's still a murderer out there, and we can't let ourselves forget that."

Angus looked at her curiously, but seemed pleased by the compliment.

"I'm usually around anyway, but I'll make sure I'm here tonight. I'll keep an eye out for anything that looks wrong." He shook his head and rolled his eyes. "But a séance? Balls! I'm sorry, and I get that you have to try everything, but . . . balls."

They thanked him for his willingness to watch for trouble, then headed back toward the house.

"I told you that would be his reaction," Scarlet said.

Jane nodded. "That's all right. At least we know he'll hang around in case the killer makes a move or something."

Inside, everyone from the main house — except Matt and Meg, who were already on the road — was just finishing up breakfast, the giant moose head seeming to look down at them as if it agreed with Angus about the idea of a séance, which they were animatedly discussing.

"We'll do it. We'll do anything you want," Ben said. "I have to admit, I think it's silly. But if you guys think it'll help, Trish and I are in. Aren't we, honey?" he said, turning to her.

She put her hand on his arm and nodded.

"Well, I'm afraid I'm not in," Linda said, smoothing back her hair before pouring coffee for Jane and Scarlet. "I'm sorry, but I think it's absurd. On the other hand," she added with a smile, "I will admit I don't want to miss the fun. So I'll stand guard and make sure the candles don't set the house on fire."

"So long as you're quiet and don't

interfere, that will be fine," Jane said.

"I'm definitely in," Terry said with his usual enthusiasm. "To be honest, I think it will be fascinating."

Scarlet was surprised when Clark Levin spoke up next, seemingly intrigued. "A séance? That could be interesting. At the very least, it will be amusing."

"Amusing, Clark?" Gigi asked, batting him on the arm. "It's ridiculous — and in extremely poor taste."

"It's never in poor taste to try to find a killer," Jane said.

"I'll sit at the table, if that's what required, and if Clark thinks that we should. However, I still feel that it's in poor taste, as if we're mocking the dead."

"I agree with Jane. There's nothing disrespectful about trying to help," Gwen said. "I think it's exciting."

Gigi made a tsking sound, glaring at Gwen, it was as if she believed all the evils in the world came from a younger generation that could be excited by such a prospect.

"How did you find a medium on such short notice?" Charles asked.

"It wasn't a problem," Jane said. "I'm the medium."

"Oh," he said, surprised. "I thought you

were an artist?"

"An artist, an FBI agent — and a medium," Jane said. "I really know how to multitask."

"So what do I need to do?" Trisha asked Jane.

Jane smiled and shook her head. "Nothing. We'll plan for about eight o'clock tonight, then."

"Something to look forward to," Gwen said with enthusiasm.

"I have some email to catch up on," Adam said. "And some work to do, but I'll be around, if anyone needs me. And I'll definitely see you all tonight."

"And I've got reading to finish back at the museum," Scarlet said.

"I'll go with you. See the rest of you later," Jane told the group with a smile.

As they headed outside, Scarlet asked, "Do you really think we can pretend a ghost is telling us about a murder and get someone to confess?"

Jane looked at her and shrugged. "Maybe a ghost really *will* tell us about a murder. I don't know, but we have to try anything we can at this point. Forensics hasn't come up with a thing. Whoever's doing this is hiding his identity with more than that mask. He wears gloves and takes care not to lose so much as a skin cell at any of the scenes."

"So we have to become creative," Scarlet said.

Jane nodded.

"What if Angus or Linda is the killer?" Scarlet asked.

"Do you think so?"

"No, but I can't figure out who it is, so I have to consider everyone a suspect."

"If we understood why, we might discover who," Jane said. "Maybe all those journals of yours are important. I'd like to do some reading, too."

"Sounds like a plan," Scarlet said. "And later, if there's a chance, I'd like to spend some time at the shooting range."

When they returned to the museum, Diego was on the phone with Lieutenant Gray, and Brett and Lara were checking out the displays together.

When he hung up he recapped the call for them. "Gray has had people out on the street night and day, trying to find anyone who saw anything. They've followed up on all the calls that came in and talked to our leads from the Twisted Antler, but when it comes to useful information, his people are drawing blanks. I've told him about tonight, and he'll be on call, ready to step in if anything happens. Believe it or not, Lieutenant Gray likes our idea of a séance. He's feeling tremendous pressure from the mayor to solve this. He told me that for the first time in his life, he was glad for the Bureau to take over."

"Brett and I are going downtown to follow up on Cassandra's story. Maybe we can find something in that alley. He had to move fast there, so maybe he got careless in a way he hasn't, at least so far, at the kill sites," Diego said. He looked questioningly at Jane.

She smiled and told him, "Scarlet and I are going to read. Don't worry, please. I can handle myself in a fight."

Diego grinned. "I have no doubt, though I also doubt it will come to that. Just be careful and don't trust anyone. My gut says our killer's going to be one of those scary guys everybody likes and no one suspects. Let's face it, if some guy was running around town dripping blood or spouting threats, someone would have noticed him by now."

"We'll stick to each other like glue, and we won't trust anyone," Scarlet promised him.

"Good. We'll meet back here for dinner around six, then head over and 'séance,' " he said.

"And I'd like to read Nathan's journals

with you guys, if you don't mind," Lara said, coming up behind them.

Scarlet found the day not only interesting, but also actively fun.

Jane talked about working as a sketch artist for Texas law enforcement before joining the Krewe, and Lara talked about how Meg, who she'd known since they were kids, had gotten involved with the Krewe and how that had ultimately led to her own involvement — and to falling in love with Brett.

"I'm not law enforcement — I'm in PR and I plan to stay in PR — but the Krewe sometimes hires civilian experts, so who knows?" Lara said. "If the Bureau tells Brett he has to move one day, maybe I'll end up working for the Krewe, too. Right now, Brett can work from Miami — there's a need for a Krewe presence there, trust me — and I can stay on at the Sea Life Center. But if he has to move, you can bet I'll be going with him, because more than anything I want to spend my life with Brett. It's hard to play second fiddle sometimes, but when someone's life is at stake, I get it. It's made me pretty tough and resilient, actually. I might actually make a good agent."

"There's no way to tell what the future will bring any of us," Jane said. "I'm just lucky to be married to another Krewe agent.

I guess when you're blessed — or afflicted — with a sixth sense the way we are, it's a real plus when you fall in love with someone who can see ghosts, too."

"Hey," Lara said, frowning as she delicately pried apart pages in one of the journals. "I think there's something in here. Do you know what it is?"

"No," Scarlet admitted. "I never even noticed those pages were stuck together."

Lara handed her the journal. Scarlet dug around in her desk for a tiny tweezers and carefully extracted the folded note stuck between the pages.

"It's a note," Scarlet said, delicately unfolding the fragile paper. She looked up at the others. "It's a note written by United States Marshal Tom Vickers — his eulogy to his daughter."

Scarlet began to read aloud.

" 'Did ever a child bring greater light to a parent's life? Could any man be prouder of a daughter's beauty, that which shone on her lovely face, and that which eternally radiated from the sweet glory of her heart? Her child, her boy, is all that is left in life that matters to me, and by my daughter's soul, I swear I will raise that boy to know of her beauty, and I will raise him in happiness and that blessed light which Jillian bestowed upon all others.' " She looked at Jane and Lara, and said softly, "Wow. Sure doesn't sound like the words of a man who killed his daughter and her husband."

"I really don't believe Marshal Vickers killed his own daughter," Jane said. "Admittedly, he doesn't mention Nathan in the note, but it's obvious he truly loved his own child and his grandchild."

Scarlet smiled suddenly, "I just realized — if I'm a descendant of Nathan Kendall, then I'm also a descendant of Marshal Vickers."

Maybe she didn't want to believe Tom Vickers had been a murderer because she didn't want to think badly of a relative, however distant, or consider the possibility that a killer's blood ran through her own veins.

"Diego said he's been studying the murders, too, and that he could be proven wrong, but he's never thought it was Jillian's father," Jane said. "That leaves us with one of the outlaws Nathan Kendall ran with right after the war."

"Or someone else we've never thought of, even some stranger passing through," Scarlet said, shaking her head.

"But why?" Jane asked. "What motive could a stranger have had? All the evidence says Nathan Kendall was killed for a reason."

"The only other person I can think of," Scarlet said, "is Rollo Conway. But he sold Nathan the ranch. Nathan did him a favor, really, since Rollo needed the money so he could keep looking for gold. Why would he kill Nathan?"

"Jealousy?" Lara asked. "Resentment?"

"We've thought about that," Scarlet admitted. "But it doesn't really make sense, and it's not as if Rollo would have gotten the ranch back if Nathan and even Jillian died. There was still their son, and the killer could easily have gone into the house and killed him, but he didn't. Rollo just doesn't fit."

"Was Nathan Kendall wealthy?" Jane asked. "Maybe someone was trying to torture him into giving up the location of his money."

"I don't think so," Scarlet said. "One reason people back then suspected his fellow outlaws was the theory that they'd made a big score somewhere along the way and Nathan was hiding the money, even that he'd stolen it from them when he left them for a normal life. But if you read Nathan's journals, it's hard to believe he was hoarding anything of value."

"I guess we keep reading," Lara said.

"There's a mention here about the death of a friend," Scarlet said a little while later, looking up at the others. "Nathan doesn't give a name, but I have a feeling it was the last of the outlaws he ran with. He says, 'Goodbye, old friend; goodbye to the past. Gunned down in Missouri. I guess it was fitting. You died in what was once the Old South, just as you would no doubt have wanted. And yet you were just here with me, as were the others. How quickly we are going. You died fast, they said. Before you hit the ground. More than any of us deserved, perhaps. Rest in peace.' It has to be Jeff Bay. So if all the outlaws died before Nathan was murdered, then it's obvious none of them killed him."

"I still don't believe it was the father," Lara said.

"I don't, either," Scarlet said. "But that takes us right back to Rollo Conway," Scarlet said. "And we've already agreed that he doesn't make sense, either." She shook her head. "No, the killer wanted something. That has to be it. He wanted something."

"But what?" Jane asked.

Scarlet looked around. "Something that might still be here?"

She rose, walked over to the window and looked out. She had the sudden sensation that someone was watching the house, and a shiver raced along her spine.

It was different from what she felt when a ghost was near. It was the same feeling she'd had that night when she'd come back after a night in town and found out that two people had been murdered right here on the ranch.

"Don't think I'm crazy, but I feel like we're being watched," she said, looking back at Jane and Lara. "It's not the way I feel when a ghost is around, it's . . . creepy. But maybe ghosts make you guys feel creepy?"

"Not me. I'm not afraid of them at all," Jane said. "I think there's a real and noticeable difference between the feeling you get when the dead are trying to reach you and when the living are watching you, stalking you. Like I said, I don't fear ghosts, but I definitely fear the living."

"She's right," Lara said. "Ghosts — they're just lost souls and they need help. But the living . . . yeah. They can be terrifying."

"They can be the true monsters," Jane said, joining Scarlet at the window. "Unfortunately, I think it's very likely that we *are* being watched."

Lara joined them, shuddered and said, "By the living."

■ ■ ■ ■

Diego and Brett walked all along the streets of downtown Estes Park and spoke to dozens of people.

"I thought I heard a scuffle," the owner of Louie's Lounge, Louis Richmond, told them.

"Where? Where did you hear it?" Diego demanded.

"I was on my way to my car, and I was coming up on the alley a few doors down from here," Richmond said.

"Did you see anyone?" Brett asked.

"No, I looked when I got there, but it was dark, and there's a Dumpster in the way. I figured it was just a cat going after a rat or something."

They thanked him and left, hurrying toward the alley in question. It was the same alley Cassandra had mentioned, and they'd been saving it for last, but now, with Richmond's confirmation, there was no reason to wait any longer before checking it out.

"So," Brett said, "Cassandra left the Twisted Antler and passed this alley on her way to her car. Whoever grabbed her knew she would be coming this way. He was ready."

"And since people would notice a guy wearing a bag over his head, he had everything timed and didn't put it on 'til the last minute. And that strongly suggests he's familiar with the area and knows exactly where to hide if need be."

"Yeah, like this damn alley," Brett said.

They began searching it inch by inch. They'd been at it for nearly an hour when something caught on a brick facade snagged Diego's attention. "Check this out," he said.

"What?" Brett asked, walking over to join him.

Diego inspected the tiny fragment of material he'd found caught on the brick, then looked over at Brett. "Burlap," he said. "I think we've just found part of the killer's mask."

"I think it's time for Lara and Scarlet to leave," Diego said, taking his seat at Scarlet's kitchen table.

Matt and Meg were still gone, but they weren't expected back until later, probably not until the séance was long over.

Scarlet ordered pizza for dinner, and when it had arrived, she realized that the delivery boy was scared and eager to get away as quickly as possible. Obviously the Conway Ranch had quickly gained an unenviable reputation. She had sympathized, tipped him well and hoped, for Ben's and Trisha's sakes, that reputations could be unmade just as quickly.

Everything — pizza, salad and cold drinks — had been ready when Brett and Diego returned. Diego had told them right away about the scrap of burlap, which had already been sent to the lab for analysis.

She hadn't expected such news, much less his announcement sending her away, and she suddenly felt as if they were in a war zone, and she and Lara were noncombatants who had to be evacuated as quickly as possible for their own safety.

She was ready at first to plunge right into an argument — what could happen to her when she was surrounded by agents? She even thought about getting personal and pointing out that Diego's macho determination to be chauvinistically protective of her — when he'd actually been home, that is — had helped to end their marriage.

Except that it wasn't true. Not really. His way of keeping her out of danger hadn't been by bullying, but rather, was his silence.

She suddenly envied Meg for being an agent. Jane, too. No one was sending *them* away.

The thing was, Scarlet realized, she had

no death wish. But neither did she wish to leave. She was in this up to the gills. The ghosts had come to *her*.

She poured iced tea into a glass and looked at Diego. "Let's discuss this," she said. "The thing is, the ghosts come to *me*. If I leave, they might leave, too, and you need them. Plus, when I'm here, I'm with you and the rest of the Krewe, and you can keep me safe. If I leave, I'll be a walking target, because we don't know that the killer's limiting his murders to Estes Park." She met Diego's eyes with all the firmness she could muster. "You need me here."

Brett looked at Lara, who shook her head stubbornly. "I've already been through the wringer. If you're here, if Diego and the others are here, I need to be here, too."

"The killer has been targeting Nathan Kendall's descendants," Diego said flatly. "And that puts you in the line of fire."

"And we both want the killer stopped," Scarlet said, an edge to her tone. "So I'm not going anywhere."

Tension hung in the air.

"Love the pizza," Jane said enthusiastically, and everyone turned to stare. "Who knew Colorado had such great pizza?"

Scarlet knew Jane was just trying to lighten the mood — not to mention change the subject — but she wouldn't let herself be distracted and continued to stare at Diego across the table.

"We can discuss it after the séance," he finally said, then excused himself and headed down the hall toward Scarlet's bedroom.

She excused herself, too, and followed him.

She burst into her room to find Diego standing by the window, looking out on the stables. He turned to face her.

"You're not being logical," he told her. "This killer is after descendants of Nathan Kendall. You or Ben or Gray or Terry could be next."

"But *you're* here," she said.

"This is what I do, Scarlet."

"But that doesn't make you immune to danger. And it doesn't mean that you can protect the rest of the world from everything that could go wrong. Things happen. Bad things. But I can't hide from who I am and, even more important, don't want to hide from it. I know this place, Diego. I know its history. Yes, I'm afraid, but I still believe I have to be here."

He shook his head. "Jane told me that you felt you were being watched today. And it's likely that someone *was* watching you.

Watching to see if you left — and if you left alone."

"I wish she hadn't told you. It was probably nothing."

"We're Krewe and this is a murder investigation. She had to tell me," he said.

"I understand that. I really do. But I don't care. I still wish she hadn't said anything."

He let out a soft groan of aggravation and walked over to her, taking her by the shoulders. His eyes were dark and intense as he looked down at her. "Scarlet, I didn't want what happened between us, but I'm okay as long as I know you're out there in the world somewhere, alive and happy."

She looked up at him. "What if the alive-and-happy part included you?"

He froze, startled. "Scarlet," he said finally, "*you* were the one who filed for the divorce."

"I never really wanted to. I know you thought it was your work, but it wasn't. It was the fact that you never shared your life, not really. I didn't want to be protected from it, I wanted to be part of it. So please don't push me away now — especially since this situation includes me."

"I don't want you to become one of the ghosts of Estes Park!" Diego said.

There was a tap at the door. "Yes?" Diego

said, still staring at her.

She heard Brett clear his throat before he said, "It's time. We need to head over."

Scarlet realized that the sun was rapidly falling.

"All right, we're ready," Diego said.

He released his hold on her and walked to the door.

Scarlet was suddenly struck by the way the dying sun lit the stables. She walked to the window and stared out at the ranch that was her home. She was in the midst of such beauty, here on the mountaintop. She could see the rise that led up the mountain to the cemetery. Along the way, she knew, were streams and a few old shafts where miners had searched, mostly futilely, for gold.

Diego was frowning, waiting for her at the door.

"We think it's possible that Rollo Conway killed Nathan Kendall," she said. "We just don't know why."

"What?"

"Process of elimination, with help from the diaries. It wasn't one of his fellow outlaws, because they all died before he did, so it looks like the mask is a coincidence, not a lead. And it wasn't Jillian's father. We found the eulogy he wrote to his daughter, and I just don't think he could have done it. That leaves Rollo. What if . . . ?" She paused as an idea formed in her head, then went on. "Okay, Rollo sold this place so he could afford to search for gold on his property to the south. What if he wanted this place back because he still thought there was gold here, so he killed Nathan and Jillian? We kept getting stuck on the fact that even if they were dead, their son would inherit. But Rollo hadn't been living around here for years. What if he didn't know about the baby, so he figured the property would be forfeit and he could homestead it? Or maybe he thought it would go up for sale and he had just enough money to buy it."

"But by law Marshal Vickers would have inherited."

She stopped for a moment, stymied, then said, "Rollo wouldn't have cared. Vickers didn't live here, and he was off doing his marshal thing all the time anyway. That would have left Rollo Conway free to explore and find the gold he thought was here. Maybe he even believed Nathan had already found the gold, and he tortured him to get him to say where it was. There's nothing in the journals to indicate Nathan even looked for gold, much less found it, but Rollo didn't know that."

She walked over to him to be sure she had his full attention. "I think we've had it all wrong, Diego. We thought we might be looking for someone related to Nathan, but I think we need to be looking for a descendant of Rollo Conway."

Chapter Fifteen

Night came quickly, with a rich deep color that seemed to wrap the house and grounds like a mysterious blanket.

Darkness reigned, except for a glimmer of moonlight playing over the mountaintop. The forest seemed filled with shadows, and the wind moaned as it found its way through the trees.

They reached the main house to find the candles had been lit and the lights were low, and with the mountain now in darkness, the city of Estes Park shone like a beacon from below. An aura of something magical pervaded the old ranch house.

A clock struck the appointed time, and the séance began.

Jane had gathered them around the dining room table, the moose head looking down on them with an expression Scarlet found unreadable in the flickering shadows.

There were eleven of them: Jane at the

head of the table, and then, moving around the table clockwise, Ben and Trisha, Adam, Gigi and Clark, Diego and Scarlet, Gwen and Charles, and finally, completing the circle, Terry. As she'd said she would, Linda stood in the doorway, quietly watching.

Scarlet had seen the dead before, but this situation felt very different.

It was dark, for one thing. The brightness of the candle flames rendered everything beyond their reach so dark as to be stygian.

There was an edginess, a tension, that was palpable about the table. On the one hand, most of them were amused and even felt a bit silly. But on the other hand, they were also nervous, even those who didn't believe were somehow touched by the power of the moment.

Even Jane's face — usually so beautiful and animated — seemed different. There was something eerie in the way the candlelight caught her reflection.

Scarlet couldn't help thinking that she was about to announce that someone among them had been stricken by the curse of the werewolf.

But Jane didn't speak like some gypsy in a horror movie. She smiled at everyone and said, "None of us knows what, if anything, we may learn here tonight. But so far, every clue we have leads to a dead end. The purpose of a séance is to connect — to connect with the dead. I know that many of you at this table doubt the possibility of such a thing, even thinking about the dead creates a connection with them. And of course, beyond connection and communication, we want justice for them, so even though we may not connect with the dead, we may connect with our own deepest thoughts and memories, and come up with an idea that could help in the quest for truth."

"We didn't even know the Parkers," Gigi said, shaking her head as if she felt she had truly been drawn into insanity.

"Are we all supposed to close our eyes and concentrate?" Trisha asked.

Gwen giggled. "Or stare into the flames and think deep thoughts?"

"Nope," Jane said. "Just hold hands loosely and think about helping those who need help — and being helped in return."

There was silence for a moment, and then Gwen whispered, "The guy who was killed up on the mountain — his last name was actually Kendall?"

"Yes," Trisha said. "Hush now."

"Kendall," Charles Barton said, and shivered. "I'm glad I'm not a Kendall."

"You could be," Gwen said. "So could I. It's not like we ever checked into any of those ancestry sites."

"Well, I *am* a Kendall," Terry muttered. He suddenly didn't seem to be having fun. "Maybe I should check out and go home."

"I'm thinking we all should," Gwen said.

Scarlet cleared her throat and suggested, "How about we stop worrying for now and see what happens?"

There was silence again.

"Okay, let's keep holding hands and concentrate on the flame burning in the center of the table," Jane said.

"Isn't this kind of a big table for a séance?" Gwen asked.

"Concentrate," Jane said. "Candace, Larry, we're all here in hopes of helping you. Your lives were lost not far from where we sit, cruelly stolen from you. If you can help us, please make yourselves known. Cassandra Wells, we want to be there for you. And Daniel Kendall . . . you were taken first, but we swear to find justice for you."

"Do the cops even know if Daniel Kendall's death was a murder?" Clark Levin asked. "I haven't seen anything about that in the media. Maybe the guy was just a klutz, and he fell down and hit his head or something."

The table shook violently. Scarlet had to lower her head so no one saw her smile. She hadn't seen Daniel in the room earlier, but he was there now, his hands on the table as he stood between Jane and Terry, his expression angry.

"What was that?" Gwen gasped, jerking her hands free.

"Just a trick," Charles told her.

"Oh, my God," Gigi breathed.

"Someone kneed the table, that's all," Charles said.

Ignoring them, Jane lowered her head and said, "Daniel, is that you?"

Of course, Jane knew perfectly well it was Daniel, Scarlet thought.

"If so," Jane went on, "would you kindly let us know — without doing anything with the table?"

Scarlet looked up to see Daniel staring around speculatively. He grinned suddenly and moved over to the doorway, where Linda Reagan stood and rapped the wall hard, right next to her head.

She jumped. "What the hell?" Angry, she stepped into the room. The candle glow caught her face, turning her into an evil queen out of a fairy tale. "You rigged this house!" she accused Jane.

"Turn on the lights," Jane said calmly.

"Let's see if this place is rigged."

Ben turned on the lights as the others got up and started looking around the room.

Charles was down on the ground, searching under the table.

Clark began tapping the walls, while Gigi remained in her chair, arms crossed over her chest. "Is this going to go on long? I'd like a drink now, please."

"I don't know," Trisha said, looking at Jane. "Would that change things?"

"Yes, it will put some *real* spirits into play," Gigi said drily. "Honestly."

"This is interesting," her husband told her. "It's not as if we had anything else to do."

"I'll get my own drink," Gigi said.

"I'll get it *and* I'll join you," Linda told her. They headed into the kitchen together.

"What should we do?" Scarlet whispered to Diego.

"Just sit here and watch," he said, smiling. He indicated a big upholstered chair in the corner of the room.

Daniel was sitting there, studying his nails thoughtfully, as if he was just waiting to see what would happen next, too. He saw Scarlet looking at him and grinned.

She wanted to ask him if he'd seen Cassandra again, but since he was across the room, she didn't.

His wry smile, however, made her realize that he was plotting what he was going to do next.

"What do you really think we'll get out of this?" she said quietly to Diego. "Will Daniel spur someone into a confession? Could that really happen?"

"It could, but there's no guarantee. Maybe nothing at all will happen. My guess is that the killer is feeling pretty safe, since he always wears a burlap bag when he commits his crimes. I don't think he expected any real ghosts. So assuming he's here and believes a ghost is, too, he's probably somewhat unnerved but not terrified. Because the ghosts didn't see him, either. We'll just have to wait and see."

Jane waited patiently. In a few minutes the group tired of looking for wires and other tricks. One by one, everyone — even Gigi — came back to the table and sat down again. Linda reclaimed her post in the doorway. Ben turned off the lights, and everyone joined hands again.

"Communication is the key," Jane said quietly. "If there's someone out there in pain or in trouble, someone who wishes to be known, we're here to help you. Please, join us, communicate with us and let us help you as you can help us."

Daniel stepped up between Gwen and Charles and waved a hand through the air. Gwen jumped; the candles flickered.

"Stop that," Gwen whispered heatedly to Charles.

"I didn't do anything," he protested.

"Shush," Terry admonished them.

"I sense that someone's here," Jane said. "Were you murdered on this mountain? One rap for yes, two for no."

Daniel reached over to rap on the table, then suddenly stopped, his hand stopped in midair.

A single rap shook the table. Everyone — including Scarlet — jumped.

Even Jane seemed startled. Then she turned to stare past Charles and asked, "Were you murdered on this mountain?"

A second rap slammed down hard on the table, and Scarlet turned, then barely stopped herself from gasping aloud.

Jane had summoned the ghost of Nathan Kendall himself.

He looked like the statue come to life. In fact, he almost could have been a statue, he looked so solid and real.

The candles flickered violently. Nathan stood stock-still, looking solemnly over the group gathered at the table, before smiling at Scarlet.

She heard something like a hoarse rustling, and then the rustling became a voice.

"Mur . . . dered."

"No," Gwen whispered. Then, voice rising, she screamed, "No, no, *no!*"

Scarlet realized that the other woman was able to hear Nathan, too.

"Murderer . . . among you," Nathan said, his voice harsh and unearthly.

"Do you know who murdered you?" Jane asked.

The wind blew from out of nowhere; the curtains rustled. The candles flickered, and two went out.

Another sharp rap sounded at the table.

The wind blew again, and the rest of the candles went out.

"Scarlet . . ."

Chills shot down Scarlet's spine as Nathan said her name; she thought at first that she was being identified as the murderer!

But then he continued.

". . . knows . . . Scarlet knows . . ."

Gwen Barton let out a terrible, high-pitched scream.

"It's Scarlet!" Terry cried. "The ghost says she knows!"

"I don't know anything," Scarlet said

quickly, trying to digest the fact that Terry, too, could hear Nathan.

"It's a trick. There is no damned ghost," Clark said, all his earlier sense of fun gone.

"All right, that's it," Linda snapped, flicking on the dining room lights. "I've had it. You people claim to be professionals, but this is absolutely ridiculous."

"But who was it?" Gigi demanded, white-lipped. "Was that poor Larry Parker?"

"I'll tell you who it was. One of these so-called agents," Charles snapped. "Linda, you had it right. This whole thing is smoke and mirrors. We just need to look harder to prove it."

"There's got to be a wire or something somewhere," Linda said. She began tapping on the wall by the moose head.

Suddenly something flew out one of the moose's giant nostrils.

Linda screamed in surprise and terror.

The projectile flew with the speed of a bullet, cutting through the air with an audible whoosh.

Diego lunged for Scarlet, bringing them both crashing to the floor. He shouted out to the others, "Everyone get down!"

Scarlet heard a thud as a silver arrow embedded itself in the back of the chair she had just vacated.

Ice filled her veins.

She was about to rise when she felt the pressure of Diego's hand on her shoulders.

"Stay down!" Adam shouted.

Another whoosh and a second shaft hit the seat of her chair.

"What the hell?" Ben thundered from the ground as more arrows flew around the room.

"What the devil are you doing to us?" Clark yelled from under the table. "Séance, indeed!"

"We could have been killed," Gigi said, practically sobbing.

"We still could," Gwen said.

But then there was silence. Scarlet had tried to count. She thought she'd heard six arrows fly.

Was that it?

Diego quickly stood, but his hand on her back kept her where she was. "Everyone keep low," he said in a warning tone. He looked down at her, and she nodded. With that assurance, he dashed across the room, stood on a chair and tore the moose head from the wall. It appeared to be a surprisingly easy task. Plaster seemed to explode everywhere as the mounted head fell to the floor with a massive thud. Staring, Scarlet realized that the wall had been hollowed out behind it, where the support beams stood.

"Don't move," Diego commanded everyone, jumping down to investigate the head. "We don't know if it's safe or not yet."

It was easy for Scarlet to obey his words, because she realized her muscles were frozen.

"How the hell was the damned thing triggered?" Adam murmured, rising carefully and stepping to Diego's side.

"The wall — Linda tapped the wall," Gigi said, her voice quavering. "I'm not related. Whoever is doing this, I'm not related to Nathan Kendall!"

"I don't think I'm related, but I won't move anyway," Linda said.

Suddenly, someone groaned.

"Oh, my God. I was — I was hit!" Terry called out. "I'm bleeding. And I *am* a descendant of Nathan Kendall. Oh God, oh God!"

Scarlet's muscles suddenly started obeying her again, and she crawled over Terry. She saw a tiny trickle of blood on his shirtsleeve. She pulled his sleeve up to survey the wound. It was barely a scratch.

"I'm going to die," he said.

"No, Terry, you're just going to need a bandage," she said reassuringly.

"Is the damned thing disarmed yet or not?" Clark growled, irritated. "I've stayed through a lot, Kendall, but my wife and I are out of here now."

"I understand," Ben said.

"I don't know why you're so worried, Levin. It's obvious *I* was the target," Terry said peevishly.

"If you'll notice, Terry, my chair was skewered — twice," Scarlet said impatiently.

"If I'll notice?" Terry protested. "I'll tell you what I noticed. According to the ghost, you know everything."

"And I'll tell you again, I don't know *anything,*" Scarlet insisted.

They heard the front door burst open, and Brett came running in, his Glock in his hand.

"Oh, my God, he's going to shoot us!" Gwen shrieked.

"Don't be ridiculous!" Gigi snapped at her. "He's law enforcement."

"Who on earth trusts law enforcement?" Gwen asked her.

"What the hell?" Brett demanded, shaking his head. "I saw the candles go out, so I had Lara set the alarm and lock up after me. I ran over, and then I heard screaming. Lieutenant Gray and his men are coming, too. Diego, what's going on in here?"

"Someone rigged the moose, turned it into some kind of crossbow," Diego said, rising. "Brett, give me a hand with this thing, will you? I'd like to get it out of the way, just to be safe. It was set on a spring system — Linda's tap on the wall set it off. We need to get some engineering techs on this to figure out just how it was rigged."

"Gotcha," Brett said.

"So we're safe now?" Clark demanded, rising and running his fingers through his short gray hair. "Gigi, get up. We're going to our room right now, and then we're out of here in the morning."

"No one is out of here until they've been questioned," Diego said, his voice ringing with authority.

"What? You can't believe that Gigi or I had anything to do with this," Clark said angrily. "We're — we're *retirees*!"

"Sir, you were here all day and you come here every year. I'm afraid you'll have to answer questions just like everyone else," Diego informed him.

"That's preposterous," Clark said, drawing himself up. "In fact, it's criminal of you to even keep us here."

"No, murder is criminal," Adam said in a tone that brooked no argument.

"Did anyone call an ambulance?" Terry

asked, his voice pathetic.

"Terry, you don't need an ambulance," Gwen said. "I've had worse mosquito bites."

"You weren't hit," Terry protested. "They weren't after you, they were after me."

"Medical help is on its way," Brett said, heading over to Diego and the offending moose head. "All of you, give us some space."

"Everyone into the parlor, please. Follow me," Adam said, quietly but firmly taking charge.

Clark put an arm around Gigi's shoulders and turned to stare at Ben. "You! You're responsible for all of this. You found those bodies because you put them there! What was this? Your attempt to create a haunted house and compete with The Stanley? You're a psycho. We're out of here tonight." He spun on Diego. "Arrest us if you want, but we won't stay in this house a minute longer than you're pointless questioning takes!"

Trisha stepped forward. "You're right. You *will* get out of my house. My husband is not a psycho, much less a murderer, and you're a complete ingrate. We've given you discounts, free nights. You outeat every guest every morning, and this is how you repay us? I can't wait for you to go."

"Trisha," Ben said, "just let them go. We should have closed down as soon as we found the Parkers."

"Everyone, please," Adam said. "Let's all be civil and head to the parlor. *Now.*"

Scarlet noted the strength in his voice and the ice in his eyes.

Adam was normally mild, calm and the complete opposite of pushy. But right now, when he spoke in that tone, no one was willing to argue with him.

Clark, his arm still fiercely around his wife's shoulders, headed for the parlor. Terry, holding his arm and looking ready to collapse, left next, followed by Gwen and Charles. Ben looked at Adam and then said, "Trisha, my love, that means us, too."

Gwen suddenly spun around, her expression shocked. "Oh, my God! Clark's right — it *is* you, Ben! You were in here today, plastering or painting or something."

"Painting. I was painting. Touched up some nicks and scrapes, which was probably only necessary because someone has been messing around with my house," Ben protested.

Linda was still sitting on the floor, leaning against the wall, looking incapable of getting up under her own steam. Diego offered her a hand, and she managed to stand with his help. She stood there for a moment and looked around.

"I have to clean up this mess," she said.

"Not now," Diego told her. "Not now. Just go ahead and join the others."

Still looking distressed and disoriented, Linda left.

Adam glanced at Diego, then followed the group into the parlor. Once he was gone, Diego closed the door to the dining room and walked over to where Scarlet was standing.

His expression hardened when he saw the small silver arrows that had pierced the chair right after she had vacated it.

"You all right?" he asked, catching her by the shoulders and searching her eyes.

"Yes. Fine," she assured him.

"The arrows don't appear to have been aimed at anyone specifically," Brett said.

"Despite the fact that Terry and Scarlet appeared to be targets, I agree with you. The perp couldn't have known where people would be sitting — except maybe that Jane would probably be at the head of the table — or even that the weapon would be tripped tonight," Diego said. "What do you think? Set to go off a while ago or only configured today?"

"No idea," Brett said. "Maybe forensics

can figure something out."

Diego reached into his pocket for gloves before pulling one of the arrows from Scarlet's chair and studying it. He shook his head.

"What?" Scarlet asked.

He turned to show her the arrow. The shaft was some kind of silver metal, but it was tipped with what looked like an old Native American stone arrowhead.

Brett walked over to study the arrow with them. "Our killer certainly seems to be fixated on history," he said. "What do you think? How complicated was it, rigging that moose head?"

"Someone knew what they were doing with a trigger mechanism. I haven't pulled it apart to check out the whole thing, but it looks like it was set with industrial-strength rubber bands. But that's not rocket science. Anyone familiar with archery — especially crossbows — could have done it. When Linda knocked on the wall in the right place, she set off the firing mechanism, and the way the arrows were set, they followed one after another automatically."

"But until now the killer seems to have chosen his victims carefully, and even this method was obviously no guarantee," Scarlet said.

Diego didn't look at her. "I don't know. You were nearly hit, and Terry Ballantree actually was."

"And let's not forget that this *is* Ben's house, so if anyone knew about the space behind the moose head where a weapon could be set up, it's him," Brett said.

Just then they heard the front door opening, followed by someone shouting, "Police!"

"Lieutenant Gray," Brett said. "He said he'd be ready for our call, and he was."

Diego nodded and headed to the dining room door, then stopped and looked back at Scarlet, a question in his eyes.

"Yes?" she said. She was loathe to leave the room.

Nathan Kendall had been there tonight. She had heard him, and she hadn't been the only one. But it was her name he had spoken, and he'd said that she knew who had killed him. If only that were true, she thought.

"You can't stay here alone. Come with us," Diego said.

"Yes, of course," she said with a sigh.

She knew she couldn't allow herself to be vulnerable, but she didn't want to leave the room. She wanted to see if Nathan would return now that things had calmed down.

Brett walked past her on his way to the door and threw an arm around her shoulders. "Come on, kid, the fun and parlor games are just beginning."

She nodded. "Yes, of course, I'm coming."

But still she paused.

The dining room was different now. The glare of the electric chandelier fell differently on the antique furniture, the arrow-riddled chairs and the downed moose head. Despite the destruction, the room didn't feel at all spooky. The magical aura of the séance was gone.

And yet . . .

They had found Nathan Kendall. Or rather, he had found them.

He had said that she knew who had killed him, but he hadn't ruled out the possibility that he knew his murderer's identity, too. So, did he know? And could he help them?

They had expected something to come from the séance, and it had, though it certainly hadn't been anything they'd expected.

She wasn't Krewe or any kind of law enforcement, but the ghosts of the Conway Ranch were coming to her. And that had to mean something, right?

Brett and Diego were waiting expectantly

for her to join them, but she ignored them both.

"Nathan," she said softly to the room. "Nathan Kendall. We need your help. Are you still here? Will you speak to me?"

She didn't receive an answer in words.

But she could have sworn that a gentle hand touched her cheek.

"Scarlet?" Diego called.

"Come on," Brett urged gently.

Reluctantly, she joined them as they went to greet Lieutenant Gray.

As Brett had said, the fun and parlor games were just beginning.

CHAPTER SIXTEEN

"This is ridiculous. Why are you question-ing *us*?" Gwen asked indignantly. "We just came for our honeymoon. We stayed on after what happened because we didn't want to be like rats deserting a sinking ship. But to suspect that Charles and I could be guilty of any of this is — is *preposterous*!"

"And I was nearly killed," Linda said, toss-ing back her blond hair. "You can't possibly believe I was stupid enough to rig up a weapon and then let it kill *me.*"

"No, *I'm* the one who was nearly killed," Terry said, staring at her and holding up his wounded arm.

A paramedic had already seen to his injury, applying antibiotic ointment and, as Scarlet had predicted, a small bandage.

Lieutenant Gray was in the parlor, watch-ing, listening, questioning. A crime-scene unit had been called, and they were work-ing throughout the house, with a focus on the dining room.

Gray was standing by the mantel. He had the look of a man who had unexpectedly found himself in the middle of a freak show.

Brett had headed over to the stables and asked Angus to join them, so the grizzled old stable master was there now as well, his expression clearly saying that he thought he'd landed in the middle of an asylum.

"We didn't do this," Ben insisted to Gray. Trisha, sitting next to him, nodded.

"Don't look at us," Clark said.

"As far as I'm concerned, we're through with Estes Park," Gigi said firmly. "The area's absolutely ruined for us now."

"Thank the Lord Almighty I wasn't here for that idiotic séance," Angus muttered.

"There's absolutely no reason to hold us all here. If anything, we're victims, too. What about Scarlet? She's the one who had those awful photos on her camera. She's the one who brought in her quote-unquote friends. Some special agents, nearly getting us all killed. She's far more suspicious than anyone else I can think of."

"Scarlet was seen in town by dozens of people the night the Parkers were killed," Lieutenant Gray told them. He looked at Ben almost apologetically. "While you and your wife were here. Yes," he said, turning

378

to stare at Gwen, "and so were you, Mrs. Barton, along with your husband. So if any of you knows anything, now would be the time to talk to me."

Diego didn't blame Gray for being angry. He felt as if he had stepped into an Agatha Christie mystery himself, except that there would be no drawing-room conclusion tonight.

The people at the Conway Ranch were all behaving like rats confined too long in a cage that was far too small, attacking one another with a vengeance.

He walked into the center of the room. "Could I see whatever's in your pockets, please?" he asked. "And your purses, ladies."

"Certainly not," Charles Barton said angrily. "This is America."

"Yes, where everyone is subject to the rule of law, which would be me. Let's take this from the beginning. I want to know who moved the statue of Nathan Kendall up the stairs at the museum the other morning," Diego said.

"What?" Trisha said.

"Someone was in the museum the morning after Candace and Larry Parker were killed. That someone carried the statue of Nathan Kendall up the stairs and set it at the foot of Scarlet's bed for reasons unknown, maybe hoping to give her a heart attack, or maybe to scare her into leaving. At the moment the why doesn't matter. I need to find out the who," Diego said.

"The museum is kept locked," Gwen said, shifting closer to her husband and taking his hand. "How could any of us — other than Ben and Trisha and Scarlet — have gotten in and done something so bizarre? Maybe they're in it together — Ben and Trisha and Scarlet. They could have moved that stupid statue just to make it look like someone else was behind everything."

"Until recently, the museum had no alarm system, and it wouldn't have been all that hard for someone to 'borrow' the key and make a copy," Diego said. "Someone has that key. So, please, your pockets and purses."

"Do you have a warrant?" Clark demanded.

Gray stepped forward before Diego had a chance to respond and said, "Since you're interested, I *do,* so," he said, reaching into his jacket, "I'll let you all know now that it includes the house and grounds, all buildings on the grounds, and all vehicles parked on the grounds. In other words, it covers pretty much everything here. You're all welcome to read it at your leisure."

"Let me see that," Gigi said, leaping to her feet.

Lieutenant Gray politely passed her the warrant.

"Take care with that," Adam warned her quietly.

"I don't know why you're looking so hard for a suspect when you have several right in front of you, as Gwen has pointed out," Clark said. "Ben has both a key and the physical strength to move a mannequin. You don't even know that the incident with the statue is connected to the murders. Maybe it was Ben's idea of a joke. Or maybe Scarlet did it herself. Look at her history, excavating graves, for heaven's sake. Maybe all that death drove her crazy."

"Mr. Levin, trust me, I am not crazy," Scarlet said with quiet dignity.

Diego glanced over at her, trying not to smile. She was completely controlled. She really did have more inner strength than he'd ever expected when they first met.

"No, Scarlet is not crazy," he said, before turning back to the others. "We've already acknowledged that three people had the key legitimately. But copying a key is one of the easiest things in the world to do. In fact, Lieutenant Gray, perhaps in the morning you could check local hardware stores and find out if anyone in this room has been in recently to have a key duplicated. Now, for the last time, pockets and purses."

For a second there was silence. Then Clark stood in aggravation. "Look, here's me, emptying my pockets. I have keys to my house, my Lincoln back home and my room here. That's it. Pat me down, feel me up, search wherever you like."

"Here, my purse," his wife offered. She stood up from the antique sofa where she'd been sitting and dumped the contents of her little over-the-shoulder handbag onto the coffee table. A packet of tissue, a lipstick, reading glasses, and a little leather case that held ID and credit cards fell out.

"My pockets," Charles said, rising and pulling them out. Change fell onto the rug and rolled across the hardwood floor.

"My purse is upstairs," Gwen said.

"Since I live here, so is mine," Linda said.

"Then you won't care if we search your rooms, right?" Lieutenant Gray asked.

"Go ahead," Charles said, his tone furious. "Knock yourselves out. You want a strip search, too?"

Angus grinned and looked over at Jane. "You can strip-search me — as long as it's one of the pretty agents who does it."

Gigi made a disgusted noise and shuddered.

"Sure as hell wouldn't want it be you, you old prune," Angus said.

"Enough!" Gwen said. "I'll go up and get my purse for you. I assume you'd like to send someone with me to make sure I don't take anything out of it first?"

"Thank you, Gwen," Diego said. "Jane will go with you." He addressed the room again. "People nearly died here tonight. I would think that anyone who's innocent would want us tearing the place apart."

"You go right ahead and tear our room apart," Gwen said. "Because Charles and I are leaving."

"Not before Gigi and I do," Clark said.

"You're not leaving until Lieutenant Gray says you're leaving," Diego said firmly.

"You're not leaving," Gray said.

"Arrest me, then," Clark said, daring him.

"All right," Gray said, "you're under arrest for murder."

"What?" Clark demanded.

"Let's just sit down and wait," Gigi begged him.

As if on cue, one of the crime-scene techs came in, his countenance grim. He walked straight over to Lieutenant Gray and whispered to him. Gray nodded toward

383

Diego, who joined him for a quick sotto voce conference.

"Apparently," Diego said to the group, "they've found something in Mr. Ballantree's room."

Terry leaped to his feet. "I didn't put it there."

"You didn't put *what* there?" Diego asked.

"That key — that wretched key."

"What makes you think they've found the key?" Diego asked.

"Well, I — I . . . We were talking about the key, so of course I assumed —"

Diego smiled. "Well, Terry, they did in fact find the key in your room."

Terry exhaled in surrender. "Okay, I admit it. I did it. I moved the statue up the stairs and into Scarlet's bedroom. But, that's it! It was a joke, just a joke. I kind of had a thing for her, and I figured she'd freak out and maybe come to me for protection or something. But she didn't. And then you guys showed up and I realized it was pointless anyway, she was never going to look at me twice. But I didn't *murder* anyone. I was in town when the Parkers were killed, too, so I couldn't have done it."

"You will come down to the station, and we will talk further," Lieutenant Gray said quietly.

"But it was just a joke. I didn't mean any harm," Terry said, his voice high with fear and his face ashen.

"And I guess you didn't mean any harm tonight, either, right?" Linda demanded. "You might have killed all of us!"

"I had nothing to do with tonight. I swear it," Terry said. "For God's sake, I'm the only one who got hurt." He turned back to Diego and Gray. "And you don't understand. That key *can't* be in my room. It's impossible. I threw it in a stream. I'm not stupid. I got rid of the damned thing immediately. So if you found a key in my room, I'm telling you now, it's not the key I had made."

"Listen," Clark Levin said. "You've got your man, so for the love of everything holy, can the rest of us go?"

"Oh, good God!" Linda suddenly announced. "Trust me, Terry didn't kill the Parkers."

"And how do you know that?" Brett asked her.

"Because he was my date that night," Linda said, shaking her head.

"Why didn't you tell us that earlier?" Diego asked her.

Linda shrugged and glanced at Ben. "There's an unspoken rule here that we don't date guests. I was afraid of losing my job."

"I don't understand why you're wasting time with any of this," Gigi complained. "This is Ben's house. Obviously he's the one who booby-trapped the moose."

"I'm afraid that's not obvious," Lieutenant Gray said.

"Why not?" Clark demanded, gruff as a bulldog, ready to defend his wife.

"Because we base our conclusions on evidence, not supposition. The forensic team and the techs back at the station will be able to tell us more about things like the way the trigger mechanism was set, and when. That information will help us home in on a suspect."

"But this is Ben's house," Gwen said. "I don't go into other people's houses and start excavating behind their walls."

"Most people don't," Diego agreed. "But most people don't commit murder, either."

Diego could see that they weren't getting anywhere. Accusations were flying. Lieutenant Gray arrested Terry Ballantree for stealing the key and breaking into the museum, but that wouldn't get them any closer to finding their killer.

For the moment, he had to pin his hopes on forensics. With luck he would get something useful from that scrap of the burlap, as well as from tonight's search of the house and grounds. Additionally, with Gray's help in the manpower department, they had the ability to follow everyone here. Earlier they'd wanted to bring them all together to see how they reacted at the séance, now they needed to see who would do what once they were apart.

"With the exception of Mr. Ballantree, none of you is under arrest or even being held. Mr. and Mrs. Barton, Mr. and Mrs. Levin, you are free to check out and find another hotel, but I must ask you not to leave the immediate area. Terry, suggest you do the same once — or if — Lieutenant Gray releases you," Diego said.

"Instead of a hotel, you might want to check into the hospital for that arm, don't you think?" Gwen said derisively.

"All of you, out," Diego said, thoroughly sick of every single one of them by that point.

"We'll be escorting you into town to ensure you find room at a hotel of your choice," Jane said.

"Well, I, for one, am happy to be leaving this place," Clark said, rising and reaching a hand down to his wife.

"I'll escort you," Brett told them.

"Just remember," Lieutenant Gray said, "don't leave the area and be sure we have your contact information in case we need to get in touch with you."

"Our lives will be at your convenience," Gigi said, not even bothering to hide her contempt. "Clark, let's go."

"What about us?" Gwen asked. "Who'll go with us?"

"I will," Jane said.

"Great, we get séance lady," Charles muttered.

"I'm sure Lieutenant Gray has a uniformed officer who can assist you instead," Jane said.

Diego lowered his head to hide his smile. Jane was a master of holding her cool no matter what. All that mattered to her was getting the job done. He was going to like being part of the Krewe.

"I'd like to come back as soon as the police let me go. You're not going to close the place, are you, Ben?" Terry asked.

Ben just shook his head, looking shell-shocked. "Who knows what will happen?"

For a long moment everyone in the room just stood there silently.

"Freedom. We're out of here," Clark said, turning to Brett. "We'll be packed in ten minutes."

Terry and the Bartons followed quickly on the Levins' heels. Adam excused himself at that point, too, saying he wanted to do the paperwork on that night before the details started to fade.

"What now?" Trisha asked, looking at Diego.

"We'll see what the forensic crews turn up," he said. "The killer will make a mistake somewhere."

Scarlet walked over to him. "I know you have work to do here, but I should get back. Lara is still at the museum — alone," she said softly.

Brett heard her and walked over. "Lara is fine. Meg and Matt drove up just as I was running over here earlier, so they went up to hang out with her."

Scarlet smiled. "Still, I'd like to get back home."

"And there isn't much reason for me to be sitting here anymore," Angus said, evidently listening in. "Horses are much safer — and most of the time much nicer — than people."

"I'll walk Scarlet and Angus back to where they need to be, and then head back here to help Clark and Gigi find a hotel," Brett said.

Diego looked at Scarlet. She seemed surprisingly fine, considering she'd nearly been skewered earlier, but he could see the question in her eyes.

What happens now?

"I won't be long," he told her. "We'll get the guests out and situated, and I'll be back."

After she left with Brett and Angus. Lieutenant Gray came over to him and said, "I'll have men watching their movements. You can leave that to me."

"Thank you," Diego said. "Whatever the killer is after, he hasn't found it yet. Someone will be on the move."

Gray nodded in agreement.

Ben rose on shaky legs. "What do we do?" he asked. "I'm starting to wonder — should I leave, too? Burn the place to the ground?"

"For tonight, go to sleep," Diego told him.

"But will we be safe?" Ben asked.

"Meg, Matt, Jane and Adam will all be here," Diego said.

"Safer than leaving, then," Ben agreed. He looked up the stairs, where the last of his guests were gathering their things to leave. He shivered suddenly. "Much safer than leaving."

"Are you really okay?" Brett asked Scarlet.

They'd seen Angus safely to the stables. He'd assured them that he would be fine;

he had his shotgun, and he was damned good at watching out for vermin.

Then they'd headed to the museum, reset the alarm after entering and called up to Lara, Matt and Meg to let them know that they were downstairs.

But Brett had paused to question her before going up.

"Surprisingly okay," she assured him. "I just wonder, how could anyone have rigged that moose head? I don't want to believe Ben is doing this, but it has to be him. He and Trisha bought the heads. It's their house. He was working in the dining room, painting, today."

"I'd say this has all been in the works for a long time. Daniel was killed months ago, and we don't even know for sure that was the beginning. That means any number of people had the chance to rig the moose. Not to mention there's been nothing resembling security around here until this week, and there's still no alarm up at the main house. In a way, the fact that so much evidence points at Ben suggests that he's being set up." He hesitated.

"What? What else?" she asked him.

"We talked to Will Chan today. He's still working on your camera, but he thinks someone did mess with it, that they took

391

pictures of pictures in a book and then hacked the workings so they'd be erased two minutes after being viewed. So it's almost certain that the killer rigged both your camera and the moose head."

"Actually, that's a relief," she told him. "Because I just don't think Ben could have faked his reaction to those pictures."

"I agree. We're moving forward, we really are."

She studied Brett. "I keep wondering . . . The pictures on my camera, they were an illusion. Do you think it's possible that something else is going on here, that it's all really an illusion? That the murders of Nathan Kendall's descendants are a smoke screen for something else? I mean, this far down the line, how do we really know who's descended from Nathan and who's not? Someone might have fooled around outside of marriage, so there could be descendants who aren't on record, or supposed descendants who really aren't. How can we ever know the truth?"

"We can't, not really. But if the killings *are* a smoke screen, we still have to figure out for what. I don't know. Maybe there is something here at the ranch that someone wants. But it's late now, and none of us will be any good without sleep. Are you ready to head up?"

"In a few minutes. I just need a little time alone first."

"All right," Brett said. He walked over and made sure that the door was locked and that the "armed" light on the alarm was blinking as it should be.

When he was gone, she stood alone in the museum. She looked around at the display cases and the many mannequins.

"I'm so sorry," she said softly, thinking of all the tragedy that had invaded Nathan's life and the lives of so many of his descendants now.

She felt Daniel's presence even before he spoke to her.

"Do you play the slot machines?" he asked her.

"Pardon?" She frowned as she stared at him. He was good; he looked as solid as any man on the street.

He smiled. "Slots. I love them. Loved them, that is. And they have all kinds of bonuses that really increase your payoff. But the thing is, there's no way to walk into a casino and know that a slot machine is ready to give. You can sit at one forever and ever, and that bonus just won't kick in. Other times, you just sit down and the bonus triggers and triggers and triggers.

And the thing is, life is like that. Some men just touch money and it makes more money. They get sick, but they always get well. Some people do atrocious things to others and get away with it. Sometimes your life is like the machine that pays off nonstop. Other lives, there just isn't going to be a bonus. That was me, Scarlet. And Cassandra," he added softly. "We just weren't meant to have a bonus."

"Oh, Daniel, I'm so sorry. But," she said, and then hesitated. "You *are* here — as a ghost, true, but still you're here. We're talking. You met Cassandra. Maybe life *is* like a slot machine. Your first life wasn't your day for the bonus. But now you have another life, and maybe this time you'll get the bonus."

He grinned. "I wish I could give you a hug," he said. Then he went quiet and nodded toward the stairs and the pedestal where Nathan's statue stood. "He's here," he said quietly.

Scarlet turned and stared at the mannequin. As she watched, Nathan Kendall stepped around it and started walking toward her.

"Hello, Nathan," she said quietly.

He looked at her for a long moment. Then his eyes narrowed as he turned and stared at Daniel.

Daniel grinned. "Hey, Gramps!" he said.

Scarlet ignored Daniel and addressed Nathan. "You've been here all along, haven't you?"

He nodded.

"Do you move the mannequin?" she asked. "Not up the stairs — we know Terry did that. But when it fell over, that was you, wasn't it?"

Nathan seemed to wince. He nodded. She realized that he'd been there for years and years, watching and waiting, but apparently he'd never tried to communicate before. He might be an old ghost, but he wasn't at all a practiced ghost.

He was a ghost, just as Daniel was. But the spirit that remained was the essence of the man, and some men were outgoing, like Daniel, and others were introverted, dealing privately with the demons that had plagued their lives, and clearly Nathan was the latter.

She smiled and moved closer to him. "You've been trying to help us, haven't you? You pushed your statue over because you were trying to tell us that what's happening now is connected to what happened to you."

"Yes," he said, and his voice was like the wind blowing over brittle leaves in winter.

"I can push," he said, and he almost managed a smile. "But I cannot carry."

"It's all right, we know that Terry moved the statue upstairs," she said. "But what we don't know and hope you do is who killed you. Was it Rollo?"

She knew that it was painful for him to speak, but she felt she had no choice but to press him. This was important. Crucial.

"I don't know. I never knew, I only knew that I was going to die. All I saw was the burlap bag he wore over his head," he said, and winced. "A mask like the ones we wore when we were robbing banks and stagecoaches. I did bad things, things that hurt people. Perhaps I deserved what happened to me, but . . ."

"Did you recognize his voice?" Scarlet asked.

"I felt as if I should have, but . . . I didn't. He might have disguised it. I don't know."

"Do you know what he wanted from you? Was he looking for the gold?"

He nodded. "Yes. He kept demanding to know where it was. I tried to play for time, but the pain . . ." A shadow crossed his face as he remembered. "I prayed that someone would come, that Jillian and the baby would escape." His voice grew stronger as he spoke. "But she must have heard, and she rushed out and surprised him, so he turned and shot her, and for the love of God, all I could do was scream her name until . . . Until I realized I wasn't making a sound. That was when I realized I was dead."

"Why didn't you just give him the gold?" Scarlet asked.

"Because I never knew where Jillian had hidden it," he said softly. "I found it by accident, after a hard rain that revealed a vein of pure riches — what Rollo was looking for, I imagine. So I dug it out and gave it to her, told her to put it where I wouldn't know and couldn't be tempted. Maybe she left it with her father, I don't know. It was for a rainy day, for our son."

"It was Rollo — it must have been Rollo," Scarlet said. "I can't believe it was your father-in-law." She'd meant the words as a statement, but they came out sounding more like a question.

The ghost of Nathan Kendall shook his head sadly. "Never Tom Vickers. He may not have liked me, but never would the man have killed his own daughter."

"Do you know if the gold is connected to what's happening now?" she asked. "Could someone know you found gold and that it's somewhere here, on the ranch?"

"I wish I'd never found it," Nathan said.

He looked at Daniel and shook his head sadly. "So much tragedy because of man's greed."

"Well, I didn't have any gold. I wasn't worth more than what I had in my pockets," Daniel said.

"I think every bit of this has been planned — starting with your death, Daniel," Scarlet said. "The killer is looking for the gold, pure and simple, but he wants it to look like someone has gone crazy and started killing descendants of Nathan Kendall. I think his original plan was for Ben to be arrested for the murders, but when it became clear that wasn't going to work he switched tactics and started finding ways to ruin Ben's business, like that trick with the moose head. Either way, the business would end up closed down and the place would be abandoned, maybe forever. But even if it was only temporary, while Trisha tried to sell the property, the killer would be free to rip it apart from stem to stern until he found the gold."

Nathan Kendall nodded and looked at Daniel, but he was fading. "I'm so sorry," he said. He was almost gone, but before he faded entirely he approached Scarlet, who felt a gentle touch on her cheek.

Then he was gone.

Daniel met her eyes and asked, "Did you hear him?"

"Just now?"

"Yes."

"I heard him tell you he was sorry."

"Perhaps the dead hear the dead speak more clearly than the living. Because he told you to be careful. He's afraid for you, Scarlet. So am I."

"You don't need to be, either of you. I *am* careful," she promised, then thought about the past — and the present.

"And I have Diego," she said.

But did she?

Maybe not forever. Maybe he was only here because he was an honorable man who had sworn to serve and protect.

"Daniel," she said.

But he was gone, too.

She looked around the quiet museum and a chill settled into her bones.

She prayed there were no more horrors to come.

But as she ran upstairs to join the others, she knew in her gut that her prayers would go unanswered.

CHAPTER SEVENTEEN

It was getting late. Diego saw to it that the guests left — escorted — and got rooms at a brand-new name-brand hotel down by the highway. Lieutenant Gray promised that officers would be assigned to watch both couples and Terry Ballantree, tracking their movements 24/7. He shook his head like a sad old bulldog when he took his leave. "Hope you know what you're doing, Agent McCullough. Hope you know what you're doing."

"Lieutenant Gray, I always hope that myself," Diego said drily.

After Linda, Ben and Trisha went up to bed, Diego joined Matt and Meg, who had returned to the main house, along with Adam and Jane. They sat up late, discussing the events of the night and their plan to keep watch through the hours ahead.

"I was here most of the day, and other than Ben, I didn't see anyone in the dining room," Adam told them. "It would have taken a while to set up such an elaborate weapon, so my money is on it having been in place for a while."

"Yes, but until today," Jane said, "no one knew we were going to have a séance."

"True," Diego admitted, "which means whoever rigged that moose head was playing the long game."

"And that points to Ben," Adam said.

"Too conveniently?" Matt suggested.

Diego turned to Adam. "Scarlet believes that Nathan Kendall was killed by Rollo Conway, the original owner of this property. She thinks Rollo was bitter about having to sell, certain that Nathan had found the gold Rollo had spent years looking for with no luck. Rollo never found anything worthwhile on his other property, so it must have burned him up to think Nathan had gotten rich on what should have been *his* gold. So Rollo tortured Nathan to get him to give up the location of the gold. I think Rollo wore the burlap bag over his head to look like one of the thugs Nathan had ridden with. He probably didn't know they were all dead at that point. If that theory's true, our killer might not have any connection to Nathan Kendall, he might be distantly related to Rollo Conway. Can we get our researchers on that?"

"I'll make the call now," Adam said.

"I think it's about three in the morning back East," Diego said.

"The Krewe never sleeps," Adam said lightly.

Meg grinned at Diego. "Our tech office is staffed 24/7 — just waiting to hear what we might need."

"Nice," Diego said.

The Krewe of Hunters. He liked it. What the hell had he been thinking, not to jump right on immediately with Brett?

He'd been thinking that if he just stuck to his comfortable life in Miami and worked hard, somehow he would learn to live, really live, again without Scarlet.

"Do you think we'll find out that someone in our suspect pool is a descendant of Rollo Conway?" Matt asked.

Diego mulled that over for a moment. "I don't know. But there's real logic to the theory, so let's just say I wouldn't be surprised."

"I keep wondering if we should have cleared this place out at the start," Adam said.

"I don't think we'd have saved any lives," Diego said. "In fact, I think we would have made it easier for the killer to search this place for the gold or whatever it is he's after, and that he still would have killed people, because that's his cover for what he really wants. Anyway, I'm hoping we scared our killer tonight, and a scared killer makes mistakes."

"Ready to run, or do something desperate because he believes the ghost really saw something and Scarlet knows what it is?" Jane asked.

"Except that if she *does* know something, it seems pretty clear she has no idea what it is," Meg said thoughtfully.

"I have no idea whether she knows anything or not," Diego said, "but after tonight everyone will think she does, and I have to admit that worries me."

"We're missing something — something we should know from the journals," Jane said.

Diego nodded, feeling his throat tighten. "I need to get back," he said huskily.

"Brett and Lara are at the apartment with her, and the alarm is set. She's all right," Meg said firmly.

"I know. I just need to get back anyway," Diego said.

"Go," Adam told him.

Diego nodded. He headed for the door and then paused. "Tomorrow I'm going to talk to Lieutenant Gray about taking Ben and Trisha in."

"So now you *do* think they're guilty?" Jane asked.

"No. I think they're innocent. But I think they're in danger — just as Scarlet and Terry and Gray himself are — and making it look like we suspect them is the best way to protect them. Ben will understand if you explain it and if it means he's helping the investigation, not to mention I think he's finally realized his wife might be in danger, too."

"What about Linda Reagan?" Meg asked.

"I think she bears watching," Adam said.

Diego nodded.

"Then we'll watch her," Jane said.

"See you in the morning," Adam said to Diego.

"In the morning," he agreed, then left.

He was ready to reach for his Glock as he walked toward the museum.

He looked over at the stables. The drapes were open, and he could see Angus sitting in his chair, probably watching television. His shotgun was at his side.

Diego reached the museum and was ready to key in the alarm code as soon as he opened the door, but he didn't need to. The door opened and Scarlet was there, with

Brett and Lara right behind her.

Scarlet blushed slightly. "We just wanted to make sure you got in safely," she said.

Behind her, Brett shrugged. Diego knew his partner well. The shrug meant, *What was I supposed to do? She was worried about you, and I wasn't about to let her come down here alone — or leave Lara upstairs alone.*

"Thanks. I'm safe, I promise. Now we're locking up, going through the whole place and getting some sleep," he told her, then looked at Brett.

"I've checked, but it never hurts to check again."

"Nathan was here," Scarlet said, following close behind him as the four of them walked through the museum.

Diego stopped short and turned to face her. "What did he say?"

"He didn't move the statue of himself upstairs, but we knew that. He *did* knock it over, though. And, Diego, he *did* find gold, and that's why his killer was torturing. He wanted to know where it was. Nathan would have given it to him, too, but he didn't know where it was himself. He would have done anything to protect Jillian, except that he'd given her the gold to hide for the future, for their son. Oh! And his killer wore a burlap bag over his head, just like our killer. I told him I thought it was Rollo, and why — did Matt and Meg explain when they got up to the house?"

Diego nodded. "They did."

"Good. Anyway, I think Nathan agrees with me about Rollo, even though he never saw his killer's face and didn't recognize his voice."

"We're tight as a drum down here," Brett said.

"Good. Let's try to get some sleep," Diego said.

They headed upstairs, where, by rote, he and Brett went through the apartment, even though someone had been there all night.

In the hallway, they said their good-nights and went to their separate rooms.

The minute the door was closed behind them, Scarlet turned into his arms. There was a sweet rush of urgency about her. They didn't speak as they struggled out of their clothing, and when they fell into bed, he thought he might drown in the silk of her flesh and the fall of her hair. The night was electric. They should have been exhausted after everything that had happened, but they made love as if it might be the last time, as if the earth might open and take them away with the morning's light.

As in fact he feared it might.

After they climaxed, when they lay replete, Scarlet didn't speak and he thought that she might have fallen asleep, curled against him, her head on his chest, one long leg draped over his body. He thought about their marriage and the way it had been destroyed, and he wondered again how they had managed to tear each other apart so completely.

And then she spoke.

"I understand now," she said softly. "I understand how you can't walk away from a case like this."

"No. It's not right — it will never be right — for a job to take precedence over a marriage," he said. "Most people would have thrown me out long before you did."

She sat up and looked down at him, a hand on his chest. "In case you haven't noticed, I'm not most people." She grinned slightly. "Though I might have been stupid and acted as if I was."

He only meant to hold her, but the minute he pulled her into his arms the urgency returned, the feeling that they had to cling tightly to one another because the cataclysm was coming and it would try to pull them apart.

They made love again. Afterward, when she curled up against his side, he held her close and they slept.

Diego began to dream, and in his dream the old Cuban refugee woman was back. She walked up to him through a sunlit field, and he realized he was standing on the mountain, and in the distance he could see the Rocky Mountains tipped with brilliant, sparkling snow.

"You're a good man," the old woman said. "But sometimes that isn't enough. You have to listen, listen with your soul. Only then will you know how to survive."

She smiled as she stopped speaking and faded into the sunlight. He stood on the mountain alone as a chill breeze began to blow, flattening the grass around him. In seconds the daylight was gone and it was full night. The white mountaintops began to move closer, but they weren't mountain peaks dazzling with snow anymore.

They were gravestones.

He woke with a start and realized that his phone was vibrating under his pillow.

It was Lieutenant Gray.

"They've lost Charles Barton," he said without so much as a hello. "My men watched the damned hotel all night and never saw him leave, but his wife called us this morning, crying hysterically, saying he was gone. I've got her down here right now.

You want to come talk to her? She's a mess — certain the killer got hold of him somehow."

Scarlet was still feeling the effects of a very deep and comfortable sleep when Diego woke her to tell her what was going on.

Charles Barton had eluded the police, and they were torn between suspecting that he was a victim, or the killer. Gwen was a basket case down at the station, and Diego was going down to question her. He explained that he was going to take Ben and Trisha down with him, which the group had decided on the night before.

Linda had gotten dressed and gone out very early; Jane and Adam were following her. Meg and Matt were watching Angus, while the police were still assigned to keep an eye on Terry and the Levins.

Scarlet said she would be fine with Brett and Lara, but he promised that if he was going to be detained long at the station, he would send someone to pick her up and bring her down to be with him.

She nodded vaguely when he left her.

She started to drift back to sleep and then woke with a start. She looked around, suspicious that someone was in her room, but it seemed to be empty. Still, she decided to shower and dress, then head into the kitchen.

Company would be good right now.

The company of the living.

She found Brett and Lara at the kitchen table. They'd brewed coffee, and cereal, milk and juice were on the counter. Lara was working on her laptop, and Brett was pacing back and forth by the window that looked out on the stables.

Lara grinned at Scarlet and told her in a whisper, "He hates sitting around watching. He's an action kind of a guy."

"I heard that," Brett said. "And I'm absolutely fine."

"We're supposed to stay right here, right?" Scarlet asked.

"Unless there's a compelling reason to be somewhere else," Brett said. "If there is, I let Diego know I'm taking eyes off the stable, then stick to you like glue. He's really afraid for you, Scarlet. You know that. And he's not being overprotective. You *are* in danger here."

"I know that," she assured him. "Want to help me help you?" she asked.

"What are you thinking?"

"The morgue. I'd like to go to the morgue."

"I don't know what happened!" Gwen said. "I was having one of my headaches, so I took a pill — like the one I took the night the Parkers were killed. When I take those pills, I don't hear anything. I'm so afraid. Charles has been acting so strange. He's afraid — and he has a right to be. I mean, we're not used to wide-open spaces and people carrying guns everywhere."

She was sitting across from Diego in an interrogation room, though everyone had tried to make the place comfortable for her. She had a cup of coffee right in front of her, and a plate of Danishes sat untouched nearby.

She stared at him. "Fat lot of good you all have done us. He disappeared — even though there was a patrol car right outside the hotel. Someone came in and kidnapped him right out from under the cops' noses."

"Gwen, I can't help but feel that there's something you're not telling me," Diego said. He waited a moment and then added, "It's very unlikely that kidnappers walked into that hotel, then managed to walk out with your husband without being seen."

"Well, he was there, and then he wasn't.

Obviously he left somehow."

"That's true," Diego agreed, "but it's easier to slip out unnoticed than it is to be forced or dragged out with potential witnesses everywhere."

Gwen gasped. "You think that Charles . . . ! But I told you. Charles and I were together at the Conway Ranch when the Parkers were killed."

"And you had taken one of your pills that night," he reminded her. "You just told me that they knock you out and you don't hear a thing. How do you know *where* your husband was?"

"I *had* taken a pill," she murmured thoughtfully. "But . . . he's my husband." She sat back, her cheeks burning, stared at him for a moment and then looked down at her hands. "I'd know, wouldn't I?" she asked, her voice breathy. "I'd know if my husband was a homicidal maniac. Wouldn't I?"

He realized that the last question was a plea.

"Has he been behaving lately as if he was . . . a different man?" Diego asked.

She looked away from him, staring at the wall as if it was a window and she was looking out. A little sob escaped her.

"Not until we got to the Conway Ranch," she whispered.

CHAPTER EIGHTEEN

Scarlet had never been to a morgue before; to be honest, she'd never thought she ever would be.

She'd certainly never thought she would ask to go to one.

She hadn't expected the reception area to resemble a doctor's office. But to everyone who worked there — photographers, technicians and office staff, as well as the MEs — it was just the place where they went every day to earn a paycheck and everyone was pleasant. While they waited to see Dr. Robert Fuller, she eavesdropped as the staff talked about family and friends and plans for the weekend.

Life always went on, she thought. Even when you were surrounded by the dead.

Diego had been silent when she'd told him that she wanted Brett to take her to the morgue. For a moment she'd been afraid he would use his authority as lead agent and forbid her to go.

But while she was certain he wasn't happy about it, he hadn't protested. He'd warned them that Charles Barton had disappeared despite police surveillance, and that the man's own wife had admitted to being unaware of his whereabouts during the time of the Parkers' murders. But, he'd pointed out, whether Charles Barton was a victim or the killer, someone was still out there. She needed to be careful at all times.

Brett assured him that they would be careful. And then he, Lara and Scarlet had set the alarm, locked up and headed out.

Scarlett was impressed with Dr. Fuller when she met him. He was young and bright and enthusiastic. He was also curious that Brett wanted Scarlet to see Candace and Larry Parker's bodies, but given that she was in the company of a federal agent, he didn't object to letting her in.

She realized that for some reason she'd expected the medical examiner to be older, matter-of-fact if not actively chilly, and definitely a bit strange.

Instead, Dr. Robert Fuller seemed like a regular guy. A regular guy whose job involved corpses on a daily basis.

"Have they found that murder weapon yet?" Fuller asked Brett.

"You mean the 1849 Colt pocket percussion revolver," Scarlet said. His look of surprise prompted her to continue. "I'm the curator of the historical museum at the Conway Ranch. And just such a weapon disappeared from our collection."

"So I'm right!" Fuller said, pleased.

"Yes."

"Hot damn," he said. "I do historical reenactments, so if you're ever interested, let me know. We have several events coming up." Then he blushed, as if realizing that he was digressing, and said, "Well, come with me. Mr. and Mrs. Parker are shelved at the moment. Lieutenant Gray hasn't released the bodies yet, since the investigation is still open."

They accompanied him down a hallway to what looked like a safety deposit vault with very large boxes. He checked the notepad he pulled from his pocket, escorted her over to one drawer and opened it.

Candace Parker lay there, a sheet covering her so that only the top of the Y incision made at the autopsy was visible.

Scarlet wondered how people ever said that the dead looked as if they were asleep. They didn't look as if they were asleep, because sleep implied life and color and breath. The dead had none of those things, and no one with eyes would ever mistake them for anything but the corpses they were.

She stared at Brett in surprise when he set a hand gently on Candace's shoulder. He looked at her and nodded toward the body, a clear suggestion that she do the same. She carefully avoided glancing at Fuller, who must have been thinking they were all crazy.

She touched Candace but felt nothing. Nothing at all except for an inanimate coldness, as if she was touching a rock in winter. Nothing more.

"Are you guys mediums or something?" Fuller asked.

"Me?" Scarlet asked, turning to face him. "No, not at all."

Fuller looked at Brett. "It's fine with me if you are, just so you know. Whatever works for you, go with it. Okay, let's go see Mr. Parker."

He rechecked his pad, but Larry Parker turned out to be in a shiny silver drawer right next to his wife's. Fuller pulled it open.

Larry Parker had been about forty, graying a little and balding. In death his chin had sunk into his chest, and the top of his Y incision was visible, as well.

Scarlet thought he'd had a nice face; he had a lot of laugh lines.

He, too, was cold, and she wondered why she'd even wondered if it might be otherwise as she laid a hand on his shoulder. She looked down at his kindly face, vaguely listening to Brett and Lara talking with Fuller in the background about recent developments in the case.

She didn't realize she was still touching him until . . .

His eyes suddenly flew open, and he sat up and grabbed her arm. When he spoke, his voice had the same sound of dry, rustling leaves as Nathan's.

"You know," he said. "You know!"

Scarlet backed away and blinked hard, startled.

When she opened her eyes, she realized that Larry Parker hadn't really moved. She had imagined the entire scenario.

And she'd backed right into Dr. Fuller.

"I'm sorry," she said quickly.

"It's okay. Are you all right?" he asked her.

"I'm fine," she said, and forced a smile, then felt ridiculous for trying so hard to smile.

In the morgue.

Lara looked at her with concern, but it was Brett who spoke.

"You all set?" he asked.

"Are you okay?" Lara asked.

"I'm all set. Dr. Fuller, thank you."

"I hope you find the killer soon," Fuller said, and led them out.

As they left the morgue, Brett looked at Scarlet with concern. "Did something happen in there? Did you get a sense that Larry or Candace was still there?"

"No. There was a moment when I got spooked and thought Larry was coming back to life, like something from a cheap horror movie, but that was it. Thank you for bringing me, even if we didn't learn anything."

"Well, you never know 'til you try," Brett said.

His phone rang just as they got to the car, and they waited while he answered. Scarlet could tell that he was talking to Diego.

As soon as he hung up he said, "They've found Charles Barton and they have him in custody."

"And?" Scarlet persisted.

"He's denying everything, but . . ."

"But what?" Scarlet asked.

"They found bloody fabric in his car. Lieutenant Gray thinks it's from a jacket Cassandra Wells had at work but wasn't wearing when she was found. As unfathomable as it may seem, it looks like Charles Barton is our killer."

■ ■ ■ ■

Charles Barton sat in a chair across from Diego. He was belligerent, still, after several hours, denying that he had killed anyone and swearing that he had no idea how the bloody fabric had ended up in his car.

"Why in God's name would I have come out here for my honeymoon and then started shooting a bunch of total strangers?" he demanded. "And that moose head! I wouldn't begin to know how to rig it up to shoot arrows at people. And don't forget I have an alibi. On the night the Parkers were killed I was with my wife, remember?"

"Your wife doesn't really know where you were. She took one of her headache pills, *remember*?"

"And so did I!" he exclaimed. "I was out like a light. Or do you think I kill people in my sleep?" He groaned suddenly. "I shouldn't have said that. It's probably happened, or at least someone's probably used it as an excuse in a courtroom. But I swear to you — I didn't do it! Get Gwen in here. She'll tell you I'm not a killer. I'm a quarterback, for God's sake."

Diego decided against telling him that being an athlete didn't make a man innocent.

In fact, given recent events, it might even make things more difficult for him.

Charles leaned forward suddenly. "It's an inside job. Can't you see that? You have to look at Ben Kendall. It's his place. He knows his own damned walls. I'm telling you, this is a setup."

"So why did you elude a police guard?" He saw Charles's shocked look and said, "That's right. We had people watching your hotel. So where were you? Where did you go this morning?"

Charles reddened, then quickly looked away.

"Wherever the hell it was, it's better to tell us. Otherwise it looks as if you were out planning to ditch evidence or even kill again," Diego warned him quietly.

"I — I can't tell you."

"You'd better tell me."

Barton looked down at the table. "If I do, can we keep it a secret?"

"Charles, we're talking about multiple murders."

Barton remained silent. Then his shoulders fell. "I was with a woman," he said.

"What?"

"I was with another woman," he snapped, then let out a breath. "Yes, I know, I'm on

421

my honeymoon. But with every passing minute, I know . . . well, I know I made a mistake. I have no excuse. I just . . . I couldn't help myself," he admitted lamely.

Diego sat back, skeptical and wary. "Who is this other woman?" he demanded.

Barton didn't answer.

There was a knock at the door. Lieutenant Gray had been watching the interview, so Diego excused himself and stepped outside, expecting to see Gray in the hallway.

It wasn't Lieutenant Gray, however, who had knocked at the door. It was one of his men, a young detective.

"Lieutenant Gray asked me to tell you that the men following the Levins tailed them into town, then lost them somewhere around the old water wheel. Lieutenant Gray has headed out to the Conway Ranch. Ben and Trisha Kendall are here, and Gray thinks Scarlet and Terry Ballantree — who went running right back after we questioned him — should be here, too, for their own safety. The lieutenant's going to ask Agent Cody and fiancée to come along, too."

Scarlet was staring at the pile of journals on her desk. Lara was sitting across from her, while Brett kept circling the statue of

Nathan Kendall.

She was edgy, Scarlet realized, starting when Brett's phone rang. He looked over at her immediately, and she knew it was Diego again.

Brett spoke in monosyllables. "Yes" and then "No," and then "Yes" again. When he hung up, he looked at her.

"Lieutenant Gray is on his way. We're all going down to the station with him," he said.

"Why? Do they know something new?"

He nodded, then turned his attention back to the mannequin. "So strange," he murmured.

"What is?" Scarlet asked.

He looked at her and grimaced. "Life and death," he said. "We have Daniel Kendall, nice easygoing guy, killed relatively recently, and all of us can hear him. Then we have poor Nathan Kendall, who's been around well over a hundred years, and we needed a séance to hear a few words from him, though he did manage to talk to you later, at least. You'd think he would have found peace by now."

"They say they stay for a reason," Lara said. "He probably wanted to see his son grow up, but that was years ago now."

"I wonder about Jillian," Scarlet said. "We

don't really even know what she looked like. Her mannequin is gone, and I haven't seen a likeness of her anywhere."

"You think he's looking for Jillian?" Brett asked. "Why? She's buried next to him."

"Yes, but let's face it," Scarlet said. "Nathan has difficulty as a spirit. Maybe he just can't figure out how to leave."

Her eyes traveled to the side window and she jumped up, a scream tearing from her throat.

Angus was there, his face pressed to the glass, blood dripping from a wound on his forehead. He seemed to be trying to cry out for help.

Diego walked back into the interrogation room and leaned over the table to stare Charles Barton in the face. "Who?" he asked. "Who is the woman you were seeing?"

"Look, it was stupid. She just came on to me, that's all. And Gwen is . . . I was supposed to marry Gwen. We'd been together forever. But she always has a headache. You know that joke about having a headache at night? Well, it's no joke with Gwen, it's the truth. It was like I put that ring on her finger, said 'I do,' and she *did* everything known to man to emasculate me. So when this beautiful woman was interested in me . . ."

"Charles!" Diego said sharply. "Your marital problems are your own problem. Who is the woman you've been seeing?"

"Linda," Charles said. "Linda Reagan. I was with her the night the Parkers were killed, too, and pretty much every night since I've been here."

Diego stared at him in shock for a long moment.

"If you were with her when Candace and Larry Parker were killed, how could she have been in town with Terry Ballantree?" Diego asked.

Charles shook his head. "She wasn't. She probably just said that because Gwen was getting suspicious. Or to help Terry out because of the key the police found in his room, and she likes him and doesn't think he's guilty. Or maybe she hates Gigi and Clark Levin and wanted to cut them off at the knees. I don't know. I *do* know that she was with me that night."

"In that case, do you know where your wife was?" Diego asked him.

"Sleeping through the night. She had to be sleeping, because she took one of those stupid headache pills, and they always knock her out. It's how I was able to sneak away

425

without her knowing."

Diego had the feeling that everything was starting to fall into place, he just had to re-arrange the pieces a little more.

He'd learned something about people and interrogation over the years, and he was convinced that Charles Barton was telling the truth right now, which meant that he was innocent. Ben and Trisha, he was convinced, were also victims, although the incident with the moose head proved that he'd been right from the beginning. This was indeed an inside job, he just didn't yet know who the insider was.

He stood suddenly. He needed to get to the Conway Ranch. Linda needed to be questioned, as well.

Lieutenant Ernie Gray was also a descendant of Nathan Kendall, but whether that meant something or not, Diego didn't know.

He *did* know that he wanted to be with Scarlet — now. He didn't want to wait for Gray to get back to the station with her.

He wasn't even sure he wanted Gray to reach her first.

Scarlet's scream brought Brett and Lara quickly to her side.

But in the split second it took them to

reach her, Angus had disappeared and all that remained were the horrible bloodstains dripping down the pane.

"It was Angus. He was hurt, bleeding . . ." Scarlet said.

"All right, you two stay here. Lock the door and set the alarm behind me," Brett said. Then, Glock in hand, he was out the door.

Diego dialed Brett's number as he headed to his car.

There was no answer.

He tried Scarlet.

No answer.

Last, he tried Lara.

When he received no answer from her, either, he floored the gas pedal and sped through town, his heart thundering.

Scarlet's phone started to ring in tandem with a thunderous knock at the door. She jumped, startled, and looked over at Lara.

Before either one of them could react, the visitor announced himself. "Scarlet! It's Lieutenant Gray. I'm here to take you down to the station. Diego knows I'm picking you up. You shouldn't be out there with just one or two people around. You need to be at the station, *surrounded* by cops, where you'll be safe."

She disarmed the alarm and swung the door open.

Lieutenant Gray was there, looking anxious.

"Diego called Brett to tell us you were coming, but . . ." She paused. She wanted to tell him about Angus and Brett running out to find him, but then she saw the apparition of Nathan Kendall standing behind Lieutenant Gray and gesturing frantically.

Scarlet saw the danger coming, and something inside her sprang to life. She couldn't save herself, but Lara was still inside.

She slammed the door behind her.

And then the killer fired.

She screamed and stared at the man standing in front of her and wielding the antique gun that had killed the Parkers, the gun that had just been fired at Lieutenant Ernest Gray, who now lay on the ground with a pool of blood forming beneath him.

Scarlet hunched down instinctively to see if she could help the lieutenant.

She wondered what this man had done to Brett Cody, and she prayed that Lara wouldn't rush out, fearful for her fiancé.

"Get up, Scarlet. Leave him. Now. Unless

you want me to make sure that he's dead. You know — put another slug in him."

Scarlet got to her feet. The Colt was still pointed at her. She thought about the hours she'd spent at the shooting range when she was still with Diego back in Miami and the vast array of historic weapons just inside.

He was wearing a burlap bag over his head with roughly cut holes for the eyes. But she knew who it was. Knew by the sound of his voice, and his height and build.

"If you're going to shoot me, shoot me," she told him, amazed at how calm she sounded.

She couldn't see his mouth, but she knew he was smiling. "Now, Scarlet, I've learned to judge people fairly well. You're going to come with me, because you know that I'm perfectly willing to shoot people. And I'll be happy to shoot your friend."

"I've just closed the door."

"Which has to be locked from inside."

"Do you think Lara is an idiot?" Scarlet demanded. "She'll lock the door. And there are dozens of guns in there."

"That need the right ammunition. Why take a chance with her life? The poor woman has been through enough. Come with me," he said.

"Where?" she asked.

Nathan Kendall was still there, gritting his teeth in concentration and trying to fight him. But Terry Ballantree was entirely unaware of the apparition at his side. "We're going to take a ride," he told her.

"Where?"

"Up to the cemetery."

"Why?"

"Because I've figured out that's where it is — where it has to be! I've searched everywhere else, and hell, where do you bury things? A graveyard. I just don't know *where* in the cemetery. But you do, and you're going to show me."

She shook her head. "The gold? I don't have any idea where the gold is. That's the truth. And why did you attack Angus? He had no part of any of this. He's not a descendant of Nathan Kendall."

"No, he's not, and I don't really care. He was just a means to an end. And it's not as if the scraggly old coot has anything to live for anyway. You think ancestry is so important, don't you? Well, yeah, I learned about the gold because I'm a descendant of Rollo Conway. I heard about the gold and how it was stolen from us my whole life. I needed specifics, though, and all those ancestry sites were perfect for that. You like the burlap bag? I think it's a nice touch. I know it's what Nathan Kendall and his friends wore when they robbed people, and I thought it would help muddy the waters." He snorted derisively. "This place is called the Conway Ranch. It should be mine, but it isn't. I don't really give a damn about that, though it was fun to watch you all go crazy looking for the connection to old Nathan. It was such fun to find and kill the right people to get you all hot on your research. I know you read those diaries cover to cover — and I know you found the gold. Now let's go."

"Brett Cody is here, and I can guarantee you'll lose in a shoot-out," Scarlet said.

"Not to worry. Agent Cody is off following Angus's bloody trail into the woods. He'll come back eventually, of course, and then I'll shoot him. Lara, too, when she comes rushing out to see what's going on. And, of course, if you don't come with me nicely, I'll start shooting you in some of your less vital body parts. Hurts like a mother, but you'll stay alive long enough to give me what I want."

"You idiot. Brett Cody called for backup," she said.

"I figured he would. And Agent McCullough, your dear ex, will be first in line, rushing heroically in to save you — and I'll shoot him," he said. Once again, she knew that he was smiling. "That will actually be a pleasure. Come on, Scarlet, no more playing for time, hoping for rescue. I have the horses ready. Blaze for you, of course. Come. *Now.* Or stay here and wait for the bloodbath. And then, once I've gotten what I want anyway, I'll make sure that you bleed out slowly yourself, watching life, in all its beauty, disappear before your eyes."

She was still stalling, desperately trying to decide what to do, when he shot at her foot — close enough for her to feel the burn and watch the leather of her boot rip.

"Don't think I caught flesh yet," he said cheerfully, "but next time . . . I will."

"Let's go," she said, heading for the stables.

She could play for time there just as easily. Pretend she couldn't mount Blaze, adjust the girth, mess with her stirrups . . .

There were all kinds of things she could do.

And then she felt the gun in her back and heard him whisper coldly into her ear, "Don't even think about wasting any more time or this gun goes off and I'll find the damned gold on my own. Do. You. Understand?"

She realized then that he was on the verge

of losing control and she'd run out of time to play games.

Lieutenant Ernest Gray was alive — just barely.

But even as he hunched down by the man, doing his best to stop the flow of blood from the hole in his side, Diego could hear the ambulance siren, along with the sirens of half a dozen police cars.

Lara had burst from the museum the minute he arrived, speaking as quickly as she could. "The killer attacked Angus, and then Angus disappeared, so Brett went out to look for him. Then the killer shot Gray when Scarlet opened the door. I called 911, and then looked, but I couldn't find the bullets for any of the guns. Diego, he's taken her somewhere, I think on horseback. The horses are all running loose, and I don't know why he would let them out otherwise."

"Lara, put pressure on this wound," Diego told her.

The minute she knelt down and replaced his hand with hers, he took off on the run, heading to the stables. As Lara had said, the horses were all gone. But even as he stood there raging against the time it would take him to try to find their trail and follow on foot, he saw that one of the horses was loping back toward him.

He blinked. The horse appeared to have a rider.

Yes, there was a ghostly rider astride the black gelding. Nathan Kendall was bringing him a horse.

Had Nathan Kendall seen what had happened?

The apparition pulled Zeus to a halt in front of Diego.

Nathan's voice was as raspy and faint as it had ever been, but he said very clearly, "The cemetery."

Time. Time meant everything now. The killer had a gun. But he also wanted something, information he thought Scarlet had, and that meant he wouldn't kill her right away, not until he got what he wanted, or was convinced she would never give it to him. Diego prayed the time she had left was *enough* time.

Diego's mind had been racing during the drive to the ranch. He'd gone over everything he knew about the psychology of killing. This murderer combined disorganized and exceptionally organized skills. He was a sociopath, putting his own needs above the slightest concern for others' lives. He'd thought he had it all figured out, and in a way, he had.

But now the killer had Scarlet.

And he wasn't working alone. The way people were always covering for someone else, the logical conclusion was that two people were in on the killings, with one always covering for the other, so they could cover their tracks with alibis.

Diego swung up on the horse and realized he'd paid no attention to the ghost, who hadn't dismounted.

Nathan Kendall was riding with him.

CHAPTER NINETEEN

"Everybody thinks they know everything these days. All those ancestry sites! Thing is, all you find online is what someone knew before you decided to write it down. So if you look at those sites, I'm a descendant of Nathan Kendall. That's because I hacked a few historic documents. And once you write something down, it becomes fact, so if anyone checked, they would see the connection."

Scarlet was in the lead on Blaze, but she knew there was no point in trying to escape. He had the Colt trained on her, and he was perfectly willing to shoot.

She turned around to look at him. Once they'd started up the mountain he'd shed the mask. His expression was filled with glee and that same enthusiasm he'd always shown for everything, but now it wasn't goofy and kind of endearing, it was unhinged.

"You'll never get away with this, you know," she said. "They'll figure out it's you and you'll fry, or spend your life locked up in prison, which is even worse."

"Oh, I've got that all figured out. I won't be me anymore. You just shift a few records — well, find the right dead guy, take his name and move on." His smile deepened. "There really was a Terry Ballantree. He's just not with us anymore. He was my first. I suppose it wasn't very fair of me to steal his life so I could have his name, but, well, I needed it. And anyway, life isn't fair. Was it fair that Rollo had to sell this land before he found the gold he knew was here? And that Nathan found it? Rollo knew it, too, even though Nathan would never admit it."

"So this has all been about revenge?"

"No, not really, though I admit I really do want the money, because, well, it's mine. Mostly, though, it's just been a fun challenge," Terry told her cheerfully.

She wondered what his real name was as he moved up to ride beside her, the gun still aimed her way.

"All of it was fun, really," he went on. "Especially when it came to you. Watching you. Stalking you. You were just so . . . uninterested in me that it was a pleasure making your life miserable. I loved getting

437

hold of your camera and sneaking those pictures onto it. That was truly priceless. And the mannequin! That was the best, even better than hacking your camera. I only wish I could have hung around to see your reaction. You were terrified, weren't you? Go on, admit it."

"I was terrified," Scarlet said.

"Only thing is, I really did throw the key in the river! How the hell it got back in my room, I'll never know."

"One of the ghosts?" she suggested.

He laughed at that. "Ghosts! You guys are good, though. That voice we heard, that was the old guy, right? Adam Harrison."

"It was a ghost," Scarlet said. "And the ghosts know the truth now."

"Scarlet, you're just too funny with all your ghost talk. They obviously weren't watching or they would have found a way to stop me by now. I started with that stupid hiker months ago. I'd come out here to check out the lay of the land, and I heard him talking in one of the bars. I thought I'd follow him and just see how difficult it might be to kill him. Piece of cake. That was when I started watching Ben and Trisha. I thought about killing them, and I guess I would have gotten to them eventually. But after I ran into Candace and Larry

Parker, it seemed to make a lot more sense to use Ben and Trisha and make them look like murderers themselves than to kill them — at least for the time being."

"Why did you kill Cassandra Wells?"

"Everyone thought she was so perfect. It made me nuts. Beautiful girl, though."

"So why did you kill her?"

"I didn't." He gave her a secretive grin.

"There's another killer running around the area, killing in the same way?

"Wouldn't you like to know?" he asked softly, and then shrugged and laughed. "Well, you *will* know. You're about to find out. Now quit talking and hurry up."

She knew they were nearly at the cemetery, and once they got there, she wouldn't have a chance, because she really had no idea where to find the gold.

"How did you rig the moose head?"

"Oh, I did that ages ago. Believe it or not, the house was full of tourists, but I did it at night. It was easy. All I did was take it off the wall so I could hollow out the plaster and make room, then move the head off the panel it was mounted on and cut through the wood. You really can find everything on the internet, you know. I read about crossbows and the rest was easy. It was perfect, don't you think? Of course, your stupid séance ruined my chance of actually killing anyone. But, still, it was a lot of fun. Some stupid kid came in when I was making the arrows, and I just gave him a lesson on arrowheads. People just smile and think you're a crazy Easterner who's really fallen in love with the Old West when you get carried away like that."

He was ridiculously proud of himself.

Maybe not so ridiculously. He was holding her at gunpoint, after all.

"Ride," he told her.

Scarlet knew she had to risk it. She looked up at the sky. Afternoon was turning to evening. The sky was ablaze with colors that would quickly fade to gray. Gold streaked over the mountaintops in the distance, making the snow glitter like pastel diamonds.

A calculated risk, she told herself. Now or never.

The weirdly freestanding wrought-iron gates were straight ahead, and if Terry hadn't been lying, a second killer could be waiting behind them.

"We're here," she said, sliding off Blaze's back. She stood tensely for a split second, waiting. The moment Terry began to slide off his horse, she gave Blaze a solid whack on the chest. As she'd suspected, he jerked backward, slamming into Terry's horse. She heard his startled grunt as his horse reared in turn, sending him flying to the ground.

She saw him flounder, trying to hold his Colt as he struggled to rise without being stepped on.

She knew she couldn't reach the gun before he could fire, so she started running into the cemetery, using the mausoleums and greenery for cover as much as she could.

A bullet whizzed by her ear, so close the whistle of its passing was almost deafening.

She kept racing, dodging between headstones, then tearing into the field of crosses, still running.

For her life.

First Blaze came racing toward Diego, followed quickly by Madrigal.

There was no way in or out of the cemetery except on horseback or on foot.

The killer was up there somewhere, and so was Scarlet. But if the horses were racing back to the stables . . .

Then Scarlet had done something to send them running.

Which meant . . .

He had to believe she was still alive.

Night had fallen in earnest. A three-quarter

moon cast down an eerie glow where the golds and mauves of dusk had so recently reigned.

"Oh, Scarlet, you're making this so hard for me. I mean, let's be honest, I can't let you live. But I know you know where the gold is, so if you just tell me, I can be quick. One moment you'll be here, and then you won't. Think about it. You love history, and now you can be a part of it. They'll make a statue of you and everything. You'll go down in local legend, and you deserve that, you really do. Believe it or not, I like you, you know, even though you never had time to look at me twice. You're bright, and very pretty."

"Shut up, you ass," a woman said, and Scarlet jumped and then, afraid she would be seen, she froze.

"Where the hell have you been?" Terry demanded.

"You told me to lead that Fed off the trail. Did you think that would be easy? And then I had to get all the way back here after leaving the police station. All you had to do was kill the cop and get Scarlet — and you've screwed that up, too!"

Gwen? Gwen Barton?

Yes, it was Gwen. And now Scarlet understood. Terry hadn't killed Cassandra.

Gwen had committed that murder. And it had probably been easy enough for her to hide her activities from Charles. She had pretended to be out cold on her headache pills, and he had borne witness to that.

"Oh, shut up and help," Terry said. "Scarlet, come out, wherever you are. I really would like to make this easy on you."

"You're not going to make it easy on her. She knows where the damned gold is, and you're going to have to make her tell you," Gwen said.

Scarlet tried to register just where Gwen was standing. Voices had a strange habit of ricocheting around the stones and mausoleums in a cemetery. She was hiding behind the Vickers mausoleum, ironically enough, and she thought the two of them were near the old wrought-iron gates, but she didn't dare look, in case they spotted her.

She had to be careful when she made her move. Terry might not be the best shot unless his victim was right in front of him, but even if she was only winged or wounded, she would be in trouble.

She started thinking about the six-shooter he was carrying. He'd obviously shot Angus, and he'd used another bullet on Lieutenant Gray. He'd shot her foot. He had three shots left.

Scarlet heard rustling and realized Terry and Gwen were on the move, and it sounded as if they were flanking her hiding place.

Was Gwen Barton carrying a gun? Did the disgustingly perky ex-cheerleader even know how to shoot?

Yes, she did, Scarlet thought. She was the one who had killed Cassandra.

Scarlet knew she might be signing her own death warrant, trapping herself, but she carefully opened the wrought-iron door to the mausoleum and slipped inside the cold stone darkness, hoping she could silently push the door shut and slide the lock into place from inside.

To her amazement, she accomplished the task with a minimum of noise — easily hidden by the rustle of her pursuers' footsteps.

Then she nearly screamed.

There was a woman inside the mausoleum with her.

The long lost ghost of Jillian Vickers Kendall, appearing at last?

No.

The woman was real — well, real as in carved from wood. The matching piece to the statue of Nathan Kendall was standing at the far end of the vault. Scarlet couldn't see her clearly, because the only illumination was the moonlight slipping through the wrought-iron door, but the workmanship looked to be as exquisite.

No one had been entombed in the mausoleum since the early 1900s, Scarlet knew. Had the mannequin been there since then?

And what the hell difference did it make? Terry and Gwen were out there looking for her, and they had at least one gun.

"Come out, come out, Scarlet, its playtime!" Terry called.

She could hear him coming closer. She *had* trapped herself.

To her left were the sealed coffins of her long gone family members. To the right, more of the same.

And at the back, the mannequin.

"Quit fucking around, Terry. She has to be in there, so go in and get her!"

"All right, all right!" Terry said, and shot at the lock.

Once. Twice.

The lock gave. Terry entered the mausoleum, and Scarlet shoved the mannequin of Jillian Vickers Kendall at him as hard as she could.

Terry screamed.

And shot the mannequin.

■ ■ ■ ■

Diego reached the cemetery and slid off his horse's back, racing as silently as he could through the cemetery, hoping that he was right about where the shots had come from.

As he neared the Vickers mausoleum, he saw Gwen Barton looking shocked and Terry lying on the ground beneath . . .

. . . a statue of a woman?

Diego couldn't be bothered to worry about that, because Gwen was holding what had to be the missing antique Colt and Scarlet had to be somewhere nearby.

"Drop the gun, Gwen, or I'll shoot," he said, his Glock aimed at her heart. He'd meant what he'd said, and he was sure she knew it.

"My, my, my, we do have a dilemma here, don't we? Honestly, men screw everything up. Terry turned out to be as big a buffoon as that idiot I had to marry to make this work."

"Why *did* you have to marry Charles?"

"Alibi, of course. He's always been a cheating idiot, so between his habits and my 'sleeping pills,' I knew I'd have my nights free. But forget all that. It's time to make a deal. You want your sweet little ex to live? Drop your gun," Gwen said.

Terry struggled to his feet. "We'll offer you the same deal we promised Scarlet. She tells us where the gold is and we kill you both quickly. We won't renege, I promise."

"Shut up, you asshole!" Gwen told him.

"Well, aren't you a bitch," he told her. "I should never have gotten into this with such a bitch. I could have managed on my own."

"You idiot — you would've been caught right away if that stupid housekeeper hadn't used you as camouflage so she could sleep with my loser husband," Gwen snapped. "It all seemed to work out — Linda so ready to lie for you so you'd both look good. She thought you were such a poor sweet innocent, she couldn't bear to see anyone distrust you."

Terry laughed. "I *was* caught — and I talked my way out of it. Of course, that wouldn't even have happened if you hadn't planted that damned key in my room."

"I didn't put the key in your room," Gwen said. "Anyway, shut the hell up. Where's the gold? And drop your Glock, Agent McCullough. What a stupid name. Who the hell names their kid Diego McCullough?" Gwen said.

Scarlet suddenly stepped out of the tomb. Her hair was a tangled mess, her clothes were dirty and her face was gray with tomb dust.

But she didn't seem to be injured.

Scarlet met Diego's eyes and said, "Shoot her."

"Go ahead — but I can pull this trigger before your bullet hits me," Gwen said. "Grab her, Terry."

As Terry moved toward her, Diego was amazed to see Scarlet react instantly, delivering a hard right hook to Terry's jaw.

"Shit!" he yelped, staggering back.

"Do I have to do everything?" Gwen demanded, wrenching Scarlet in front of her as a human shield.

"Shoot this bimbo!" Scarlet commanded Diego. "Damn it, shoot her!"

"Let's talk about this," Diego said, striding toward them. He had to get close enough to take Gwen out before she could shoot Scarlet.

"No talking!" Gwen said, pointing the gun at him.

"Go for her," Scarlet said.

For a moment he caught her eyes in the moonlight.

There was something there, a message, telling him that he had to take the shot.

"One more step and I shoot one of you!" Gwen promised.

"Nathan Kendall won't let you get away with it," Scarlet said. "The others won't, either. They're all here, you know. My God!" she added suddenly.

"What?" Terry demanded.

"It's Jillian! It has to be Jillian Kendall. Don't you see her? She's right there, next to Daniel and Cassandra."

"She's right," Diego said. "They're all here, and they'll never let you leave."

That was when Gwen made her mistake. She turned to look. And Diego was just close enough. He didn't dare fire, for fear of hitting Scarlet. Instead he threw himself across the two feet between them and brought Gwen down to the ground — and Scarlet, too.

"The gun!" Terry shouted to Gwen.

But before Gwen could reach it, Nathan stepped forward and kicked it out of her reach. Diego got to his feet, dragging her up with him. Terry took one look at them and turned to run. He didn't get far. He seemed to trip on nothing at all and fell flat to the ground.

Standing right in front of him was Jillian Kendall, smiling with pride.

"Get up, Terry," Diego commanded quietly as he secured Gwen with plastic cuffs. Then he looked at Scarlet, who was standing and dusting herself off.

"You risked your life," he said accusingly.

She shook her head. "He was out of bullets," she said. She picked up the Colt and fired. It let out a silent click.

He smiled at her. "Good show," he said softly.

She smiled and turned to Terry, who was just standing there, a blank look in his eyes.

"Guess what, Terry? I do know where the gold is," she said.

"You do?" Diego asked her.

She shrugged. "I didn't until tonight. But that mannequin . . . It's the heaviest thing I've ever tried to move. Nathan Kendall gave the gold to his wife for safekeeping. Her father apparently decided to keep it safe, too. There's going to be some kind of panel in that statue. We'll find the gold behind it."

"I knew she'd find it," Terry said to Gwen.

She told him exactly what he could do with himself.

Diego ignored her, drawing Scarlet into his arms. "I nearly died a thousand deaths, watching her holding that gun on you," he said.

She smiled. "That's because you love me. And I love you," she said softly.

"Hey!" a voice suddenly thundered.

450

The cemetery suddenly seemed to be ablaze with light. Brett rode straight toward them, followed by a half dozen cops.

Diego turned to Scarlet. "They can take it from here."

Suddenly he realized just how badly he was shaking. He'd almost lost her.

She laid a hand on his face and met his eyes. "I think we can take it from here, too."

He smiled. And he suddenly knew, there in a mountainside cemetery, in the dark and surrounded by the dead, that they had wonderful lives ahead of them — together.

EPILOGUE

It was the next day before the events were finally and entirely untangled.

John Williams, the man known as Terry Ballantree, was not only a descendant of Rollo Conway — through the bastard child back East — but also of Nathan Kendall, since his great-grandmother had headed west and met up with one of Zachary Kendall's multitude of grandchildren.

Gwen Barton had met Terry at the Twisted Antler when she and some friends had spent spring break in Estes Park, and they'd recognized each other as kindred spirits. Together they'd devised a way to get away with murder — and hunt for the gold. She hadn't known about the gold until Terry told her about it and explained how he knew, through family lore, that it existed. After that, they just needed to find it.

Her poor husband had been, in her mind,

a necessary and completely disposable pawn.

Of course, things had started to go to hell when their attempt to frame Ben failed, so eventually they'd realized that they had to kidnap Scarlet — who, they were both convinced, knew where the gold was — and escape before they were caught. Terry had managed to slip past Matt and Meg to get to Angus, but that was his last piece of good luck. He and Gwen hadn't counted on Scarlet's love of history and knowledge of antique weaponry, much less the spectral posse that had come to her assistance.

Adam and Scarlet had spent a lot of time talking about the fact that the Krewe always needed more historians and archaeologists, and they didn't have to be trained agents if they chose office work.

An understanding of life after death was always a plus.

Scarlet had to admit she liked Adam very much, along with every other Krewe member she'd met so far.

In Diego's mind, what was there not to like?

Not to mention love.

It was twilight — that perfect moment when the sun was falling and the sky was alive with crystalline color — and the Krewe were together on the porch of the main house. They had the ranch to themselves. Ben and Trisha were on an extended trip to the Caribbean, Clark and Gigi Levin — who'd been easily located having lunch after going missing — were headed "anywhere but here," and Linda Reagan was down at the station, tearfully begging not to be arrested for being an accessory to murder.

Terry and Gwen were under arrest, of course.

Angus was recovering from his head wound and accompanying concussion, thanks to Brett's quick decision to drive him straight to the hospital after finding him out in the woods. Gwen had hit him with a baseball bat and nearly killed him in her attempt to draw Brett away from the museum.

And Lieutenant Ernest Gray was alive as well, fighting for his life, but hanging on. Diego and Scarlet planned on heading to the hospital to see him in a little while.

But at the moment they had gathered solemnly with their friends, because those who had helped them were gathered before them. Nathan was at last reunited with the ghost of his wife, while Cassandra Wells held tightly to Daniel Kendall's arm.

The four of them were standing together in front of the porch as the sun fell.

Daniel looked at them, lifted Cassandra's hand and smiled. "To eternity," he said, then paused and grinned. "And beyond."

Nathan seldom had much to say, and this was no exception, but he offered Scarlet a special smile and mouthed the words, *Thank you.*

Jillian Vickers Kendall lifted a hand in farewell.

It felt as if the sun gave off one last brilliant splash of gold, all but opening the heavens, and then the ghosts were gone and dusk began to descend like a soft blanket around them.

Diego turned to Scarlet. "Where do we go from here?" he asked her with a smile.

She, too, smiled. "Anywhere you want." And then she laughed softly. "Wherever you go, I go, too. In this life," she added, "and the next."

ABOUT THE AUTHOR

New York Times and *USA Today* bestselling author **Heather Graham** majored in theater arts at the University of South Florida. After a stint of several years in dinner theater, back-up vocals, and bartending, she stayed home after the birth of her third child and began to write, working on short horror stories and romances. After some trial and error, she sold her first book, *When Next We Love*, in 1982 and since then, she has written over one hundred and fifty novels and novellas including category, romantic suspense, historical romance, vampire fiction, time travel, occult, and Christmas holiday fare. She wrote the launch books for Dell's Ecstasy Supreme line, Silhouette's Shadows, and for Harlequin's mainstream fiction imprint, Mira Books.

Heather was a founding member of the Florida Romance Writers chapter of RWA and, since 1999, has hosted the *Romantic Times* Vampire Ball, with all revenues going directly to children's charity. She is pleased to have been published in approximately twenty languages, and to have been honored with awards from Waldenbooks, B. Dalton, Georgia Romance Writers, *Affaire de Coeur, Romantic Times,* and more. She has had books selected for the Doubleday Book Club and the Literary Guild, and has been quoted, interviewed, or featured in such publications as *The Nation, Redbook, People,* and *USA Today,* and appeared on many newscasts including local television and *Entertainment Tonight.*

Heather loves travel and anything to do with the water, and is a certified scuba diver. Married since high school graduation and the mother of five, her greatest love in life remains her family, but she also believes her career has been an incredible gift, and she is grateful every day to be doing something that she loves so very much for a living.

The employees of Thorndike Press hope you have enjoyed this Large Print book. All our Thorndike, Wheeler, and Kennebec Large Print titles are designed for easy reading, and all our books are made to last. Other Thorndike Press Large Print books are available at your library, through selected bookstores, or directly from us.

For information about titles, please call:
(800) 223-1244

or visit our Web site at:
http://gale.cengage.com/thorndike

To share your comments, please write:
Publisher
Thorndike Press
10 Water St., Suite 310
Waterville, ME 04901